THE WANDERER

V. Shinilal is a contemporary Malayalam novelist and short story writer. He hails from Nedumangad, near Thiruvananthapuram and works for the Indian Railways. His major works include the novels *Udal Bhauthikam*, *Adi*, *124* and *Iru* and the short story collections, *Chola*, *Buddhapadham*, *Garisappa Aruvi Adhava Oru Jalayathra* and *Naroda Patyayil Ninnulla Bus*.

Shinilal is a recipient of the inaugural Karoor Award (*Udal Bhauthikam*), Padmarajan Award (*124*) and Makasa Award (*Garisappa Aruvi Adhava Oru Jalayathra*) in 2021. He is the winner of the O.V. Vijayan Award in 2023. His works have been translated into many other Indian languages. *Sambarkkakranthi* (*The Wanderer*) was awarded the Kerala Sahitya Akademi Award for the best novel in 2022.

Nandakumar K.’s co-translation of M. Mukundan’s *Delhi Gadhakal* (*Delhi: A Soliloquy*) won the JCB Prize for Literature in 2021. His other translations include *A Thousand Cuts* (*Attupokaatha Ormakal*), the autobiography of Professor T.J. Joseph; *The Lesbian Cow and Other Stories* by Indu Menon; *In the Name of the Lord* (*Karthavinte Namathil*), the autobiography of Sr Lucy Kalappura; *Elephantam Misophantam* (*Aanaththam Piriyaththam*), *Anthill* (*Puttu*) and *Blackened* (*Karikkottakkary*) by Vinoy Thomas; and *Zin* by Haritha Savithri. Nandakumar is the grandson of Mahakavi Vallathol Narayana Menon. He lives in Dubai and works for a shipping line as a business analyst.

THE WANDERER

V. SHINILAL

TRANSLATED FROM THE MALAYALAM
BY NANDAKUMAR K.

First published in Malayalam as *Sambarkkakranthi* in 2019 by DC Books

Published in English as *The Wanderer* in 2025 by Eka, an imprint of Westland Books, a division of Nasadiya Technologies Private Limited

No. 269/2B, First Floor, 'Irai Arul', Vimalraj Street, Nethaji Nagar, Alapakkam Main Road, Maduravoyal, Chennai 600095

Westland, the Westland logo, Eka and the Eka logo are the trademarks of Nasadiya Technologies Private Limited, or its affiliates.

Copyright © V. Shinilal, 2019
Translation copyright © Nandakumar K., 2025

V. Shinilal asserts the moral right to be identified as the author of this work.

ISBN: 9789360458461

10 9 8 7 6 5 4 3 2 1

Typeset by Jojy Philip, New Delhi

Printed at Thomson Press (India) Ltd

THE STORY SO FAR

The creature that evolved and branched into ape and man roamed the face of the earth without a destination or an objective. Roaming thus, it grew into groups. Groups slowly became tribes. Tribes became races.

Instinct compelled the creature to keep rambling. Movement gave it an identity. Defying the seasons, the journey continued over earth's crust. Peregrination is history. History was created by nomads.

They fenced lands and demarcated them as yours and mine. They patrolled the borders. Kings and kingdoms came into existence. Warring became a habit.

Those who were bounded by the Himalayas and the sea created a country which came to be known as India. Like an amoeba, this country assumed many shapes. Bloated at times and squashed at others, it keeps travelling through Time.

The earth is a spaceship, and India a country that clings to its midriff. In that, a mongrel populace multiplies with uncontrolled fecundity and behaves pompously.

The silence of a country that lay in darkness for centuries ended. Its skies were filled with the smoke of a new age. On 16 April 1853, train services started in India, heralded by a 21-gun salute.

Fourteen bogies, hauled by three steam engines named Sahib, Sindh and Sultan, carrying some 400 passengers over a distance of 34 kilometres between Bori Bunder and Thane, connected ancient India to the modern world.

A European who viewed India with empathy recorded:

The day is not far distant when, by a combination of railways and steam-vessels, the distance between England and India, measured by time, will be shortened to eight days, and when that once fabulous country will thus be actually annexed to the Western world.

The railway system will therefore become, in India, truly the forerunner of modern industry.

'The Future Results of British Rule in India'
Karl Marx
22 July 1853
London
New York Daily Tribune, 8 August 1853

Behold, the train that runs on the crust of India is a mini-India. In other words, India is a humungous train. Here, despite being swaddled in centuries of growth, a collection of humans—whose base, animal instincts have not left them—travel on the train.

To be continued ...

PART ONE

Territorial Animal

KARAMCHAND'S FACEBOOK POST

We had a dog in our village. When other dogs entered his territory, he would attack and chase them away.

We had a beggar in our village. When other beggars turned up, he would throw stones at them and drive them away.

We had a landlord in our village. If anyone entered his lands, he would shoot them with his shotgun.

We had a merchant in our village. If another trader set up shop, the merchant would use black magic to get rid of him.

8.5k Likes   6.5k Comments   2.8k Shares

REMEMBRANCES

Thiruvananthapuram

Dawn was breaking. Seated on the cemented floor of the Ganapathi temple, a man whose looks suggested that he had been travelling for a long time gazed at the railway station. The shadows and yellow light of the sodium vapour lamps that fell on the granite facade of the building gave it an ancient grandeur. The man opened his stroller bag and extricated his camera from inside it. Seated in the same spot, he clicked pictures of the railway station. Satisfied with what he saw on the camera's small rear monitor, he returned it to his bag, happy that the building's antiquity had been adequately captured.

Pulling his stroller, the man entered the station. A few lines in commemoration of Gandhi's visit to the station had been engraved on an uneven granite slab hung from the roof. Although he had read it many times before, on that morning only three days away from yet another Republic Day, he read it once more:

Gandhiji made his three visits to Kanyakumari from here.
    'The music of the waves like the sweet, tender strains of the veena will make you contemplative,' he wrote in 1925.
    In January 1937, seated facing the sea, he said, 'The view

of the confluence of three oceans from here is unequalled in the world.'

After Harijans were allowed entry into Anantha Padmanabha Swamy temple, he had visited the temple. While speaking about the Temple Entry Proclamation, he had said, 'No one is to be considered high or low. In the eyes of God, everyone is equal.'

When he climbed the footbridge going to platform no. 3, a cool breeze was blowing. He stopped on the bridge for a little while. A new thought sprouted in his mind: 'When one walks, memories start walking with him.' The thought gave him reason to smile.

The night train from the north steamed into platform no. 1. It disgorged a multitude which soon scattered and was lost in the city. 'A man is equal parts memory and physical body.' Believing that his stray thought had reached its culmination, he walked towards platform no. 3. His mind always militated against determinations.

'When a man walks, he becomes another man.' Bubbles of concepts were popping up around him through the conjoining of words and their surgical separation. 'When a man keeps walking, he turns into another man.'

A breeze had sprung up from the Arabian Sea. It was cold and dark. He tried to imagine what the city might have looked like five centuries ago. Visions of the Ananthan forest arose in his mind. The sea breeze blew unhindered over the empty, flat terrain bereft of tall buildings. 'Does a man carry his memories, or do his memories carry him?'

He took the escalator down to the platform. All the seats on the platform were taken. He found space on a cement bench sponsored by the Lions Club and leaned back on the cold lion head.

Some children were playing on the escalator, riding it up and down. That was how children grew into adults.

With their heavy suitcases, looking at each other helplessly, an old couple was waiting by the side of the escalator. Their beautiful past, untroubled by moving stairs, was mocking them like a demon.

Finally screwing up their courage, they got on the escalator and rode it down. Their fears did not come true. They stepped onto the platform in a self-congratulatory mood.

Escaping his scrutiny, behind them, countless people appeared and moved—singly, in pairs, in groups. The old woman and her dog who had turned the space beneath the escalator into their home woke up and stretched.

The sun had risen.

The railway station, passengers, bogies, rail lines, the nocturnal animals lurking beside them, and electric locomotives, surfaced out of darkness and presented themselves.

The empty rake of the Sampark Kranti Express rolled into platform no. 3. The gong sounded through the PA system. The lazily chatting throng perked up as if a live current had passed through it. People readied themselves for the dash into the bogies. As the locomotive slowly rolled past them, pulling twenty-two coaches after it, the crowd ran up and down alongside their respective coaches. The platform came alive. Newspaper and magazine vendors emerged out of nowhere with their shrill, cicada-like voices.

A steam engine attached to the rear of the train turned out to be the centre of attraction. The crowd looked at it in amazement. It was being taken to New Delhi for display in an exhibition of heritage engines on Republic Day. With its chimney that had once set the skies trembling, 'Wanderer', now aged, stood quietly behind the twenty-two coaches pulled by one of its modern descendants.

People crowded near the rear of the train to watch the grandee engine. They kept gazing at it, as if it was a demon that had emerged from the yakshi tales.

The man climbed into the air-conditioned First Class coach. He tethered his bag with a chain to the leg of the seat and padlocked it.

This was Karamchand, thirty-nine years old. He returned to the platform and was now in the process of taking a selfie with the Wanderer behind him. His stance was proof enough that the zeitgeist which renders any man disciplined when holding a selfie-stick was present in him too. To an extent he was revelling in it. The day he discovered the real meaning of the word 'narcissism' was when he reached a hundred likes on Facebook, and he kept staring at it for a long time. However, his brain was blessed with the prescience to see himself and his selfie together at the same instant.

The selfie was taken. A swipe with his finger and his bald head received a shock of hair. How facile it was to transform a selfie! 'How much of a man is in his own selfie?' he wondered. 'What role does memory play in a selfie?'

People were struggling to board the train with their luggage. On the platform, a young, newly wed couple was seated on a bench. Cold and silent, the Lions Club's ferocious lion lay between them. A dam broke in the bride's eyes, releasing a torrent of tears down her cheeks, as if signifying the quantum of each invaluable second. The man was a soldier. The girl was holding his hand tightly in her soft hands. A white man who was travelling in Karamchand's coach came up to the door and stood by it.

'Good morning,' Karamchand said.

'Good morning,' the white man responded. Then he got down and walked towards the Wanderer.

He ran his hands over the words wrought in the bell metal welded on to the belly of the engine that bore the memories of a colonial past. He stood with his eyes closed for some time. Karamchand watched him with amusement. Suddenly, a book the foreigner was holding fell down and slipped through the gap between the train and the platform on to the tracks. Its title was *India*. It now lay right below the toilet of the A1 coach. *India* could be seen lying in shit.

Karamchand, the foreigner, and a group of onlookers were standing on the platform, staring down at *India*. The jacket showed a red saree floating on a blue background. Probably attracted by the crowd, a travelling ticket examiner, a.k.a. TTE, reached there. He beckoned a porter standing some distance away. As soon as he arrived, the porter squeezed himself down through the gap between the platform and the bogie. He retrieved *India*, and wiping the shit off the jacket without the white man noticing it, handed it over. Karamchand wrote a sentence in his mind and underscored it: 'Some memories are like shit that can't be wiped off.'

The white man paid the porter Rs 100 for the job. Karamchand could not help but wonder, 'Ah, such a symbolic gesture!' *India* drops into shit. A labourer redeems it. A foreigner rewards him. As a Malayali, he was unable to ignore the politics concealed in those actions. He hurried to check the chart pasted outside the coach and read the name of the foreigner.

John   M52   TVC–NDLS

This meant they would be co-passengers till New Delhi.

The guard waved the green flag. The train whistle sounded, drowning all other sounds on the platform. The soldier stood up, hugged and kissed his wife. The train started to roll slowly, mimicking his trembling lips as he took leave of his wife to head for the remote, forbidding mountains on the country's border. Wiping his tears, he strode alongside the train and boarded it.

Unable to reconcile to modern times, the steam engine rolled behind the express train attached to it by a rusty hook. The words 'Great Indian Peninsula Railway' were inscribed on the side of the engine that carried itself with a dignity born of its eminent ancestry.

The TTE stood at the door as if anticipating a last-minute passenger who comes sprinting only after the train is in motion. His anticipation was not mislaid. A young woman came running up, panting like a steam engine. Pulling a stroller bag that appeared to be as heavy as its owner and with her ample thighs camouflaged in skin-tight leggings, she struggled to hoist herself into the train. The TTE hauled the woman and her bag into the B1 coach. She too became part of this small slice of a humungous India.

The train left the platform behind. Slipping under the overbridge on MG Road that bore toy-sized cars, the train gathered speed.

Standing at the door of the First Class AC coach, Karamchand defined the train thus: 'A train is abundant memory. Or it is a collation of tiny, small memories. That's what a train is.'

The journey starts here.

Twenty-two coaches,

3,417 kilometres,

Forty-eight hours and thirty-five minutes,

Speakers of eighteen languages ...

To be continued ...

1

THE HISTORY OF FIRE

The Sampark Kranti Express took a U-turn, leaving behind its long shadow on the Veli lagoon. Standing at the door of his coach, Karamchand was looking towards the rear of the train. Sunlight reflected off the headlight glass of the Wanderer. Suddenly the piston, coupling and connecting rods of the steam engine sprang to life. The wheels that had been arrested and silenced for decades gained speed. They woke up. The coal caught fire, spewing clouds of black smoke into the sky. Two blackened men kept feeding the gluttonous furnace of the steam engine. A white man clad in coal-blackened overalls and a black cap pulled levers and drove the train. It sped along, breaking the rules of time and space. Distance and speed perished in the heat of the furnace that was capable of burning down everything that came in its way.

Fire.

The fire spread in Karamchand's panicked mind. The universe had given all its luminosity to the fire. He travelled backwards in the company of fire. A page from an unrecorded era in history dropped into his imagination.

Karamchand saw a horde of hominids—who, progressing through evolution, had started to walk upright—traipsing through forests. Without language, the creature was not an individual but a cluster. They had just started to walk on their legs in African valleys. Many millennia had to pass for them to turn into homo sapiens. One among them was the forefather of his clan, ejaculating them into existence. He was one of the last links in the chain of millions born from the natural multiplication of that one ejaculate.

They were setting a trap for wild horses. In the shared valley of two adjacent hills they rolled in boulders, stacked tree branches and leaves and made a corral, leaving a narrow opening through which only a single horse could pass. Afterwards, they rested.

Holding stone weapons and staves, they waited on the sides of both hills for the horses to appear. Grass grew abundantly on the plains at the foot of the hills.

The sound of galloping hooves reached them. The plains were soon filled with lazily grazing horses. With slavering mouths, they grazed slowly. The hominids hiding behind rocks started to pelt stones at them; the stones started to land like raindrops. The frightened horses started to mill around and run. They had only one way to run, through the narrow gap left by the hominids. As they passed through the gap, the hominids waiting on the other side smashed heavy stones on their heads, felling them. Their blood flowed in streams. The hunters dipped their hands in the warm blood and smeared their bodies with it. They drank the blood. They ate raw horsemeat. They danced and celebrated their successful hunt. The branches and leaves turned red.

A sudden wildfire blazed. Both the hunted and the hunters got caught in it. They started to run, watching their lands being consumed by fire. The children who could not run were licked up by the tongues of flame. The lucky ones survived by crossing the river. Standing in safety, they watched the fire consume their lands and forests. They saw lowing and bellowing animals scamper around with their bodies half-burnt. The fire travelled up the hills.

When the fire died down, they crossed back the river. Cooked animal meat was waiting for the famished hominids. They ate, savouring, for the first time, meat with a different taste. They danced wildly. They sparred with one another. In their ecstasy they mated in groups. They fell asleep, stacked one above the other.

Taking the embers from a piece of burning wood, one of them made a fire-pit in the cave. The rains came. A spear-toting warrior from another tribe arrived to steal the fire. His name was Prometheus. He became an exalted member of his tribe when he managed to fight off the hordes and return with fire.

Man discovered that fire lurked inside stone. Using the sharpness of one stone against another, he rubbed fire into existence. The fire residing inside bamboo was deified as the presiding deity of yagnas. During man's peregrinations, fire was tamed like an obedient rakshasa; it was used to reduce enemies to ashes. Man made fire-pits near riverbanks and prayed, '*Om Agnim-Iille Purohitam Yajnyasya Devam-Rtvijam.*'[1]

Meanwhile, millions of generations of hominids had travelled through time and space to settle down in various corners of the world.

Fire became man's companion. He stored it in a small box. It became his faithful servant. Cast-iron vehicles sped using the power of fire. Steamboats hastened the progress of explorers.

Trains hooted and whistled like keening demons and sped over rail tracks criss-crossing the face of the earth. In eras of conquest, they ran through history, carrying men, slaves, animals and armaments.

From the rear of the Sampark Kranti Express, the Wanderer, which had borne Karamchand into thrilling memories of fiery history, now brought him back to the present day. He started to walk back into the vestibule.

The soldier was still lingering at the door of the B3 coach. His bloodshot eyes still showed pain, sorrow, despair and the pangs of separation.

The soldier opened a bottle of Pepsi, poured out half of it, poured rum into the bottle, winked at Karamchand, and as a slow smile started to spread across Karamchand's face, sipped his drink.

After rounding another bend and passing over a bridge, the Sampark Kranti entered Varkala Station.

HEAVEN AND EARTH

A procession was moving along the road running parallel to the rail tracks. Everyone was dressed in yellow. Karamchand entered the B coupé and closed the door. John was lying on his stomach, watching the sights through the parted curtains of the double-glazed window. The yellow procession was proceeding at a stately pace and marked singlemindedness. Karamchand took his seat.

A movement under the carpet caught his eye. A pair of shiny, bulging eyes appeared where the two edges of the carpet met. It was the resident mouse of the railway coach. It emerged from beneath the carpet, sat up on its hind legs, the forelegs mimicking that of a praying mantis, and surveyed the two other occupants of the coach. The sight made John scramble and pull his legs up onto the seat. Karamchand stamped his feet on the floor to scare it away. The startled mouse ran in a circle on the carpet and disappeared into the gap from which it had emerged.

John had not got over his panic. He rang the call bell and summoned the coach attendant. He took out his anger at being accosted by a mouse on the attendant. After listening to the tirade for some time, the attendant said, 'Sir, this is India, after all. On occasions, a mouse will ride in the First Class AC coach. And at other times, humans will travel sitting on the toilet.'

He went out and quickly returned with a mouse trap. 'Doesn't matter how big it is. It'll be caught.' He left after leaving the trap between the feet of the two passengers.

Meanwhile, Karamchand's selfie had taken wings. It spun around in his mobile phone as if gathering enough speed to reach escape velocity.

After swerving to the left, the train straightened and eased onto the platform of the Varkala Station. Drawn by the procession of yellow clothes, John walked to the door of the coach, with Karamchand in tow. The yellow-clothed men were clambering onto various coaches. A young couple, busily chattering with each other, got into the S1 Sleeper coach. An ear-shattering song in Malayalam that seemed to hold the earth and the soul in a bear-hug floated down from the crown of the weeping fig that stood on the road outside the station.

No longer is the soul tethered to this earth
Even to the body in which it resides
Souls alone are related to one another
An unbreakable bond between the divinity and the soul

The repetitive journeys of the soul that never cause tedium. When the train was leaving the station, John asked, 'Can you please tell me the meaning of that song?'

How can I explain it to him, Karamchand mused. After doing its last rounds on his mobile, the selfie threw a pall around Google and shot up in the sky like a bolt of lightning. Now likes would start flowing into the mobile from every inhabited corner of every continent of the world. A torrent of comments. All flummery. Yet, they gladdened one's heart. He suddenly realised that in that selfie lay the answer to John's question.

He explained, 'There's a selfie dormant in us. It is not related to our body. In the deepest recesses of our minds, intangible, it waits on high alert. It's there but it doesn't belong to us. It's a reflection that the universe has deposited in us. It's directly linked to the global web. Salvation is like the selfie merging with the network. Do you understand? To put it more simply, the selfie equals the soul, the web equals the *paramatma*. The selfie merges into the web, the soul becomes one with the *paramatma*.'

For some time, John kept looking into Karamchand's eyes. Then he jumped to his feet laughing raucously. He took Karamchand's hand, shook it, and said, 'You're a funny guy.'

'How did you land up here? In this place, how come? How did it happen?' A bewildered Karamchand blabbered.

'I'm John. I'm a professional wildlife photographer. Asian tigers are my favourite subject,' he said, turning his laptop's screen towards Karamchand to show him the picture of a tiger family. 'They're the top predators in Indian forests.' He scrolled through more pictures. Karamchand was astonished by a shot of a tiger standing on its hind legs and scratching the bark of a tall tree. 'Can you shoot them from so close?'

'He's marking his territory. Should another male come into his territory, it'll either be chased away or one of them will die.'

As Karamchand listened attentively, many territorial boundary markers flashed before his mind.

2

TERRITORIAL MARKERS

All over the world, the lines of white men's authority were marked. The skin of India was carved up between the Dutch, the French, the Portuguese and the English. They became owners of men, nature and minerals.

John's grandfather had sailed into the antiquity of Calcutta at the start of the Sepoy Mutiny. He meandered over the land, on the trail of wild animals and humans. Neither the rampant plague nor forbidding, difficult terrain hindered him. He criss-crossed this magical land.

He found territorial markers everywhere. He thought, much like the marks of the tiger's claws, the vermilion on women's foreheads were the stamps of arrogant male dominance and patriarchy. They were the impermeable and impregnable boundaries of the fortified caste system. Every journey of his corrected his impressions about the India of his imagination. His job was to shoot pictures of life all over India for the British government. That was the beginning of his fascination with tigers. The genes carried it through the generations. The pictures in John's laptop bore testimony to the power of this penchant.

The train entered Kollam Junction. Passengers who alighted from the slow train that had reached the next platform bulldozed their way into the Sampark Kranti's Unreserved coach. They were people from Tamil Nadu, fleeing to the north Indian metropolises. The women carried infants on their hips and the men, bundles on their heads. It was a demographic efflux from one end of the subcontinent that had been tipped up by the weight of people to the other end that had been tipped down by the weight of its riches.

The Sampark Kranti glided out of the station. Its TTE stood at the door. He resembled a white dwarf island—white shoes; sparkling white trousers; a stiff, spear-like necktie; a white peaked cap hiding his baldness.

Lying on the lower berth, John was lost in *India*. Karamchand's eyes were glued to the sights outside, keeping pace with them. The TTE entered their coupé. The badge pinned on his chest announced him as Louis Fulton Carvalho. John handed over his passport and the ticket. When he was checking Karamchand's ticket, Carvalho's face took on a look of superiority. The reason was that he viewed him as a freeloader who had received an upgrade from the Sleeper Class to First Class AC. Karamchand could recognise the look. He showed the TTE his Aadhaar card.

Government of India
Karamchand S/O Mohandas
Year of Birth: 1979
Male 3863 6538 8875
Aadhaar—A common man's right
Unique Identification Authority of India
Address:
C/O Mohandas, Nadavazhi, Karinthapuram,
Thiruvananthapuram, Kerala 695701

Karamchand placed his finger on the phrase, 'A common man's right', calling Carvalho's attention to it. A wordless communication took place between them.

'Sir, until which station are you on duty?' Karamchand asked.

'Till Chandigarh.'

'Ah, my reservation is till Chandigarh too, though I have not decided where to get off.'

'That's good. What's your occupation?'

'I'm a traveller. Journeying is my occupation.'

Carvalho gave him a long, searching look. In his long service in the Railways, he had seldom met someone who travelled solely for the sake of travelling. Men travel with some purpose, and to a predetermined destination. Although those who travel on vacations can be dubbed as travellers, throughout their journey, their words and thoughts revolve around their jobs. When he saw one of the very rare breed of genuine travellers, he felt happy. After checking the tickets, he left, closing the door behind him.

Karamchand was an itinerant. His pastime was losing himself in crowds and visiting historical places and removing himself from the present time. The ruins of the Babri Masjid in Ayodhya, the Muslim ghettoes of Gujarat, the sectarian trouble-spots of Assam, farmers' agitations, anti-reservation protests, localities of agitating Meenas and Gujjars in Rajasthan—few were the places that he had not visited. He was a traveller who had visually lapped up our times. Many are the readers who wait to read his travelogue.

Once, after accepting an award for the best travelogue, he wrote, 'I'm an itinerant seeker. My travels are not flights from my own home or a nostalgic retour. I travel to travel. An itinerant has his feet planted in at least two eras. In the present and in the past eras of the place he is in. In reality, a traveller who is in Kodungallur or Hampi simultaneously travels in parallel in another era. At the same time, a taxi driver or a shopkeeper of that place lives only in the present.'

In another post, Karamchand narrated the story behind his name:

I am Karamchand. Many ask me how I got this name that is quite uncommon for a Malayali. This post is to answer them.

This name is a memento of my grandfather catching a glimpse of Mahatma Gandhi in 1924. My grandfather had driven a bullock cart to Thampanoor to meet Gandhi who was on his way to Kanyakumari. A large crowd had already reached there, thronging the station. As he stood atop the bullock cart parked behind the crowd, Gandhiji appeared before him as a fleeting, quickly receding bald head. In his uncontained excitement, my grandfather leapt off the bullock cart. The spooked bullock set off at a wild run, occasionally looking back at my grandfather. Is he a bit unhinged? Just so, believed the animal. Possessing a remarkable sense of responsibility, it did not rest till it brought my grandfather to the gate of his house.

The euphoria of sighting Gandhiji never left my grandfather. The man who constantly sang *Raghupati Raghava Rajaram* was known—much like Frontier Gandhi and African Gandhi—as Rustic Gandhi. Bifurcating Gandhi's name, he gave his son, born to him many years later, the first part of the name. The second part that had been kept in reserve was given to me by that son of his. That was how I ended up as Karamchand.

Karamchand walked up to Carvalho's cabin. He was talking on the mobile. Karamchand scanned the names on the reservation chart that had been left face up on the seat. He was amused by the names that bore witness to the diversity of India. Every name was a piece of history. Karamchand's eyes widened.

'Behold, two people of different castes, who otherwise would not share a space, are seated next to each other.'

That made Carvalho laugh aloud. 'Not only that. Something that would be deemed indecent and illicit elsewhere is happening here. Two strangers attempting a woman-on-top sexual encounter with the young woman prone on the upper berth and the young man lying on his back in the middle berth.' As he spoke, he removed his peaked cap, revealing a shiny bald head that had even given up on the memories of the hair that had once adorned it. His pate had slight discolouration in some places and his face bore black spots.

His name was a memorial of the gene that had started its journey from Portugal. The sun's rays bouncing off the waters of the lagoon and shadows of the tall trees on the open plains sneaked into the coupé. Karamchand made a mental note: 'The colour of the skin is a souvenir gifted by the seed.'

3

JOHN

The month-long journey had exhausted John. Lugging his bag and cameras, he travelled between two valleys of the Western Ghats that lay at the border of Kerala and Tamil Nadu. Setting off from Yakshiamma Kovil in Nagercoil, he had walked through Thovala, past Aralvaimozhi and Pandipathiram to reach Kallar. A rogue tusker, Kolakolli, that had killed twelve men was on the loose. Giving up on his plans to go further north, John billeted in Kallar. There he ran into Lakshmikutty, a shaman from a tribe named Kani. The granny was the last link of the traditional forest curative regime passed down through multiple generations of her tribe.

During the days he lay in wait to take pictures of Kolakolli, Lakshmikutty narrated stories of the people of the forests of the south. 'You people of open lands have your king. We from the forests have our chieftain. My grandfather Mathan Kani ruled over all of this Ponmudi forest, as far as your eye can see.'

John showed Karamchand Lakshmikutty's photo on his laptop. A smile as natural as Mother Nature. Standing among the trees, she looked like a plant. John flipped through more photos. Put together, they showed the current condition of the Western Ghats.

Huge trees, vines, forest streams, wild flowers, birds. Next was a video of two emaciated men, swaying to and fro, singing chattu hymns in proto-Malayalam to the accompaniment of the kokkara, a metallic musical instrument of the Kani tribe.

Two blazing eyes among the vines and foliage. The long tusks visible only on close scrutiny. Kolakolli. The photo seemed to come alive. The bellowing trumpet made Karamchand tremble.

'How did you manage to shoot him from so close?' Karamchand asked.

'The lenses I have bring it close to me,' John said, laughing.

Stretched out on his berth with *India* lying on his chest, John spent most of the journey flat on his back. Wherever the train stopped, he opened the book to read up on the attractions of that place. What he could not find in there, he googled. He chose to sleep away his tiredness. In his waking hours he typed his travelogue on the laptop. He was amused by Karamchand's ways. John was observing him throughout the journey. He noted down his observations. Later, this profile was published in *The New York Times*.

4

KARAMCHAND'S HEAD

I write about a rather quaint man I met on my last trip to India. His name is Karamchand. He hails from Kerala. I was travelling between Thiruvananthapuram and New Delhi. We shared a coupé in the First Class AC coach of the Sampark Kranti Express. I was asleep most of the time. However, he was, all the time, walking up and down the train chatting up everyone.

On the second night of the journey, he startled awake and screamed, 'Nooo ... don't kill me ...' I was woken up by the scream, and in the dim light of the cabin, I saw him look sheepishly in my direction. From the beginning, I had this impression that he was a man weighed down by many secret sorrows. He opened the door silently and went out.

I was as much under his scrutiny as he was under mine. Two pairs of eyes watching each other. While I was observing him and the train, he was observing me, the train and the whole world.

He was an extraordinary man. I realised that his mind was a whole nation. People were being born, growing up, living and dying within him. For them, he started schools; factories; hospitals to treat them, to which he brought doctors from far-off lands. In his mind you could find rivers, lakes and roads. Boats were plying on the river; vehicles on the roads. The rivers ran into the sea; the roads into cities. His mind was noisy from the thrum of the cities.

His mind was home to a number of garment factories. He clothed every person in a different attire. Many gods also lived in his mind. He built temples and shrines for them. Prayer meetings of many denominations and faiths took place; sometimes religions fought one another. Some religions gained dominance over others. Many gods and religions disappeared into oblivion.

His mind had many layers of time. History lay like striations upon them. In some places were black holes of ignorance. At times gruesome battles took place in them; fighter jets and intercontinental missiles screamed across them. When the battles peaked, he himself would arrange round-table conferences and sue for peace.

A primitive tribe would be busy in some corner of his mind, trying to discover fire.

People would fall in love and make love in his mind. His mind would tremble with moans of pleasure and giggling grunts. Lyricists would write, singers would sing, authors would write and readers read inside it. As a burglar fled with his loot, from another corner of the brain a policeman might appear. The searchlight he switched on would flood the brain with a blinding light.

He would divide his land into provinces and then he would stitch them back together again. At other times, a sudden tsunami would obliterate the land completely.

In a time-warp and a condensed globe, Gandhi, Socrates, Michelangelo and Genghis Khan may sometimes sit across the table and parley. Some men he gets killed off. He resurrects those who are killed. Some people he exiles. Some of the unluckier ones he forgets altogether.

As is the case with most of us, Karamchand too knows only the two generations that preceded him. Nevertheless, he keeps searching for his forebears in historical texts and libraries. He discovers them in the backstories of famous paintings. The thought that the man in front of him and he himself have sprung from the same primeval seed from times of indefinite antiquity and have been flung apart to travel through time turns him into a philanthrope. His intellect has told him that all the people in this world were, once upon a time, a single human being.

See, he is an itinerant. 'Social Science nomad' is a better description of him. He keeps travelling, carrying unconventional thoughts in his head.

To onlookers, he's merely a slim, slight, ordinary-looking man.

[As published in The New York Times *along with Karamchand's photograph]*

5

THE CHART

The Sampark Kranti Express had three TTEs, including Carvalho. While Karamchand was seated in Carvalho's cabin, the other two TTEs arrived.

Carvalho introduced one of them, a young man with curly, oily black hair. 'This is Elvindas. He takes care of coaches S1 to S4.' Elvindas smiled at Karamchand as he took off his jacket and tie and hung them on a wall-hook. He then leaned back against the berth and started to read a Tamil newspaper. Karamchand ran his eyes over the reservation chart of the Sleeper coaches. It was another gene pool of diversities. A mélange of no distinct design. No one had any form of ascendancy. A magic chart that seated eight possibly complete strangers facing one another. Men who may, despite travelling together for days, not speak a word to one another. And sometimes those who struck up strong friendships.

Reservation charts are reminders that there are more people one is not acquainted with than there are known to one. When Karamchand scanned through the chart, his eyes caught on one of them. A red-hot bullet pierced his heart as he read the name. He read it again:

Narendra Dabholkar   M73   MAQ-BRC

'When will we reach Mangalore?' Karamchand asked.

'Midnight,' Carvalho replied.

'Aiyyo! Midnight?' Karamchand felt a sense of dread. His palms started to sweat. 'Is the old man going to come alone in the cover of darkness when all lights are extinguished?' he asked himself.

He left the TTE's cabin.

John was asleep, clutching *India* to his chest. An oblong piece of bronzed sunshine was stuck on his yellow-tinted face. Karamchand desired to shoot the scene on his mobile phone. However, deeming it impolite to take a picture without John's permission, he desisted.

6

ENGINE

The train galloped over the land like a horse and skimmed over waterbodies like waterfowl. In the engine room that had turned muggy, looking into the distance at the signal, indistinct in the bright sunshine, Devadas, the loco pilot, called out to his assistant, 'Distant signal proceed.' His assistant echoed the instruction for reconfirmation, 'Distant signal proceed.' As the speedometer needle hovered above the 110 kmph mark, the engine room shuddered. Devadas was intoxicated by the thrill of speed. When the needle touched 120 kmph, his assistant reminded Devadas, 'Sir, the section speed is only 105.' Devadas caressed the brake lever with his finger. The graphite brake blocks jammed against the circumference of hundreds of screeching steel wheels. The needle stayed steady at 105 kmph.

A contented Devadas hummed a tune. In keeping with the speed of the train, the tune touched high and low pitches unimagined by its music director. The green of the distant signal was now clearly visible. Rattling over a small girder bridge, the engine sped past the distant signal. It went past the home signal and a station at increasing speed. The aged station-master, turned hoary and grey-haired by solitude, stood on the platform listlessly holding the green flag. Raising his own green flag, Devadas saluted him. From the brake van, the guard too waved the green flag. On the guarantee provided by the reassurances exchanged between the three men, the train sped along.

Every Friday, Devadas was the loco pilot and the grey-haired old man was the station-master. Although they had never met, they were acquainted. A train runs thanks to an extraordinary acquaintance between thousands of strangers.

A movement in the distance between the shimmering, gleaming rail tracks caught Devadas's eye. He alerted his assistant. A figure was walking down the middle of the tracks towards them. He kept his hand pressed on the air horn. The two blasts split the air but the figure, a woman, did not step aside.

'Close your eyes,' Devadas told his assistant. By then, the train had reached her. As she stood with worshipfully folded hands, Devadas and she watched each other. At the instant of the collision, their eyes locked on each other's. Her head was covered with a black dupatta. In the next moment, she was transformed into shreds of flesh and fragments of bone as the wheels rolled over her corpse. Devadas exhaled deeply. One more life had been extinguished in front of his eyes.

The guard called on the walkie-talkie, 'Can you smell burnt flesh?'

'Oh yeah. Possibly a goat. A herd of goats was grazing on the tracks. One of them must have been run over.'

Laughter rang out from the walkie-talkie. 'Really? Was one of the goats wearing a churidar-kameez?'

Devadas spoke to the assistant, 'Open your eyes, man.' It was the assistant's first experience of a train running over a human. His bulging eyes were filled with bewilderment and fear.

Devadas's eyes had grown numb to the sight of such deaths. What he failed to understand was, when there were so many methods to kill oneself, why did people choose the only one where another human being was compelled to become a witness to their end.

Once a woman was cutting vegetables in the kitchen. The rice pot was on the boil. Suddenly she had the urge to commit suicide. She heard the train's whistle in the distance, as if stoking her desire and inviting her. The rail track was a few steps away from the edge of her yard. Seated in their living room, her husband was watching TV. She could not wait. Leaving behind the vegetables and the pot on the stove, she went out, hurried towards the rail tracks and stood in the middle.

Her husband went to meet the loco pilot of the train that killed her. He asked only one question, 'What was the expression on her face in that instant?'

'Her face was filled with an immense peace,' Devadas told him.

He then remembered one Vishu[2] day when he had to witness two deaths.

MEMORY ONE

It was a bright, clear day. He was the pilot of an empty goods train rake from Mettur Dam to Chennai port. Speeding through the gradients and downhills of the Sathyamangalam range of hills, the rake entered a ravine. Cattle grazing on the side of the tracks were spooked and ran. Unfazed by the train, some of the bulls continued to graze. Only one bull started to run ahead of the train. It was visible from the engine room, running with its tail held high. Its flight was a movie of desperation. At some point in its despair, it decided to take the oncoming train head-on. It stopped and swung around. For a single instant, Devadas's and the bull's eyes locked. Then came the sounds of splintering bones. However, those sounds were drowned by that of the thundering train.

It was a track that stretched for miles, glistening in the bright April sun. C and DK stations with droll names kept disappearing behind them. Bommidi. Moolakaraipatti. Buddireddipatti ... An obese man was walking lazily inside the down tracks. Suddenly he trotted across the tracks and stood in front of the speeding train with folded hands. Again, their eyes met for an instant.

When faced with death, both humans and animals have the same look in their eyes. At the moment of inevitable death, the eyes are filled with a helpless detachment. Devadas had seen the look in many pairs of eyes.

MEMORY TWO

One midnight a family—husband, wife and two small children—appeared in front of the train. The children were asleep on either shoulder of the father. The wife stood with her head resting against his chest. Devadas could not stop himself from crying out, 'Aiyyo! Aiyyo!' The man's deadpan face was burnt into his mind like a mural.

MEMORY THREE

A young man who pushed his lover onto the tracks and fled.

MEMORY FOUR

The vendor whose leg was caught under the rail while crossing the tracks, causing him to fall.

MEMORY FIVE

....

MEMORY SIX

....

Gradually, death ceased to shock him.

7

THE 'ZHA' SYLLABLE

The train stopped.

'What station is this?' John asked sleepily.

'Ambalapuzha.'

'Ambalapura.'

'It's *zha*. Not *ra, zha* ...'

'*ra ... ra ... zya ... zhya ... zha* ...' John managed to pronounce the syllable after a few tries. His tongue found it difficult to reproduce the phoneme *zha* found in *puzha* (river) and *mazha* (rain).

A long rake of oil tank wagons trundled by rhythmically on the next track. Karamchand sat by the window, looking at the tireless procession of steel boxes. Silence reigned in the coupé. The sights through the window had become monotonous. Trees with poisonous fruits swinging from them; hedges and copses; storks meditating on one leg in shrimp-farm ponds; men sitting on their haunches in front of their huts whiling away their time ... humans may have discovered meditation by watching storks. Storks in turn, by watching fish. Slipping into these reveries, Karamchand gradually fell asleep.

The train left Alappuzha Station behind. The lighthouse that warned seafarers disappeared behind the crowns of the tall coconut trees.

8

VENICE

'Alleppey,' declared John, opening the chapter on the city of Alappuzha in *India*.

'The Venice of the East,' Karamchand said. 'Holding on to the coattails of the monsoon winds that link two continents, the Arab dhows arrive, trailing the fragrance of attar.' Karamchand said, as if to himself.

The national highway ran parallel to the rail tracks. The felicity with which the roadside sellers of tender coconuts wielded their choppers amazed John. A tiny slip and they could hack off their own hands. When the chopper descended in an arc through the air, slices of coconut peel would fly off in another arc.

Possibly considering the tedium that a long journey may occasion, a conversation sprang up between the usually taciturn John and a sociable Karamchand.

'They returned, having filled these dhows with spices and slaves kidnapped from the coastal areas.'

'In the meanwhile, one day ...' John started to narrate, 'the Arab dhow loaded with dates, attar and horses capsized in the high seas and broke apart.'

Karamchand took up the narrative, 'From the capsized vessel, sailors and slaves were flung into the deep waters. A shiver of sharks swarmed around them. The men's screams dissolved in the salinity of the water.'

John continued, 'Clinging to wooden planks and their hopes, a few had started to swim. Caught in the strong currents, whirlpools and high winds, they also fell prey to the sharks.'

'However, the monsoon winds scooped up only one of them and mollycoddled him. The winds carried the plank to which he clung. The winds sang lullabies to him and brought him safely ashore.'

'Aha! He was a boy. On land, by the time he drank the first drop of water and reclaimed his life, he had forgotten that he was the son of a slave couple who had perished in the shipwreck. He had a destiny to fulfil.'

'He grew up. He had long limbs, a narrow neck and curly hair.'

'He who infused African blood into the gene pool of Alleppey had no history.'

As soon as he concluded, they both burst out laughing, sprang to their feet, and embraced each other. They continued to smile after they resumed their seats. Among the many insinuations that that smile bore was this one too: 'Oh boy, you are not what I thought you were.'

9

SLAVE

He had been washed ashore. The sun was merciless. In other words, the sun had no obligation to be merciful. Occasionally, a wave arrived and tickled his legs. The first one to see him was a girl who was waiting for her father to return from the sea. She ran up, mistaking him for a large beached fish. When she realised that it was a human child, she was unnerved.

'Appa,' she called out to her father. Having tethered his catamaran to a coconut palm, he was getting ready to head to their hut. The boy opened his mouth like a fledgling. The fisherman let a few drops of water fall into the open mouth. The moisture brought life back into the boy. The fisherman carried him into his hut.

His growth was rapid, in amazing spurts. He stood head and shoulders above his peers, making him instantly recognisable. His phallus grew faster than his body. An unbridled libertinism suffused his loins as they swung between his thighs. He was fascinated with the sea; like a turtle born on land, he crept towards the sea all the time. Driven by an unknown instinct, he spent all his waking hours trying to fashion a boat. Once, carving up a log of cotton tree that had washed up ashore, he made a toy boat. He climbed into it and rowed alone into the sea. At the age of sixteen, for all practical purposes, he was an adult. His name was eponymous with his colour—Kariman.

Once, a sailing ship with a group of Saurashtrian traders headed for Ceylon berthed in the harbour. Among them were a few Buddhist monks on a pilgrimage to the Shri Pada mountain. A monk walking along the wharf asked Kariman, 'Where can we find the Ebony kid?' The well-hung Kariman was walking back from the beach, hauling along his dangling organ. He directed the monks to a field, 'I heard he's somewhere in there.' The monks wandered all over the fields but could not find the Ebony kid. However, a mantra that had been suffusing the atmosphere for centuries flowed out from the fields. It rose and spread as an aria from the compacted swamp, and the monks, standing around the swamp, chanted the mantra in a chorus: 'Buddham saranam gachchami ...'

On the way back, the monks gifted Kariman with a loincloth. Twisting it thrice around his waist, he wore it to swaddle his shame.

Around that time, a landlord from the hinterland, borne on a palanquin, turned up along with his family to enjoy the sea. Two boys were also in the entourage, carrying a mortar and pestle and other accoutrements for preparing paan. Kariman watched them with curiosity as they pounded the catechu, lime, betel nut and areca nut to prepare the paan. However, the boys paid him no attention. One of them held the mortar; the other pounded the ingredients together and offered the landlord the folded paan.

Seated on the palanquin, the landlord spat betel juice far into the distance. When he leaned out to accept the fresh paan, he noticed the tall, well-muscled Kariman striding beside the palanquin. Seeing his height and physique, the landlord realised that he was an excellent specimen. Were he to be unleashed in the fields, he could do the work of two oxen. A slave at par with two bulls. It was a marvellous bargain. He bought him from the fisherman for two chukrams.[3] In honour of his magnificent physique, the landlord named him Onnara, meaning 'greater than one'.

The lands he owned stretched far, with indeterminate boundaries. When he visited his fields, he took Kariman with him. 'He's an outsider. There's no local blood in his veins so he won't pollute.' Free of the stigma of being a polluting low-caste man, Kariman enjoyed unfettered access to the landlord's manor.

While walking among the fields, the landlord would sometimes give him strange looks. Only the caretaker understood the import of those stares. Sometimes the caretaker would also look strangely at Kariman. But Kariman was unaffected by such behaviour. He walked one hundred paces ahead of the landlord and the bellows in his stentorian voice made the polluting castes move out of the way with alacrity. On the sly, he liberally deposited the seed bearing his African genes into the begging bowls of lustful women in the landlord's manor.

The monsoon roared in fury. The water level in the lagoon rose and overflowed. In the night, the mud levee around the fields collapsed in one place. Kariman and the caretaker ran to the fields. The landlord followed at a more sedate pace on his palanquin. Standing on the ridge near the breach in the levee, the landlord gestured to the caretaker who carried a round wooden club. There were no logs available nearby to fill the breach and stanch the flow with. The landlord winked at the caretaker—let Kariman's seven-foot frame fill the breach. All that was needed was a whack on the back of his head followed by a few kicks, and the breach would be filled.

After that, everything happened in a flash. Kariman lifted up the landlord along with the palanquin and smashed everything down into the breach. The landlord's potbelly dammed the surging water. Before he could think that a Pulaya[4] would not have done this, the caretaker found himself flung down atop his landlord. Mud was shovelled over them both and the breach was truly sealed. When the landlord's henchmen came running, Kariman screamed at them, 'I'm not your Pulaya slave.'

What followed was a dead run. He galloped in the direction of the roaring sea and soon reached the seashore. His legs still had the power to continue. The night was still young. He saw the light from a big lantern moving in the outer sea. Gradually he could make out the shape of a sailing ship. Jumping into a catamaran he found on the beach, he launched himself into the sea and started to row. In the pitch darkness brought on by the storm, no one saw him leave. The ship was making slow progress towards the North. He reached it and started to row alongside it. Neither the cold wind, the roiling sea, nor his own blazing hunger fazed him. He kept rowing till dawn broke.

The sun came out. It was an Arab dhow. The sailor keeping watch on the deck saw Kariman rowing the catamaran. He informed the captain and, together, they hauled him up using hawsers.

'What's your name?' the Arab captain asked.

'Kariman.'

'From now on your name is Kareem,' said a sailor with a beard.

'Aiyyo! My name is all I have.'

'A slave with a name?' the sailors laughed. They were slaves who answered to only numbers or to monosyllabic grunts. In a single instant, Kariman lost the name that was his own.

'Umm ...' he grunted deferentially. He started his life at sea as a slave in one of the dingy cabins of the dhow that had stacks of crocks filled with black pepper, redolent of the mountains on the east. His station in life nosedived from being a landlord's productive resource to one with the utility of a mere beast of burden.

10

THE BIRTH

When he heard some passengers bustling down the passage, Karamchand emerged from the cabin. The TTE followed the passengers into the Sleeper compartments. Karamchand trailed them. A small crowd had gathered near the vestibule between the First Class AC coach and the S1 coach. The toilet door was open. A woman lying inside the toilet, naked from the waist down, was the exhibit.

Karamchand took only a glance. The blood oozing between her thighs had seeped down making a red sketch on the steel commode that had turned yellow from the shit that had passed through it. Carvalho was describing the scene on the phone to someone. The woman's moans rose and fell like background music. Someone tried to reach up to pull the emergency alarm chain. A forbidding look from Carvalho was enough to make them stand down.

With nothing to do, time stood still inside the speeding train. The spectators near the toilet turned static, like subjects in a mural. 'Give way.' An elderly lady appeared from inside the coach and pushed her way through the immobile onlookers.

The mural sprang to life. It turned into a talkie. The men hungrily switched on their phone cameras. Without taking anyone's permission, the elderly lady entered the toilet.

'Sir, I had come to pee when I heard the cries from inside the toilet. I knocked a few times. At first I thought someone was humping inside. That's not unheard of these days, no?' A middle-aged man was explaining to the TTE. 'When whoever was inside didn't open the door, I got these people. Together we kicked open the door.'

'It wasn't easy breaking down the door,' a man joined in. 'What did we see? She was sprawled on the floor, her legs spread wide. Like a felled tree.' His exaggerated gestures made the crowd laugh.

The woman massaged the woman's lower belly vigorously. 'Give me some water,' called out the woman who must have been a mid-wife sometime in her life. Someone handed over a bottle of water. A bloodied sac suddenly popped out from the bulging belly of the woman and dropped. The men closed their eyes and turned their faces away. The woman shrieked in pain.

The sac slid over the slippery commode and slipped down its hole onto the tracks. It was the placenta, the life-twin of the embryo it had nourished. Having served its purpose of life, it was returning to mother earth. A range of emotions flitted over the crowds' faces. Those whose curiosity had been quenched slowly drifted away.

'She's a gypsy. Usually as soon as it's born, they strangle the baby,' said the matron, emerging from the toilet and washing her hands at the washbasin. Carvalho was busy making arrangements to deboard the new mother at the next station.

At that instant a question was born in Karamchand's mind. 'Where's the foetus that led the way for the placenta?'

That little specimen of life—which was alive for only a moment on this earth—shifted its domicile to Karamchand's mind. Cuddling it, Karamchand returned to his coupé.

11

THE BABY WITH NO HISTORY

Weakly pulsating with life in the blazing sun, a tiny specimen of the human species was lying on the tracks. The blood on it had not dried; it glistened in the sun. The odour of tender blood attracted a stray dog. The dog circled the piece of meat. It sniffed and nuzzled the form. It licked the still wet blood. Having tasted human blood, the dog lifted its head, looked at the sky and barked. Pleased, it howled.

'Shoo ... dog, shoo ...' a feebly thrown stone bounced near the dog. Just as it was going to sink its teeth into the flesh, another stone fell smack on its back. Startled, the dog ran into the bushes by the side of the tracks. Holding a sickle in her hand, an old crone came running. When she saw it was a human baby on the tracks, she broke down.

'What is this that I'm seeing? Whose wages of sin is this?' The baby's body was still warm. By some miracle, a scintilla of life which could have been snuffed out at any moment, was still pulsating in the frail body. The old woman scooped up that slimy form from the tracks. Two bloodshot, ravenous eyes were watching the baby hungrily from the bushes.

The old woman carried the baby to her hut. She laid him down on a grass mat. Dipping a cloth in cool water, she sponged him clean. She tickled his tiny willie. She fed him a few drops of life-sustaining warm water. Life that refused to wither in the harshest circumstances started to throb again. He started to cry. His lips sought her shrivelled breasts. The spring that had gone dry ages ago showed signs of moistening. She milked the goat and brought in the milk. She let the drops of milk drip onto his lips. He smiled, displaying pale gums. She laughed with him.

He started to grow inside Karamchand as one with no lineage or history. With no baggage of religion, caste, denomination or genealogy. Karamchand searched for the baby on Facebook and on WhatsApp. Had anyone posted a picture of a newborn torn to shreds by stray dogs? Had anyone written a maudlin feature about some old woman finding a newborn and caring for him?

His selfie posted on Facebook had crossed 1,000 likes. Karamchand went to the door and stood there. The Sampark Kranti sped over the mangrove thickets, fracturing their tranquillity. Its roar alarmed the black-bellied whistling ducks and they flew up in droves. Crownless after being entombed in the floods of 2018, trees sped past and disappeared from view like bizarre installations. Karamchand saw the shipyard crane loom above the treetops like another bird.

As the train approached Ernakulam Junction, it started to slow down. Standing at the door, Karamchand gazed towards the west. He watched the choppy Arabian Sea as it heaved and rolled beyond the tall apartment buildings and factories.

The sailing ship that Kariman had boarded too had reached Kochi. Buffeted by high waves, pitching and rolling in the open seas, the dhow turned towards the shore. It had to take on black pepper from the warehouses. On the dhow's crude crow's nest atop the main mast, which was nothing more than a crucifix, Kariman stood watch. He had tied himself to the swaying mast. Here and there a few fishermen's skiffs and catamarans could be seen. Broken tree trunks and branches that rivers had discharged into the sea were floating around.

Kariman saw another sailing vessel approaching theirs. When it was close enough, he could see a shiny crucifix on top of its mast; when it drew closer, the mouth of the cannons; and eventually the flag bearing the pirate's flag with skull and bones. He recognised the threat the vessel posed. In a moment, battle-ready Arab sailors were arrayed on the deck, swords and spears in hand.

No battle ensued. It was a Portuguese caravel captained by a man called Almeida. His name was enough to make boats and skiffs in the Arabian Sea tremble with fear. One of the cannons spat fire. A cannonball shot through the dhow. As the sailors in the dhow surrendered without a fight, the Portuguese soldiers swarmed over them. The captain and the sailors were decapitated and thrown into the sea. Having smelled blood in the water, sharks made a beeline for the dhow. After chomping through human heads and torsos, they kept circling the dhow. Sensing the possibility of more corpses falling off it, they swam along Almeida's vessel like a parallel force. Flames shot up from the dhow and turned into a ball of fire.

Tied to the main mast, Kariman was the only survivor. A soldier pointed his arquebus as Kariman fixed him with a fearless, level stare.

Almeida stopped the soldier. 'He is not an Arab. He's a slave. Get him down.'

The soldiers brought him down and transferred him to the caravel as a captive, along with the cargo of the dhow. The six-and-a-half foot young man was transformed into a porter.

When the caravel set sail again, Almeida impaled and tied the burnt body of an Arab to the prow of his ship. With horrific eyes that bulged in the throes of death, the corpse continued to scare seafarers for a long time.

12

LOUIS FULTON CARVALHO

I am Louis Fulton Carvalho. My name commemorates the Portuguese incursion into India. Part of the roots of my name stretch back into Europe. I am the captain of the Sampark Kranti Express. A job in the Railways was a tradition in my family. My papa was an engine driver. I have photos of him taken in the open cabins of formidable steam engine behemoths. He was a titan. And handsome.

We are part of the history of Indian Railways. They started to hire Eurasians in larger numbers after the Sepoy Mutiny of 1857. My great-grandfather became a Railway employee following this. Till India won Independence, for the so-called Anglo-Indians—though many of us have less Anglo-Saxon and more Latin blood in us—the Railways was a traditional employer. The way a carpenter's son becomes a carpenter.

My great-grandfather used to drive the Boat Mail Express, one of the more important trains in India at the time. Traversing a route unimaginable in the India of today, it connected Madras to Colombo in Ceylon. The Pamban Bridge across the sea between the mainland and Dhanushkodi was an adventure in those days.

The journey from Dhanushkodi to Talaimannar was completed aboard a steamer. From Talaimannar to Colombo, it was by train again. When Dhanushkodi was destroyed in the 1964 cyclone and the Pamban Bridge went down, the legendary Boat Mail and its journey came to a hault.

The Eurasians had a strong connection to the Railways. The first person to be sentenced to death for a Railway crime in India was Morris, an Anglo-Indian.

It was the first murder on a train. In 1921, Morris received the death sentence for the murder of a Railway pay-clerk and peon at Manmad in the First Class compartment and for robbing the Rs 32,000 they were carrying from Bombay. His accomplice, Donnison, a British citizen, received a life sentence. If it comes to that, there is so much history that I can narrate.

All my brothers and sisters have migrated to Australia. So have my wife and children. I alone chose to stay back. I decided that I don't need a life minus the delectable toddy, the pearl spot fish from Ashtamudi lake, the boiled tapioca and roast beef seasoned with black pepper.

An old steam locomotive is attached to this train. My papa used to take care of it like he would care for his own child. He was an expert on steam locomotives and knew, by rote, their history till Antim Sitara, the last one to roll out in 1970.

On some days, he would take me along into the cabin. He used to cook many kilos of mutton in the scalding steam of the locomotive. He and the firemen would polish it off in one sitting along with the fresh, unfermented toddy they procured along the way. The taste of mutton those days was something else.

The locomotive was named the Wanderer. My mummy's own translation for that in Malayalam was 'the nomad'. The name fitted the running staff of the Railways. Before it became part of the South Indian Peninsular Railway, the Wanderer was in the private collection of the Rajah of Mysore. Those days, my grandfather was its driver. Once, on the Dudh Sagar section between the Castle

Rock and Kulem stations, it nearly derailed. The Dudh Sagar Falls was roaring down its 100-feet drop. When my grandpa looked, the bogie behind the engine seemed to be sliding off the rails. The train shuddered. My grandpa was tremendously gutsy. He managed to haul the rake over and beyond the bridge.

As soon as the train stopped, someone leapt out of the saloon car and dashed towards the engine. Who was it? None less than Chamarajendra Wodeyar, the Maharajah of Mysore. To this day, I have kept safely the gold medallion he awarded my grandpa that day.

I have been doing this job now for twenty-five years. Every journey on duty brings some incident to keep in memory. I don't have a habit of logging them. What we forget doesn't belong to us. What we need gets stored in our memory without conscious thought. This morning, just as the train was about to leave, I saw a lady running to catch the train. To be honest, the sight of her bustling body parts bobbing up and down made me laugh. All the fat she had consumed in her thirty-plus years was threatening to burst through her salwar-kameez. By the time she reached my bogie, the train had started to roll. I managed to somehow pull her onto the train.

There were no vacant seats in the AC coaches. I asked Elvindas to accommodate her in the S1 coach. Her name is Sameera Fathima. I spoke to her for a little while. She lives in Dubai with her family. While on vacation in her ancestral house in Kodungallur, she had joined a one-month yoga course near the Neyyar Dam. She was returning after discontinuing the course for some reason.

Every day, we interact with many people, all sorts of people. If you take an average of three hundred passengers a day, at a hundred thousand people a year, I would have stood face to face with two-and-a-half million people. You may consider that I have enough experience to gauge the character of a person just from reading their name on the reservation chart.

Malayalis are generally the stay-at-home type; people who celebrate bandhs and hartals. Once they board a train, they discuss politics, mock others and generally express disgruntlement and irritation. These days, religion has entered the fray; discussions mix religion and politics and turn into an omnium gatherum. Men who travel with families look as if they are war commanders. These are a few of my observations.

There are many things that can be discussed. But we have just started the journey. So many people are yet to join. So many incidents are waiting to happen. We shall wait and watch.

Till then, goodbye for the nonce.

13

S1 COACH

Ernakulam Junction.

Watching the train roll in, the throng of passengers on platform no. 1 stood silently to the side. The sight reminded one of a flock of birds, all with their heads turned in one direction. The rate of breathing would go up; from a primordial flight response, the blood circulation in their legs would shoot up; even if they were seasoned travellers, doubts would creep into their minds; out of an unknown anxiety, their eyes would flutter; they would see their co-passengers in their imagination; they would hold mental conversations, perhaps even debate; threats such as 'You don't know me. I'll finish you,' might emanate; men would fantasise about women; women would dream of men; at such times, they would don the mask of respectability and smile genially.

Karamchand and John stood at the door and watched the crowd. Passengers and their helpers were running up and down, dragging their baggage. Some of them ran into one another. Even though they had met one another only moments ago, they entered into arguments. A porter arrived in front of their coach, A1, dragging a trolley filled with suitcases and bags. An old lady, about eighty years old, was seated atop the luggage like an inanimate object. After getting off the trolley, the white-haired, bespectacled, aquiline-nosed lady dressed in all white stood haggling with the porter about his porterage.

She entered the coach and installed herself on seat no. 9. She chained the suitcases and bags the porter brought in to the seat legs. After that, she pushed up the spectacles she was wearing for cosmetic reasons and surveyed everyone around her and wondered, 'Where are all these people scurrying to? Why don't they stay home? On the way, if this train has an accident, won't all of them die?' She then looked at her watch and muttered, 'Umm ... already it's three minutes late. Indian Railways will never run on time. It never used to be like this before we won Independence. My father used to say that there was even a saying in those days that a Rolex watch may miss the hour, but the Frontier Mail, never. Ah, but then, the white men ran things at the time.'

The reservation chart in Carvalho's custody showed her name as Devika Rani and her destination as New Delhi. Diverse passengers of diverse complexions, languages and styles of dressing clambered aboard and found their places.

A group of university students boarded the S1 coach.

The train started to move. Those who had come to see off passengers started to trudge back. With the entry of university students, the S1 coach had its full quota of passengers. The silent and lifeless coach suddenly sprang to life. It turned boisterous like a festival ground.

Karamchand sat down on seat no. 7 in the S1 coach, the seat allotted temporarily by Carvalho to Sameera. While watching the students, bursting with youth, Karamchand thought of his own youth that was vanishing at lightning speed. An unexpected flutter ran through his heart.

Who isn't shocked by ageing? Leaving behind the youth who was thrilled by the prospect of challenging everything, he was entering the torpidity of middle age that sought harmony over everything else. Brightly dressed young people who face the world with positivity were in front of him. Faces that shone with the verdancy of life. Intellects in which progressive outlooks took shape. Throbbing voices; uncontaminated blood. Happiness reflected on every face. Carefree chatter and loud ringtones brought a new youthfulness to the bogie. Split into small groups, they used steel utensils and the walls of the bogie as drums and sang: 'The universe throbs with youth ...'

Their leader had an unruly head of hair. He tapped a heady rhythm with his right hand on the damru held high in his left hand, and his companions accompanied him on their improvised drums.

With their music, they heralded the way for the Sampark Kranti Express.

14

SAMEERA FATHIMA

Following the twists and turns in the rail tracks, the sun kept entering and exiting the bogie through the window and painting curly patterns on Sameera's face. She had been dialling her phone continuously. Every time she dialled, her eyes would widen with anticipation, and when there was no response, they would narrow again. Seated across her, Karamchand watched this happen time and again.

The train rattled as it entered Aluva Bridge. The Periyar river coming down the mountains flowed gently under it. Although increasingly hemmed in and throttled by the apartment buildings that encroached its banks, its flow was steady. Sameera dialled again. When there was no response again, she was furious. She smacked the window bars with her closed fist, saying, 'Shit!' All at once the train shuddered. In an instant, her iPhone slipped out in-between the window bars and plopped into the Periyar. The river invaded her privacy.

The sunshine that until now had brightened her face disappeared. It now reflected the agony of losing a limb. The river had swallowed the private moments that would show up on the phone screen at the touch of her finger in a pictorial language. She looked helplessly at Karamchand. He instinctively offered her his phone. With that in hand, she started to trawl the depths of her memories. However, no number showed up. She could not recall anyone's telephone numbers.

'I never had the need to keep anyone's numbers in my memory,' she said. 'When we lose a phone, if we are not careful, we also lose a number of people from our lives forever.'

'Where are you headed?' Karamchand asked. When he spoke, he always wore a natural, attractive smile.

'Mumbai. My brother lives there. I haven't met him in two years.'

'Have you been trying to reach your brother?'

'No, my husband. I've been trying him for two days. Whenever I called his office, I was told he was outside.'

The noise inside the coach reached its zenith after the train passed the bridge. Elvindas, the black-jacketed TTE who resembled Yama, appeared at the end of the coach. As he passed it, each bay of the compartment fell silent, even though he spoke to no one. With the reservation chart in hand, he sat down on seat no. 1.

The leader of the students approached him with their tickets. He compared them with the details on the chart. All the while he was mechanically marking the chart, his eyes were searching the leader's face. Karamchand thought that he would be able to catch the tiniest of transgressions. The silence brought on by the arrival of the TTE did not last long. The sounds that started from different corners grew louder and became a din.

'Karamchand, what do you do?' Sameera asked.

'I'm a traveller.'

'Which means you must be writing blogs and all that?'

'Ah, yes, a few.'

'That's good. Interesting for people like me who like to travel. Do you have a lot of fans?'

'Novelists and poets have fans. Who cares for travel writers?'

'Then do one thing, give me one of your articles to read.'

'I have no printed articles with me. I would have sent you a link but you do not have a phone.'

'Open it on your phone and show me. Show me a short one. It's been some time since I've read anything in Malayalam.'

Karamchand opened a travelogue he had written years ago. It was on his experience of staying in a lodge in Tirupati the day N.T. Rama Rao died.

Ramulu
18 January 1996

We came to know of N.T. Rama Rao's demise when the Kerala Express reached the Tirupati Station. As if protesting to Yama for stealing away their dear leader, the temple city lay still and cold. Dravidians, habituated to approaching everything emotionally, had unleashed their sorrow as riots. The sounds of vehicles' windscreens being broken could be heard from outside, followed by yelling and screaming. My friend and I remained on the platform.

In those days, news did not travel as fast as it does now. There were no gadgets that brought the world to you at the swipe of a finger.

We were travelling in the unreserved compartment. In those days, when no one felt compelled to update their status or respond to anyone, travellers would converse with others, get mutually introduced, and even share food.

We had, via hushed, indistinct whispers, heard that something had happened in Andhra Pradesh. The silence of the deserted smaller stations we passed through seemed to bear it out. Only a few passengers boarded the train at the way stations. By the time we passed the Tamil Nadu border, the train was half empty. Belying our youth, the two of us, twenty-something young men, killed time talking to other passengers with considerable verve. That small general compartment was a small cross-section of India. People who spoke many different languages sat together in it.

Wondering what to do next and where to go, as we stood on the platform in Tirupati, there appeared a smiling face in front of us. A young Telugu man we had met on the train was extending his hand in help.

He took us along many twisting, labyrinthine lanes. Our walk ended in the centre of the maze at the doors of a dilapidated double-storey lodge. He knocked on the door. A scrawny man opened it. Our guide handed us over to him with instructions to ensure our safety. Before he left, on a piece of paper, he drew a few squiggly, scrawly lines, one end of which was the bus terminal and the other the railway station. 'Follow this; this is the city map.' He said his goodbyes and left.

Buses were expected to start plying only in the evening. Till then we were effectively confined to the lodge. In that claustrophobic room of a cramped lodge, we sat on the musty bed covered with a threadbare sheet that smelled of stale sweat. We were the only two residents. The stick figure appeared in the corridor, carrying a pot of water.

'Where's the owner of this lodge?'

'Sir has gone for the mourners' procession,' he said. Things fell silent again; not really, sounds of some vehicle's windscreen being smashed could be heard.

Pointing to the road, the stick figure called out to us, 'Look there, you see that fat guy with an iron rod smashing the windscreens and windows? That's our owner. He's a gentle soul.'

Our callow hearts were in our throats. Before we could say anything, he took the pot and went down the stairs. When he climbed back up carrying the pot filled with water, the pictures that privation was painting on his exposed ribs surreally twisted and coiled. A personification of poverty was in front of us. Mixing Hindi, Tamil, Malayalam and English we spoke to him in a hodgepodge language.

He told us his name: 'Ramulu.' He had pointed ears like a hare's. His bones jutted out, dominating whatever flesh he had. We realised that all the privation in Andhra Pradesh was resident in his body. From him, we managed to learn how to say 'I love you' in Telugu, and some abuses and swear words to try on our friends back home. He hailed from Warangal in the north-east of Telangana. Only his mother and a younger sister remained, living on arid land still lorded over by zamindars who owned stretches of land on which only nettles grew.

My friend asked him, 'Who takes care of your mother and sister?'

'The Naxalites.' When he said that, his face showed unshakeable faith.

Ramulu turned up in the afternoon. 'Sir, do you need meals?' We looked at each other, famished.

'No.' We decided that we would go out and eat.

'Sir, you may be attacked.'

Let it happen. He's trying to earn some commission at our cost. Let him not think that he can swindle us so easily, we told ourselves.

'Sir, it costs just twenty rupees. The meals are tasty.'

In the end, we allowed ourselves to be persuaded. We paid him fifty rupees. He picked up a tall, four- or five-tier lunch box and went out. He arrived just as we were beginning to muse that the lunch would cost only ten rupees each and he would pocket the rest of the money.

He served us rice and sambar in two round bowls. We gobbled down the food along with rasam, pickle and yoghurt. Ramulu stood by, looking at us wolfing it down. We bore a grudge that he had swindled us and were determined to get as much of our money's worth as possible and leave not even a grain behind. He stood still, watching us wide-eyed. Eventually, we rose defeated, leaving behind some rice and sambar. When we wanted to throw the leftovers into the garbage bin, Ramulu stopped us.

We then witnessed something we had never seen before. He sat down on the floor in the lotus position. He put all the remaining rice, sambar, pickle and yoghurt on my plate, and mixed and kneaded them well. Then, as we watched curiously, rolling them into spherical morsels, he started to eat greedily. We watched, heartbroken. We could sense on his tongue the ravenous hunger of a wild animal that had been starving for ages. Tears were spilling from his eyes as each morsel went down.

After wiping the plate clean and licking his fingers, he rose to his feet. Then he gave us a look. Never in my life have I seen a look so full of pathos and gratification.

He picked up the vessels and went out. We sat there stunned and numb. Suddenly he returned and, pulling a ten-rupee note out of his trouser pocket, said, 'Sorry, sir, I forgot to give this back.'

By evening, buses started to ply and the city came alive. We followed the map and reached the bus terminal, and then boarded the bus to Tirumala.

As the bus climbed to the top, a cold breeze started to blow. Tyres squealing as it went around the curves, the bus was headed to the abode of the great god, the guardian of treasuries and the dispenser of prosperity. I looked down through the window at the city where the richest god had planted his feet. Our heads remained bowed.

After she had finished reading the piece, Sameera kept looking at Karamchand's face for a long time.

'Honestly, I feel a lot of respect for your point of view,' she said. 'And, therefore, I feel close to you. Don't misunderstand me. That's the power of words.' Karamchand nodded. Aided by their love for words, two strangers were drawing close.

'I'm not accustomed to this kind of heat,' Sameera said, showing discomfort. 'Shall we peep into the AC compartment?'

'Try that Anglo-Indian conductor. As far as I could make out, he seems to be an okay sort of chap.'

After completing the checking, when Elvindas stood up to go to the next coach, a young man approached him and said, 'Sir, my wife and I have been allotted berths in different coaches. If we could be given nearby berths, it would be a great help.'

Elvindas ran through the chart. 'Is Nimesha Mehta your wife?'

'Yes, sir.'

'So you both boarded from Varkala?'

'Yes, sir.'

By then his wife too arrived. They were matched like two halves of the same body.

'We've been married only for a month, sir,' Nimesha said.

'Your neighbour on berth no. 17 will be boarding from Kannur. Why don't you request him?'

'What time will we reach Kannur, sir?'

'It'll be night.'

'Please, can you also have a word with him?' Nimesha implored.

'I shall try.' He read the name from the chart, 'Kuriakose, M, 54.'

Nimesha and her husband were Parsis who had relatives on either side of the Indo-Pakistan border in Gujarat. They had chosen Kerala for their honeymoon. When they boarded the train at Varkala, after traipsing through Kovalam, Kumarakom and Munnar, Kerala had stamped itself forever on their hearts through tiny, inconsequential experiences, cool breeze, witticisms and fun times.

'Sir, is someone called Dabholkar boarding your coach?' asked Karamchand when Elvindas started to leave.

'Why?'

'Nothing. I wonder if he is the man I personally know. I saw the name in one of the reservation charts.'

'No. He could be in one of the coaches behind us,' Elvindas said, flipping through the charts. He walked to the next coach.

Sameera stood up. 'I'm going to meet the TTE of the AC coach. I can't stand this heat.' She started to walk. Karamchand accompanied her.

The sound of snoring could be heard from inside C coupé. Carvalho was sleeping sitting up. The snores rose and sank in high and low notes like the growl of an irate wild beast. The ringtone of the phone stuck into the pocket of his jacket hanging on the wall hook woke him up with a start. He ignored the slow-burning Tamil song coming from the phone. He looked quizzically at Sameera and

Karamchand, who were standing in front of him. When, with the irritation of being woken up by his phone evident on his face, he got ready to hear their case, the mobile phone rang again.

Two gave you life
Four carried you here and dumped you

The lyrics of the song that served as his ringtone were so unlike the man. Before the lines played out fully, he throttled it by squeezing its neck. It became silent.

'Sir, I can't stand this heat. Please give me a berth in the AC coach. I'm prepared to pay extra,' she spoke breathlessly.

'For the time being, you go sit on seat no. 5 in the A1 coach.' Sameera thanked him. She left for the A1 coach. Karamchand returned to his cabin. John was looking at photos on his laptop.

'Do you want to see?'

'Umm ... yeah.'

He turned the screen towards Karamchand. There were pictures of a family of tigers drinking at a forest stream: a mother and three cubs.

'They are marvellous creatures. My grandfather followed them all his life. He travelled alone in Kumaon, home to infamous man-eaters, and in the Sunderbans, home to white tigers. Far beyond what your Valmik Thapar and others can only dream of. Eventually, he reached where he was destined to reach. You've heard of Jim Corbett, haven't you? My grandfather joined the Railways to become his aide. Corbett was a fuel inspector, responsible for the purchase of coal. Corbett wrote *Man-Eaters of Kumaon* in my grandfather's presence. That was the origin of my passion for the Indian Railways and the Indian tiger.'

The next picture was that of an adult male. If the universe has bestowed all its magnificence on one beast, it is this one. The Tiger. That was how Karamchand felt when he saw the picture.

'Do you know its bite force? A full-grown tiger's? It's nearly twice that of a lion's.' Karamchand listened to John with keen interest. 'Do you know that tigers are territorial animals? Their boundaries are marked with territorial markers. If a tiger intrudes into that territory, it's either a fight to death or a quick retreat with the tail between its legs.' John was repeating himself.

15

A1

The tiger inside a human emerges when he is in total isolation or when he is part of a mob. On both occasions he ceases to be himself. A mob is an ogre-sized human. This was what Karamchand always thought whenever he observed people.

Even if a mob contains people with varied opinions, in the face of the brute strength of the majority, they become irrelevant. When he joins a mob, a man gains the courage to commit any act. He can play the hare and the hound at the same time. Great challenges are met and accomplished with ease. Laws are created at every turn and enforced. The mob is man's millennia-old, atavistic memory of life as herd animals.

The sun embraced the Sampark Kranti with its thousand torrid hands. The hooting, thundering train started to slow down and came to a halt at the platform. People crowded around the doors and created a melee. They became two groups—those struggling to disembark and those squeezing their way in. At the door of the General compartment, they scuffled.

John read the name of the station—Thrissur. He flipped through *India* and found Thrissur. He uttered a 'Wow' when he saw the photo of the arrayed caparisoned elephants and the sea of people encircling them.

As was his wont, Karamchand disembarked and stood on the platform. He saw some snowy orchids in bloom beyond the third rail track. They showed the vanity of being watered even in the summer. Possibly, some employee at the station was a nature lover. How else could they survive in a place where steel was, all the time, grazing against steel? Exhausted by the heat, sparrows and finches were perched on the orchid.

The A1 coach had attained middle-class snobbishness. Most of the passengers, cloaked by the curtains and ensconced in their private worlds, were largely silent. The only sounds were the occasional ringtones. With stiff smiles they drew boundaries to stymie any attempts from others to get acquainted. Watching them engrossed in English bestsellers, laptops or mp3 players, Karamchand felt they were a new life form separate from and unconnected to the human race. Man is what he is today due to his ability to form societies, converse and tell lies. An illustrator who has to draw the men of today shall have to draw them as part cyborgs.

Three berths of the fourth bay were occupied by a model family. Spoiling their temporary heaven, a young man boarded from Thrissur. Till then, the space, eight feet by six feet, had been their private property. The blue jacquard curtains had made them believe that it was their home. The young man's entry had, in one fell swoop, negated the pretence of space, private property and dominion.

From that time on, the father's eyebrows remained arched and the mother's face took on a permanent scowl. However, their daughter chose to keep the welcome smile she had presented him as a permanent adornment on her face. The father looked at the newcomer through the corner of his eyes. However, the young man with close-cropped hair paid them no attention and sat on his berth with his legs tucked under him. Soon, he started to read something on his Kindle. Occasionally he parted the curtains and enjoyed the view outside the window. He yawned when he felt bored. When his boredom increased, he stepped out and stood in the corridor or went to the door and hummed a song.

He went to the toilet and changed into a blue T-shirt and shorts from the full-sleeve shirt and trousers he had been wearing. As she lay on the upper berth and day dreamed, the girl felt the change in attire had given him a cute look. She threw him a sidelong, surreptitious glance. The young man also looked at her and, at some point in time, their eyes locked. On Carvalho's chart, the four of them were recorded as:

19. Mohanan Nair	M55	ERS-PNVL	413812401
20. Vasanthachandrika	F53	ERS-PNVL	413812401
21. Shaji	M29	TCR-BSR	4258446810
22. Anamika Nair	F25	ERS-PNVL	413812401

Karamchand was now seated beside Sameera. She continued to smack her head with a clenched fist and bite her nails. Karamchand asked nervously, 'I know I'm taking undue liberty. Yet, let me ask you: are you so agitated only because you lost the phone?'

'Yes,' she nodded.

'Let's try something. Give me the guy's name. Let me search for him on Facebook.' He took out his phone. The selfie had garnered 1,500 likes.

'Salim,' she said. Karamchand typed Salim in the search field. Salims of every type and shape appeared on the screen. When he was about to scroll through them, she spoke, 'Don't do it. I've been trying him for the last three days. He's not in the habit of checking FB and all that.'

The AC two-tier coach became chilled like an ice box. Condensation turned the glass windows opaque. The passengers' eyes started to droop. A few crawled under the white sheets given by the Railway staff. Sameera parted the curtains. Tumbling through the gap between the curtains, a slice of sunshine hit her kameez and lay enjoying its coolness. A tiny sliver of the sun. When Karamchand tried to close the curtains, she stopped him. 'No, let it be. Which sunlight doesn't wish for some chilly spot?' He laughed when she said that. His slim body shook with laughter. She found the naïveté of an adolescent in his laughter. She wondered how long it had been since she had laughed like that.

'I've forgotten the last time that I laughed this way,' she said. 'I have been hemmed in by ledgers. Among tables and cells, and in between figures that go wrong, one can't find laughter, Karamchand.' When he heard that, he laughed again, as if to make her envious. In the chill of the coach, the laughter resounded extraordinarily. Many passengers craned their necks to see the source of the jollity.

The old woman sleeping on berth no. 9 woke up. She parted the curtains in the corridor, stretched out her head to look at him and pondered, 'Why is he laughing so loudly? Can he laugh like this in public spaces? What is the relationship between this slim, rabbit-type man and this specimen of a conch woman? They do not appear to be husband and wife. He is a Hindu and she a Muslim. If he had to laugh out so loud, she must have said something very amusing. What could it be?' As if she had come to some conclusion, the Doubting Dowager withdrew her head behind the curtain, like a centenarian tortoise withdrawing into its shell.

'Sameera, I can hear rain pattering inside you,' Karamchand said. He was opening a guileless path to friendship.

'Aww, it's nothing like that. I've been trying to reach someone for the last two days to tell him something. It's only the minor tension of not getting through to him. It's nothing, really.'

'If it's something that can be shared with a third person, would you like to tell me? I have always believed that there are no tensions that will not ease if you share them with someone.'

'Oh, it's not so very important.' She opened her small handbag that had been resting on her ample belly like a baby. She extricated a white plastic strip from within and offered it to Karamchand. He took it, turned it in his hands and looked uncomprehendingly at the two thin red lines on it.

'Do you understand?'

'No.'

'This is a pregnancy test kit. When two red lines appear, it means that you're pregnant.'

'I've very limited knowledge of such things. I haven't yet knocked up anyone.'

'Oh, it doesn't take much skill or knowledge. It's a two-minute job.'

'Possible. However, that's not the issue here. What's there to be tense about this?'

'If you ask, really nothing. We've been waiting for a baby for a long time.' She was silent for a while. Then she spoke in a low voice, 'This news should be told first to the person who's going to become a father. But see, instead, you are the first man to be told of this. How odd is that? You, whom I have never met before, are the first one to hear the most important news of my life.'

Karamchand felt a surge of paternal affection towards her. He wanted to place his finger under her chin, tip her head up and plant a kiss on the crown of her head. He looked at her lower belly. The piece of sunshine still lay there, drinking in the chill. It had remained there for a long time. Still originating from the same source, it stayed in the same spot like a round bindi. However, was it the same slice of sunlight as before? If not, where did that sunlight go? If you can't step into the same river twice, you can't have the same sunlight touch you twice.

He quickly drew the curtains. Having been orphaned without notice, the sunlight beat a hasty retreat. Unable to countenance the indulgent affection in his eyes, Sameera bowed her head. She quickly got to her feet and walked towards the door without looking back.

The train was now entering the bridge over the Bharathapuzha river. It started to sway more than usual. The river had little water and the dry river bed was deep down beneath the bridge. Every time he passed that way, Karamchand fancied that he could hear the war cries of the *chavers*[5] who died fighting the Samoothiri's troops. He imagined that he could hear the swords clashing, steel trying to cut steel. He relived in his mind the booming beats of war drums, the whinnying of horses, the smell of fresh blood. However, now he heard none of this. He had completely lost his head in a flash episode of romantic love.

Sameera emerged from the toilet as the train was slowing to a halt at Shoranur Junction. Unbounded affection still reflected in Karamchand's eyes. Carefully navigating away from what could have turned out to be an overly sentimental moment, Karamchand said, 'Do you know that the water you just made has fallen into a parched, thirsty Bharathapuzha?'

'Ha, ha, thanks to me, the river's span has increased by at least a foot,' Sameera said. The laughter eased the tension between them.

Karamchand got down and stood on the platform. John came to the door, *India* in hand. Carvalho and other TTEs were also standing on the platform. Some passengers had a word with them and walked off.

Shaji, the young man from the A1 coach, strolled on the platform talking on his mobile phone. Afterwards, standing in the shade of a small tree, he yawned. Entwining his arms above his head, he stretched them and twisted his body. The yawning spread among everyone present. They too stretched their arms and bent their torsos like cats.

On the platform, beside the pillars of the high voltage overhead lines, stood two pruned and trimmed pipal trees. One of them had been planted by Swami Vivekananda. Crows, storks and other migrating birds were perched on the trees, resting. Beneath the trees, a group of shabby-looking banjaras were camping. They were chattering and quarrelling in an unheard language.

The station reeked of bird droppings. John and Karamchand climbed up to the foot overbridge from where they could see the whole station. The electric locomotive had been decoupled. From Shoranur, diesel engines hauled the trains the rest of the way. The ancestral steam engine was at the rear end of the train, its tall chimney rising above it.

From the overbridge, John shot a picture of the headless Sampark Kranti. Many of the passengers on the platform were impatiently looking at their watches and cursing silently.

Who would trust a headless train?

16

ONION VADA

Guruji na naam ni ho, mala che dokma
Narayan naam ni ho, mala che dokma ...

The transformation of the B1 coach into a temple had been quick. A sixty-strong pilgrims' group of seventy-year-olds had turned it into a bhajan centre. Leaving no stone unturned to attain salvation, after covering all the holy places and sacred shrines of Hindus, they were on the return leg of their pilgrimage. Their faces were serene. Seated at the far end of the coach, a short man was singing the bhajans. His contemporaries, shaking their overripe, grey-haired heads, were taking up the chorus, keeping time with the train's rhythmic clickety-clack sounds.

Shreeman Narayan, Hari
Teri leela sabse nyaari, Hari

The middle-aged tour manager bustled around, asking after everyone's welfare and attending to their needs.

'Is anyone absent?' Carvalho asked, checking the tickets.

'Yes, there's one,' the manager said. 'Manik Chand.'

'What happened?'

'Ah, he died when we were in Rameswaram. We cremated him there. He couldn't have been more blessed, could he, sir?' Every sentence he said was reinforced with a 'Ram' at its end.

Travelling on the Gandhidham-Nagercoil Express, his group had reached Thiruvananthapuram a week earlier. After completing the darshan of the Anantha Padmanabhan temple, they had headed to Kanyakumari. They bathed in the Triveni, the confluence of the two seas and an ocean. Over the next few days they had worshipped at Madurai and washed away their sins at Rameswaram. After taking all the steps to become one with the Parabrahma and the precautions to avoid being reborn and having to go through life's miseries once more, although they passed by Palani, they did not go up the mountain. They reached Palghat, whence they took a train to Shoranur. There, after completing a full loop of the southern tip of the subcontinent, the senior citizens' group became one with the Sampark Kranti Express.

When the chants and the dispassionate faces joined together, the B1 coach took on a metaphysical hue. The spread of a delicious aroma that cut through the dense cooled air of the air-conditioned coach was as sudden as it was unexpected. When the aroma reached the antique noses of the occupants of the coach, they flared and tingled. The hoary heads that were swaying in a kind of frenzy stopped. The chants of Narayana broke off in the middle or trailed off. Eyes closed involuntarily as they tried to track down the source of the aroma using more olfactory senses than visual. The taste buds woke up and the salivary glands announced themselves, moistening the tongue. Forsaking Narayana halfway, the tongues started to drool.

A youthful vendor pushed open the glass-panelled door of the coach and entered, announcing, 'Onion vada ...' Without being self-conscious, he called out in tattered Malayalam, '*Ulli vadaaayy ...*' At the sight of the copper brown onion vadas stacked on his stainless-steel tray, a wave of intemperance washed over the coach. Many hands reached out towards the salver.

The lead singer seated at the end of the coach had an unreasonable and unwarranted fear—would the vadas be polished off before they reached him? He consoled himself: 'Nah! That's not likely to happen.' As the vendor made slow progress through the coach, his craving went up; as the vadas in the tray became fewer, his nervousness increased. What if he didn't receive any? Should he stroll down and meet the vendor halfway? Galvanised by such thoughts, he even got up from his seat. However, his legs, weakened by osteoporosis, could not have carried him so far. Tamping down his craving, he remained on his seat.

Eventually, the fateful moment arrived. The vendor reached him. There was only a single vada left on the tray. Cursing his luck, the man accepted the vada. The train jerked and shuddered. The vada fell from his frail fingers enfeebled by age. He looked piteously all around him. Others were busy sinking their teeth into vadas dipped in tomato sauce. His craving lay prostrate in the depths of despondency. Cloaking his rising dismay and fury, he enquired graciously, 'Son, when will you be back with more?'

In reply, he received a discourse: 'I won't be back, sir-ji. This is the last onion vada on this train. You know, the price of onions has gone through the roof. Even these few onions were procured on the black market because our boss-man is a big politician from Marathwada and has ties with the traders there.'

With his last hopes dashed, the elderly lead singer stomped angrily on the floor with his weak right leg. Bouncing off the steel floor of the bogie, that stomp had enough power to dart through the corpses of the emaciated farmers who had hanged themselves from the neem trees dotting the arid fields of Marathwada, encircle the onion lobby in Mumbai and shake even the seat of power in New Delhi.

The vada vendor exited the coach. Suddenly, from another corner of the coach, an old woman who had sprained her jaw eating too many vadas started off: '*Guruji na naam ni ho ...*'

As a reminder of the vicissitudes of an uncertain life, the vada still lay on the floor at the man's feet. He closed his eyes. His head started to sway with the movement of the train. He started to clap and sing the bhajan:

... mala che dokma
Narayan naam ni ho, mala che dokma ...

17

THE BOY WITH NO HISTORY

The baby was growing up rapidly in the inner recesses of Karamchand's mind. A dog was his companion. When Granny went to get fodder for the goat, the dog would stand watch over him. Granny fed him, kneading folklore, stories and songs into the white rice mixed with raw eggs from country hens. As he grew, so did Granny's hopes.

'When you grow up and become a big officer will you forget your granny?' the old lady, who had no one to depend on, would ask.

'When I grow up, I will buy a big, long train. I'll make you sit inside and take you everywhere.'

'The kingdoms of the Cheras, Pandyas, Kongus, Cholas, Andhra, Kalinga, Bengal, Assam,' Granny acquainted him with the geography of the east.

'Mulaibar; the famous Konkan; Vidarbha; Saurashtra; Uttarakhand; the land of the five rivers; Kashmir, the land of the gods, redolent with the smell of saffron flowers.' When the dog heard about these lands, he nuzzled the boy's legs. 'Ah, yes, I'll take you too.'

Hooting loudly, trains whizzed past their hut. He waved at the trains. Trains made up his dreamland.

The boy turned ten. The old woman took him to the nearby Shree Narayana Vilasam school to have him admitted.

'What's his name?' the headmaster asked. Only then did it strike her that he needed a name. She looked around. She noticed Gandhi's photograph that hung above the headmaster's head. She pointed to the photo.

'Gandhi or Mohandas or Karamchand?' the headmaster asked.

'As you please.'

'In that case, Karamchand.' He put the name down on the register.

'What's his caste?'

There was another photograph hanging above the headmaster's head. 'Whose photo is that, Granny?' the boy asked.

'He, son, is our guru. Narayana Guru,' Granny explained.

'He's a child whose caste is unknown. Sir, if you can put down his caste as human, then please do,' the old lady replied.

The headmaster looked at her suspiciously.

'You crone, when I ask you something, give me proper answers. Don't try to act too smart,' the PTA president who was present chided her. He was a Panchayat member too.

'His father's name?'

'I don't know.'

'His mother's name?'

'I don't know.'

'Family?'

'He has none.'

The headmaster could not help but laugh.

Neither could the PTA president.

'Did he fall from the sky?'

'That's true, he fell into my lap.'

'Ah, whatever it is, let it be. He's a boy with no history.'

18

CASTE GAMES

The catchment area of the Bharathapuzha. The cries of the birds that try to feed themselves in the dried grasslands bordering the dry streams that snake towards the river in search of water can sometimes drown out the sounds of the thundering trains.

'You remember that pipal tree in Shoranur Junction with a lot of birds perched on it? I'm told that Swami Vivekananda planted it,' said Karamchand, hoping to start a new conversation.

'Was it on this trip that he called you people lunatics?' John's response shocked Karamchand.

'Don't be shocked. I too have read some history. However, when one hears that someone who had travelled all over India should make this comment after witnessing the caste system in Kerala, it beggars belief. It was the early seventies. My father and I were travelling from Lucknow to Jaipur by train.'

John rose from the berth, had a drink of water and continued, 'We were travelling in the First Class of some mail train. In the cabin seating four, there was only one passenger apart from my father and myself. Looking at his forehead covered in stripes of holy ash and his strange hairstyle, I thought of him as a bumpkin.

My father corrected me. He was a south Indian brahmin. I was just starting to understand the Indian caste system. The man spoke to us in excellent, unaccented English. He was a senior officer in the Railways.

'He was a scholar of the history of Indian Railways. I can still recall what he told us. Indians became punctual only after the advent of the Railways. Apparently, people started to bring order in their lives following the timetable published by the Railways.'

'That's an interesting piece of information. The speed of travel of Indians, accustomed to walking or to bullock carts, tripled in one go.'

'It must have taken decades for rail travel to become a habit. People would walk hundreds of miles with only dry rotis and green chillies for sustenance. Time was not a constraint. They were land-bound.'

'This is true. One of my forefathers travelled from Thiruvananthapuram to Kashi. He returned from there in the same lifetime. He was nicknamed Kashi Vishwanath by the people. Today he could reach Kashi in four hours if he flew, or in three days by train.'

'What made that man open up was my father telling him that his own father was a Railway employee. The man was planning to write the history of the Indian Railways as soon as he retired. He said that hundreds of workers had died of cholera and in workplace accidents during the construction of large tunnels and that he would dedicate the book to their memory. I'm not sure if he got around to writing the book. The reason I remembered him is that pipal tree, the one supposed to have been planted by Vivekananda.

'A middle-aged man got in from some station as the fourth passenger of our cabin. A dark-skinned man with curly hair. He wore a smart safari suit. With his arrival, our other co-passenger who had been voluble till then clammed up. He appeared to be agitated for no apparent reason. He also kept mumbling and muttering.

'I asked my father secretly why the man was grumbling. My father who knew India intimately told me that casteism was the reason for his griping.'

'That is true. How could he bear it? Didn't the Indian train in one stroke remove the caste quotient between them? Be that as it may, if caste is what mattered to India, colour is what mattered to you. At the Pietermaritzburg Railway Station, you pushed Gandhi out from the train. And Gandhi expelled you from the whole of India,' Karamchand said with a smile. 'There are other similar stories. Once, Ashutosh Mukherjee, the famous Bengali educationist, was travelling in a First Class compartment. A British planter was his co-passenger. He was very agitated for having to travel in the company of an Indian. When Mukherjee went to sleep, the man took Mukherjee's sandals and threw them out of the window, then smugly went to sleep.

'When Mukherjee woke up, he realised that he had lost his sandals. Without wasting any time, he threw out the white man's long coat. When the white man woke up, he asked where his coat was. Mukherjee said, "Your coat has gone to retrieve my sandals."'

John laughed out loud and narrated another story: 'Gandhi was once travelling in the First Class compartment. An Englishman was his co-passenger. He drew a caricature of Gandhi on paper and handed it over, saying, keep this, it will come in handy. Gandhi pulled out the pin that had been stuck into the paper, threw away the paper and said, 'I'm obliged, thank you. Definitely this can be put to some use.'

A dwarf palmyra tree could be seen in the distance. Despite speeding up, the train could not outrun the palm which was keeping pace with the train. What was running, the train or the palm? A man dulled by boredom catches only isolated, fleeting glimpses of things—the horn of a single cow; an electric pole; a disembodied scream; a scorched stalk of grass; the sandals on the feet of a fast-receding pedestrian; and such like. Eyes dulled by boredom are not able to tear themselves away from the trap of such singular sights and leap onto the riches of unfettered vision.

The train bursting with people sped through Pattambi, the land of dwarf palms. Karamchand returned to the A1 coach. Sameera was leaning back languidly on seat no. 5.

At that moment, a conversation was happening in the fourth bay.

'He's a Nair.'

'I don't think so. His manners are that of an Ezhava.'

'I'm certain. If you have any doubts, clear them yourself.'

'How should I do that?'

'So, you should ask him his caste. Then he will ask you, "From my looks, what do you think it is?" As we sit with our mouths agape, if he follows up with "How can something be understood from being told, when it has not been understood from seeing it?"[6] you can be assured he is an Ezhava.'

'Cheyy, that's not a nice thing to do.'

By then, the young man who had gone to the toilet returned and the couple's conversation ended. Pleasant-faced and energetic, he looked at both of them and smiled.

The twenty-five-year-old girl on the upper berth who, despite the earphones plugged into her ears and fiddling with the phone's touch screen, was lost in a parallel world was the couple's daughter. A software engineer with an IT firm in the metropolis, she was getting ready to leap into married life. Her retired schoolteacher parents were desperately searching for a suitable groom. Even though she hadn't read an entire novel or a short story in her life, an open copy of *Half Girlfriend* was lying by her side.

The mother offered the young man a quarter of an orange she had peeled. Laughing and with an, 'Aiyyo, the railway's regulation is that we must not accept food from strangers,' he accepted the orange carpels. He picked the carpels off one by one and ate them. His laughter bounced off the roof of the bogie and tickled the girl's ears.

With his innate glib cunning, the man convinced the couple that he was a bank manager, his parents had retired as officers from the State Secretariat, and his elder sister was living in France, married to a white Muslim. Although the alliance to a Muslim made the couple look at each other with a wild surmise, they consoled themselves with the thought that even if a Muslim, he was a Frenchman and it couldn't be that bad. Furthermore, they made mental notes of his head and feet positions when he was stretched out on the berth, and when the young man went to the toilet again, they took out a ruler and measured the length between those two points. Five feet eleven inches, six inches more than their daughter's height. After they found out that her body mass index was lower than the golden mean, they had also started to feed her more to bring it up to the mean. It was after they had determined that all things considered it was a good prospective alliance that they—as parties themselves involved in an inter-caste marriage—expressed two doubts.

'Must be a Nair.'

'No, he appears to be an Ezhava.'

After silent debates and experiments and observations, the husband made a suggestion. 'Let's play a game.'

Mistaking it for their code word for sex, the horrified wife pinched his thigh and said, 'What, here?'

'Silly woman, not *that* game! This is a caste game.'

'How?'

'I'll take out a book with Mannathu Padmanabhan's[7] photo on its cover and read it. You should watch him at that time, especially his eyes. It doesn't matter how progressive a Nair he is, there'll be a sparkle in his eyes. Depending on how much his eyes widen, we can even measure his progressiveness.'

'That is true. I've seen your relatives' eyes bulge like areca nuts.'

The husband took out the book. The wife wore her spectacles and readied herself to do the detective work. The subject was put under close scrutiny. He looked at the book. Without showing any emotion on his face, he looked away and kept watching the sights outside. That disappointed the couple.

'Now I shall take mine out,' the wife said softly and extricated a yellow-jacketed book named *Daivadashakam* that had Narayana Guru's image on it. Guru's serene face turned into an instrument of caste verification. The husband became vigilant. Again the young man came under intense scrutiny.

'Chetta, listen to this: "O Master mariner, your words are/Our mighty steam boat in/This temporal sea." Had he not become our spiritual guru, he would have been a great poet.'

'What's the use? They had to smash a coconut on his head to send him into his Samadhi.'

'Those are stories made up by you Nairs.'

When all these antics brought no visible change of expression to the young man's face, disheartened, they put the books away.

It was now the turn of the young man. He took out an English book, *Buffalo Nationalism*. The name, its jacket the colour of dung, and the look of the author displayed on the back jacket turned off the couple. The castles they had built in the air crashed around their ears. Their faces clouded over.

'We can now go to sleep, eh?' the wife asked.

'Yeah, let's. Engrossed in the book, I didn't notice the passage of time.'

She spread the sheets. The young man closed his book with a smile. The girl, lying on the upper berth presented him with a smile from behind *Half Girlfriend*.

19

BIOPSY SECTION

I am the S2 coach. It has been twenty-five years since I was rolled out of the coach factory at Perambur. In this country where people breed like pigs, millions have passed through my doors and reached myriad destinations. Polluted by their voices and excreta, I alone continue to run tirelessly. Aren't I a mere vehicle?

Humans are travellers. From south to north, from east to west, from the heights to the plains, from valleys to mountains, they continue to travel. Possibly because few people would have witnessed life as much as I have, the chronicler has, in what may be construed as puerile context, asked me, an inanimate object, to narrate the story.

I have borne every kind of people over the years. I was a part of the Sabarmati Express whose bogie was burnt to a cinder at Godhra. When the smell of burning human flesh emanated from the S6 coach, I was nearby. After the riots ended, I was decoupled from that rake. That is how I became a part of the Sampark Kranti Express. All these years, people have scratched out and scrawled their pervert sexual fantasies on my walls. I say that the respectability of many people is a mask that drops when they are alone. Very rarely did anyone rise above ordinary humanity. I will never forget one such—a young Tibetan.

His long, yellow-complexioned face reflected the melancholia of his race. He was from the third generation of those who had crossed the mountains. He wore blue jeans and a maroon tunic. He interacted with other passengers always with a smile on his lips. In those days, I was part of the Kamayani Express plying between Mumbai and Varanasi. Kamayani—such an attractive name, isn't it? Actually, it is named after Jaishankar Prasad's epic poem. It is the story of Manu who survives Pralaya, the Great Deluge, his isolation, his love and pangs of separation. For a poet in India, isn't a train being named after his poem the greatest honour?

The Tibetan youth stood at the door watching the scenery passing by. The air had a wintry chill. Leaving behind the stations in Madhya Pradesh, the train entered Uttar Pradesh. I fancied that the bolts that held down the tracks on which my wheels were riding were linking the two states and, through them, the whole of India. Suddenly, I heard a lament. The Tibetan youth was the singer, his voice so tender and soulful that it could melt the snow on the faraway mountains. I looked at him; his eyes were moist from some ineffable anguish.

Suddenly, he stopped singing and went into the toilet. Inside, he wept silently till his eyes melted. He took a pen from his pocket and wrote on the toilet wall.

You may love girls. But I love my Tibet. The abode of gods.

His words, among the many obscene comments on that wall, are still fresh in my memory. His heart was filled with glowing embers.

I dreamt that one day, the embers would turn into a conflagration. What can be more painful than the loss of one's motherland?

I also met a man on the Gitanjali Express that runs between Mumbai and Calcutta. In those days, I was running across the breadth of India. The train was in close touch with India's diversity.

One blazing summer day, the Deccan loo blowing into the train bursting at the seams with people made it a steam cooker. Most of the passengers were in great discomfort. The wailing of the babies and the clashes between adults turned the atmosphere deplorable.

The passengers already in the coach considered the new arrivals as troublesome infiltrators. Groups—such as those who clung to their seats, those who had standing space, those who were already in the train, those who were latecomers, those who stood on the right, those who stood on the left—were formed as a natural process. Arguments and squabbles too broke out.

A man stood by without partaking in any of these but observing everything that was happening. Unaffected by the crowding or the increasing temperature, he remained calm. His serenity drew me to him. As dusk fell, the heat came down. A cool breeze also started to blow in from the outside. People who were jostling for space with their brains on fire started to smile and share space. Gradually, amiability and friendship spread. They shared their food. They spoke to one another in whichever language that made communication possible. Everyone started to feel that those whom they had thought of as antagonists were in reality good people. People had undergone a transformation.

This man alone stayed aloof. He picked up the few dry leaves that had blown into the compartment and threw them out. When he found a place to sit down, he cleaned the area around it. He had the aspect of a birdwatcher, though he was actually human-watching. He went into the toilet and shut the door behind him. He stayed still for a little while. I have seen many types of bizarre, deviant behaviour inside. Some look in the mirror and laugh. Others cry. Still others make faces. Some act out imaginary roles, gesticulate and make speeches. Other masturbate. Toilets are witnesses to men in their real selves.

He stood pondering for a long time and then brought out his pen. When I saw such a good-natured fellow take out the pen, I felt rather sad. He started to write where many others had given vent to their frustrations and penned profanities. What he wrote was one of the most profound observations I have seen in my life.

A railway compartment is a tiny biopsy section of the Indian body.

We kept running, observing and knowing life. Railway coaches are like small nations. Powerless enough to be annexed to large trains at any point.

20

JOURNEYS WITHIN JOURNEYS

Standing in the vestibule between two coaches, Karamchand looked down through the gap. The tracks were flashing past below his feet, seemingly running in reverse. From S2, he walked to the next coach.

Two types of walking happen inside a train. A TTE or a vendor walks with an objective. When passengers walk, that is not so. They are travelling in time. Such walks do not take them to any destination. In that sense, for passengers, walking inside the train is a futile exercise.

Presaging a hot summer, bright, warm sunshine entered the coach. The majority of the passengers were drowsy, tired. The fans blew down hot air. Watching those who were nodding with magazines in hand and others lost in their smartphones, Karamchand kept walking.

When he heard conversation from one of the bays, he paused. The source and centre of attention was a lady past middle age. Karamchand sat down on the side seat, facing her. A young man with a scraggly beard was seated across him at the end of the seat, hugging his drawn-up legs and resting his face on his knees. Although Karamchand smiled at him, there was no response.

The arrival of a newcomer interrupted the woman's conversation for a moment. After assessing the newcomer, she continued to speak, 'My son-in-law will be waiting for me in Baroda.' Her companions acknowledged with a grunt. They had been drawn into the conversation unwillingly. Seated in the lotus position with the feet tucked under her, she continued with renewed gusto, 'He bought an Innova only last month.'

Another set of grunts.

'In Gujarat we don't have this kind of melting heat. Every house has AC now.' Her companions were two ladies and a man with a beard. Scraggly Beard was an unattached listener. When she saw the bearded man search for a signal on his mobile, the woman intervened, 'Back home we have uninterrupted net. That too for free.' Having had to suffer her all this while, he asked brusquely, 'Do Gujaratis use that net to catch fish?'

Everyone within earshot laughed. Even Scraggly Beard could not control his laughter. Lifting his head off his knees he too joined in. The woman looked around her. She turned towards Scraggly Beard and said, 'I know why you are laughing.' His face fell. Covering his face in his hands, he withdrew into himself.

Karamchand started to walk again. From the door of the S4 coach, he cast a backward glance. The Sampark Kranti was now a straight line running through an orchard of areca palms that had betel vines twisted around them. It was flying like an arrow towards the North.

He recalled the whistle of a goods train. The steam engine hauled a batch of steel wagons within which slogans of rebellion, turned into shrieks of agony, were interred. It started its journey from Tirur to Podannur. History tapped Karamchand's slender chest with a sledgehammer ...[8]

The prisoners were flung into the wagons. The doors were slammed shut as the wide-eyed men looked on. The sound of latches being slid into place fell upon their ears, searing into their memory.

Darkness.

In the running train, they clutched at the darkness. Crushed and packed tightly, the men screamed for air. The metallic sounds of the train masked the sound of breaking bones. In the increasing humidity the air grew dense. Gases sharper than steel split people's lungs. At the end of their lives, clawing and scratching one another and defecating on others in their death throes, they turned into mere animals. In their internal tissues, the bubbles of life kept popping. Finally, they died.

Karamchand recalled the fictional Indo-Pak border village Mano Majra created by Khushwant Singh, where even during Partition, Sikhs and Muslims were living in harmony. Nooran, the village Imam's daughter and the local thug Juggut Singh were in love. At the time of Partition, Nooran was pregnant with Juggut's child.

Despite the escalating violence all around, and thousands of corpses floating by them on the Indus, no one attacked anyone else in the village. One night, a train filled with corpses arrived at the Mano Majra station from Pakistan. With that, the peace that had prevailed so far in the village was shattered.

The Sikh youth decided to retaliate by attacking trains taking refugees to Pakistan. Their plan was to tie a steel hawser across the tracks on a bridge over the river and kill the hundreds of passengers seated on the roof of the train. Nooran was travelling on the same train. Juggut Singh, privy to the plan, sawed through the hawser with a dagger before the train entered the bridge and saved the passengers. He was shot and killed for his pains. More than twenty years after reading this Indian classic with a train as its subject, *Train to Pakistan* was still fresh in Karamchand's mind ...

The chimney of the Wanderer could be seen at the rear of the train. It stood high with the vanity of its past glory. Standing at the door of S4, Karamchand sang a ditty. None of the dozing passengers heard it. One more hour remained before they would reach Kozhikode.

21

THE BOY WITH NO HISTORY

Granny lay on the grass mat spread in the yard like a piece of rag. With her thin, feeble hands she stroked his cheeks. He sprinkled a few drops of water on her dry lips. Her eyes closed. The breath that went in refused to come out. She was dead.

He cleared the colocasia field; carried the old woman on his shoulders all on his own; made her a pyre with wood from the forest and like an unfeeling cremation groundskeeper, he kept watch on the sputtering, burning flames and the subsiding pyre. The only relative he had in the world vanished into the flames. Now, the old woman was only a smell to him.

The dog.

As it happened with the Pandavas during their Mahaprasthanika to Mount Meru, the dog stayed with him. When he tried to drive it away, it did not budge. The pyre died down. Darkness took over and shrouded everything. Like his future, the tiny bridge that he had to his past also vanished.

Without any history, the fifteen-year-old walked on without any destination. He took a dip in the Vaitharani[9] river and climbed out. The dog too now parted ways with him. He knew there must be a place where all rail lines converge. He strode ahead between the tracks.

With every step his urgency increased.

The boy with no history.

22

THE SMRITHI INQUISITION

The Kozhikode magistrate court.

A wildfire fanned by a hurricane. She descended from the jeep like a bonfire. Eclipsing and outshining everything around her, she walked with her head held high. Following a line of harlots who have shaken the foundations of many thrones. She took on various forms in the spectators' imaginations. Her radiance reduced the two policewomen with her into shadows. Her advocate had to trot to keep up with her.

She wore a smile on her face, fully conscious that all the cameras were focused on her. The spectators unconsciously emulated the smile. Ahead of her, the crowd parted. She stepped into court with unerring steps. The crowds milled around, trying to catch a glimpse of Lekha Nampoothiri's face, which had been blurred by the TV channels whenever they showed her. Hundreds of camera flashes went off. Men feasted their eyes on her.

An unbroken stream of comments darting from either side failed to wipe the smile off her face. Reaching the veranda of the court, she turned to face the crowd. In that instant, camera flashes lit up the veranda. Although she had been there many times before, she found that every time she stepped inside the court, a tide of terror rose within her. It was another place where time stood still.

The first day of cross-examination was akin to the agonising pain of her first penetration by what had felt like a barbed cudgel. Every question reminded her of the unexpected and unrelenting brutalisation of her breasts. The days and nights when, unable to suffer the corroding, blistering feeling within her, all that was inside her became liquid and flowed out. She was raped and violated again and again during the cross-examination. The merciless copulation had numbed her body and mind. Today was the last day of the seven-year-long trial—the reason for the large crowds in the court premises and the courtroom.

She had disclosed the names of sixty-six men. More than half of them had committed suicide. A few of them had absconded. Seated on the shaky bench in the courtroom, she did not look the part of the victim in a rape case that the whole of Kerala had relished in unison. Constant abrasion had made her victimhood wear thin and disappear. When she crossed her legs, the wooden bench swayed. It squealed. She sat up straight, and it squeaked again. The sounds made her mischievous. She started to move forward and backward and made it wobble. The rhythm of its squeaks and squeals appeared on her lips as a song, *'Paappi, appachcha ...'* An exquisite smile appeared on her lips.

Five minutes were left for the arrival of the magistrate. Those five minutes were as long as five years. The experiences in the court flashed through her mind like the panels of an illustrated book. Shabby wooden benches; black gowns; terrifying silences. On the first day of her cross-examination, the magistrate himself goaded the terrified girl, 'Tell us, girl, tell us ...'

She was unsure whom she was to start with. 'He had the strength of a gaur, sir.' A wave of faces started a procession inside her. Many were faceless—some had only a large nose; some only fingernails; some, nauseating body odour; some, fragrance; some, teeth abraded and stained from chewing paan; some, bald heads;

some, grey hair. Some had names; some did not. Some had gentle voices; some bellowed. There were strong men and weak men. There were ones who told stories; others who sang to her. There were those who kissed her and those who stubbed out cigarettes on her body. But all of them had one thing in common.

The ceiling fan stopped suddenly. She fell in a swoon and sweated profusely. A lady clerk sprinkled water on her face. In the depths of her unconsciousness, the droplets hit her like a cascade. She opened her eyes slowly. The ceiling fan had started again. Memories started to flood her. The magistrate kept pushing her.

'Tell us ... tell us ...'

It was an in-camera session. She began.

'Without waiting for my consent, he pushed me onto the bed. He buried a barbed knife inside me. My screams were drowned out by the unfamiliar song blaring through the room ... sir.'

'Tell us more ...'

'By the time I realised that what was moving inside my body was not a knife but that man's bestiality, the white sheet on the bed had already become bloodstained and I had slipped into unconsciousness, sir ...'

10 a.m.

There were voices everywhere. Men should be given another definition—voices. Man has created language with extraordinary variations. A word can be used as an abuse as well as an endearment. How silent the world must have been before Man invented language. The people inside the court were causing a tumult. All their conversations were laden with puns and double entendres. The mob had turned into a crow, cocking its head to see with its monocular vision.

Her reverie was broken by a snippet of conversation that blew in through the open window and swirled around in the courtroom in the breeze of the ceiling fan. Even with the crowds and commotion around her, she recognised it was an old man bitching.

'Where's the *thing*?'[10]

She looked out through the window. A spider was clinging to the window frame. Clutching her brood of spiderlings to her belly, she was clinging to the web she had woven. She was not the only spider. The courtroom ceiling was full of spiders. Lekha quickly withdrew her gaze.

'Take a look. See that sheeny thing next to the bat wearing the black gown? *That* is your *thing*.'

Another voice. 'Oh shut up you little runt! You're still suckling at your mama's teats and you want to see the bimbo?'

'Wow ... she's a real dish.' The old man could not control his ardour. 'Long ago, there was another one called Kuriyedath Thathri ...' His comment was interrupted and dwindled into a cough caught in his ageing throat. The man had come to see the trial ignoring his health and the infirmities of his age. Lekha Nampoothiri smiled when she wondered how respectable this man would be to his unsuspecting family and acquaintances. Her smile was telecast by many cameras. She was not paying attention; in her mind she was reliving another inquisition.

'Sir, when he came into the room, he was carrying a cloth shoulder bag. As soon as he saw me seated on the corner of the bed with my head bowed, he broke into tears. He ran towards me and lifted up my head and held it against his chest. He stroked my head. I could see affection overflowing in his eyes. Taking the freedom, I moved closer to him. The bag was full of books. He was a poet. And physically a weakling. His underwear gave off a musty smell. I was happy that after so many days I was meeting a decent person.

'I like poets. They always travel in other worlds that we don't get to see. Their heart is full of romantic love and their words are full of fire. They walk the earth and heaven at the same time. How drab this world would be if there were no poets. Sir, have you heard the poem: "Pain, pain intoxicates/Let me lose myself in pain." Singing it again and again, I would climb down the steps of pain and reach the abyss of agony. Do you want to hear about a miraculous thing? When you reach that point, the pain will vanish. What remains is only joy. A heaven where, in a trance, we cease to exist. I have a request, sir. You should teach all the girls in this world this poem. Cane them if need be, but teach them. This poem is so useful, sir.

'That poet explained humanity and fraternity to me. He recited his own poems too. That made me want to escape. A fervent hope surged inside me, sir. "Will you help me escape from this hell?" I asked him. "Yes, I will. I assure you." He stood up and started to sniff the four corners of the room. He stood for some time in front of the ventilator. "We'll turn into two butterflies, climb on top of the clouds and float around in the endless skies." He said that and started to cackle. Even though I knew it was utter nonsense, I enjoyed it. I like to live in the future.

'He pulled out a book from his bag and opened it. It was well-thumbed and the pages were worn out. He read it out to me. The story was titled "The Prostitute of the Poor". I listened to each sentence attentively. How naturally Basheer writes his stories! The moment he finished reading, both of us began to weep. He hugged me tight.

'"Show me your belly, let me see if it's like the belly of the girl in the story," the poet told me. His hands started to roam all over my belly. Running his hands over the contours of my belly, he started to point out: Here's Africa, here's Australia. In between, once, he gently pressed my lower belly. Honestly, at that time too his eyes were filled with kindness.

'The next moment his eyes locked on my navel. He lost control over his fingers. I had by then learnt to understand a man's intentions from the slightest of his gestures. Everything happened quickly thereafter. But he was the one who made me understand that once a man is in heat, when his loins are on fire, there is no difference between his lust for flesh and that of an animal.

'After his lust was consummated and he was spent, he lay with his head on my chest, his body cold as a corpse. And he started to weep again. My breasts became damp with his tears. He started to babble: "*Molae*, I will fight against this system that turns you into a prostitute and me into a john. I will fight through my poems."

'When I heard this, I lost all my self-control. I kicked him off the bed onto the floor. Then, from his bag, I took out a heavy book called a dictionary and hit the crown of his head. He ran out screaming. I spent my days of solitude reading the books he had abandoned.'

10:10 a.m.

The courtroom turned stuffy in the unleavened silence. Expectation turned into sighs and pulsated on the verandas. Lekha Nampoothiri felt the urge to pee. Only two minutes were left for the arrival of the magistrate. The lady advocate filled the space with a presence that no camera lens could ignore. Wearing a manufactured smile on her lips, the lady stood by Lekha as if guarding her.

'I need to pee,' she told the advocate and stood up. The advocate followed her to the toilet. Heads turned in unison to follow their progress. With instruments that could invade any privacy, the TV channel journalists followed them. When she entered the toilet and locked the door, the live telecast began.

'She has entered the toilet. The sounds of the bolt being shot can be heard. What will follow now are critical moments. Things are beyond our imagination. Today's the last hearing of the rape case whose conclusion Kerala society has been expectantly waiting for.

'In the names revealed till now, there are thirty-two politicians, including two ministers, fourteen bureaucrats, six judicial officers, eight film actors ... Let's wait for more revelations.'

An overly excited reporter stood in front of the toilet like a sentry. High emotion choked him and his voice broke. When he could no longer control his enthusiasm, he bent down and brought his nose close to the gap at the bottom of the toilet door. He sniffed earnestly for the benefit of his viewers. He lifted his head as if he had made a startling discovery and shouted into the camera, 'I have my doubts. To be honest, I have doubts. Although she has claimed she wanted to urinate, Lekha Nampoothiri has not done so. Urine doesn't smell like this. This is the smell of shit. Pay attention—this is shit. If this is so, I am posing a reasonable question—why has a person who has gone to take a shit lied and said that she had to pee? Shouldn't the country know? This alone is enough for Lekha Nampoothiri to lose her credibility.' He wiggled his finger at his audience. The instant he stopped, Lekha Nampoothiri stepped out of the toilet.

'Even if we concede that pressing circumstances compelled a person who had gone in to urinate to shit too, isn't she obliged to reveal that? Lekha Nampoothiri is walking back to the courtroom without doing so. The magistrate too has arrived. Along with camera man ...'

The magistrate made his entry and sat down on the ancient un-upholstered wooden chair. In the oppressive silence that accompanied him, the air in the courtroom became stifling.

'Is Eswaran Nampoothiri present?' the court clerk called out. An old man wearing a janeu moved out from the corner of the room and entered the witness stand. It had been long since his head had become bowed. Two dead eyes took a trip around the court from beneath a pair of bushy grey eyebrows and returned to their hollows.

'What is your relationship with this man?' The advocate and Lekha Nampoothiri rose to their feet. The courtroom resembled the court of Yama. The silence was menacing.

'He's my achchan,'[11] she said in a whisper. The distended chests of the audience deflated as they let out a collective sigh.

'Has the accused molested you?' the magistrate asked. She raised her head and so did the old man. Their eyes met. The ground under his feet splintered into a thousand slivers, the laments of millions who, driven by lust, had fallen through the cracks beneath him.

These were charged, terrifying moments.

'Tell the court, has the accused molested you?' the magistrate demanded, trying to give her courage. The audience cocked their ears. Their nostrils flared like that of rabid dogs. In a primitive craving they thrust out their greedy tongues. They growled with rapacity. They salivated, pining to drink the drops of blood that were about to fall on the courtroom floor.

'No.' Her voice was firm. The unexpected reply disappointed the audience. The old man looked up stoically. He was unaffected by what was happening around him. Murmurs started to swirl around the court.

'The accused has already confessed to the crime. Are you committing perjury to save the accused?'

'No, honourable court.'

'Then tell us in detail what happened.'

'It was the seventeenth day. I heard the pimp, Babu, talking to someone outside the room. When I listened, I realised that the voice was familiar. I felt as if a fire had been lit inside me. It was my father's voice. It had been a long time since I had heard it. I switched off the light and waited. I was trembling at the thought of my father coming in through that door. However, I overcame that fear in the next instant. I had already realised that among humans everything boils down to the relationship between man and woman.

'My instructors in this knowledge were my own uncle, schoolmaster and others. I had also realised that a man is merely an organ that goes up and down like a sphygmomanometer. Sir, from a woman with a soul I had been transmuted into an object. Sir, humans are not addressed using words such as floozy, lollipop girl, piece of ass, item, prosty, bottom bitch and the like, are they?

'My father came in! He sat by my side. I smiled when I thought he would not be able to see me in the darkness. He touched me. I felt happy. I drank in his odour as deeply as I could. He always smells of sandalwood paste and rice payasam. My father was trembling. Poor man. He had only one innocent objective: to hump a maiden. Some Tantric text, I believe, claims that doing so will increase one's longevity. Who among us doesn't have such wishes? I decided to fulfil his desire.

'What kind of fraud do you think Babu is, if he presented me as a virgin, after I had been debauched by forty men over seventeen days? Sir, I felt impish that day. Keeping my father's ear that smelt of ixora flowers close to my mouth, I whispered affectionately, "*Achcha* ..."'

In the witness stand, the startled old man raised his head.

'My father collapsed in a faint that same instant. This is what had transpired. The rest is all what the police forced him to confess using third-degree methods. Isn't that so, achcha?' She started laughing uproariously. The old man's face betrayed no emotion. He stood with his eyes focused on some distant point visible only to him.

The magistrate raised his hand signalling everyone to be silent.

Yellow sunlight fell upon the worn-out, ancient wooden furniture and fittings of the court. In that old building where rulings on justice and injustice were given, stacks upon stacks of law books came alive. Some laws and regulations, believed to have lost their relevance and therefore dead and buried, made a comeback, parting the curtains of time. The trial was on its last legs. Tomes and texts into which ancient moral codes and ways of life were crammed were getting ready to interpret the modern day.

'Allow me to have a paan,' Lekha Nampoothiri said. The advocate applied lime and catechu on the betel leaves, packed it with tobacco, slices of areca nut, and handed it over. Seated on the court bench and crossing her right leg over her left, she started to chew the paan.

'The *thing* is chewing paan. Old-timers claim that the paan-chewing on the occasion of the closing arguments of this case is making them nostalgic. Cameraman ...'

Watching the close-up of her pursed mouth moving on the TV screen, the viewers too started to masticate. Lechers gave full play to their lascivious imaginations.

Suddenly she leapt to her feet and stepped out. She hawked and spat towards the TV cameras that were pointed at her like the yawning mouths of dinosaurs. *Phthooo!* The paan juice mixed with her spittle turned the screens red on live. The viewers staggered back as if they had been slapped across their faces.

'All right, who was the last man to have intercourse with you?' the magistrate, Mahendran Elethiripad, asked.

A mischievous smile flashed in her eyes. Now she held in her palm the respectability and rectitude of at least some of the men seated in that courtroom. A word from her and the cloak of respectability they wore would be torn to shreds. She was the sovereign. The dispenser of destiny for the clan of men. Her words had the power to cast a curse on even the future generations of the accused.

She hooted with laughter. Such laughter was being heard for the first time in the courtroom where gravitas lay thick like centuries-old silt. She laughed like someone demented, the laughter powerful enough to shake the roof of the courtroom. Lizards, who believed until then that it was they who held up the roof, trembled. Spiders waiting for their prey at the centre of their cobwebs shook with fear. She looked at the wall clock above the magistrate's head. Mahatma Gandhi smiled toothlessly from above it.

There wasn't much time left now. Her eyes descended from Mahatma Gandhi and stopped at the magistrate's nose. Their eyes met and locked with each other. Her eyes were unrelenting; his were pleading.

Seated below the pankah installed by the British, the magistrate sweated. The pen slipped from his clammy fingers. The sight made her laugh again, and the laughter struck his head like a sledgehammer.

'That, sir ...' Pausing meaningfully, she looked around and continued with an impish smile, 'That, sir ... was a man who had a mole on his penis. Who, for the last time ...' As soon as she said this, the magistrate's hand flew towards his groin. The courtroom rocked with laughter.

'Order, order.' The gavel struck the sound block with the authority bestowed on it by law. The hall fell silent.

The crowd dispersed carrying diverse memories of that momentous day to narrate to their future generations. Lekha Nampoothiri made her way out through the crowd. Taking in the vibhuti smell of bell-metal vessels and warmed by the heat from the woks in which halwa was being made, her colourful saree sped through Mithai street, in between the buildings that stopped the sea breeze in its tracks. Like an ember lifted by the breeze, her pace quickened.

The cameras followed her till the railway crossing with their rapacious eyes. She crossed the tracks. A speeding train cut off her view from the ravenous lenses of the TV cameras.

23

IN THE HISTORIC CITY

The train crossed Kadalundi Bridge. The smell of rotting timber from the lagoon seeped into the train. It crawled lazily into platform no. 5 of Kozhikode Railway Station. John opened *India* again.

Calicut. Kozhikode. A historic city. Formerly part of the Madras Presidency. Vasco da Gama and his entourage, with the São Gabriel leading the armada, landed here in 1498, marking the beginning of the European colonisation.

Beypore.

'People here have been experts at making dhows since olden times,' said Karamchand.

'Beypore Sultan. A Muslim king who ruled Calicut.'

'That is not correct, John.'

'What's not correct?'

'Beypore Sultan was no king. It was the nickname of the famous author Vaikom Muhammad Basheer. Basheer, the creator of Majid, Pathumma, and Ettukaali Mammoonj. Have you heard of him?'

'Ettukaali Mammoonj, what's that?'

'That's a race of humans you can see everywhere.'

'Like Caucasoid, Mongoloid, Negroid?'

'Ah yes, you will see Ettukaali Mammoonjs among all the races in the world, those who will claim credit for anything, even that which they had nothing to do with.'

The nearest airport is Karipur. Furthermore, it is the land of halwa, and the capital of football, ghazals and Malabar.

The train squealed to a halt. Hundreds of people were running helter-skelter on the platform. It seemed to Karamchand that the base beat of all the sounds around him was *a-lu-va, a-lu-vaa*— the cries of the halwa vendors. He thought of the connection between the sound of the word and the object it named. *A-lu-va*. How soft the word was! A word that oozed sweetness.

On the platform, a dark, stocky man with the features of a buffalo approached Carvalho. He hugged Carvalho like a long-lost friend and hurried into the compartment. Someone ran his stroller bag over John's foot. 'Dangerous people,' John exclaimed, pulling his foot back.

'Indians have not changed from the time Ruskin Bond started to write,' John said to Karamchand. He looked at John quizzically.

John said, 'When you are travelling in the Third Class compartment, you will suddenly realise that you no longer own your leg. It has been usurped by a villager carrying a satchel. Your co-passenger's shabby stubble is annoyingly pricking your shoulder. The cold air grazing the nape of your neck is some asthma patient's exhalation. On your lap is someone's baby, bawling away. It will lie there till it wets your clothes. One corner of the seat you had thought was entirely yours has been commandeered by a burly Sikh with a kirpan stuck into his waistband.'

The train started to move away slowly from the platform that the crowds had pushed into chaos.

Carvalho saw a lady in a yellow saree running towards him, splitting apart the throng of people who stood waving goodbye to their departing loved ones.

'Sir, does this train go to Poddanur?' she asked him, gasping for breath as she ran alongside the train.

'No.'

'Then where does it go?'

'Delhi,' he said, standing at the door as the train started to pick up speed. She tried to jump into the train. When she stumbled and started to fall, Carvalho pulled her up. In one swift move, the man whose bloodline started from Europe, and in whom Europe lay entrenched, hauled her into the compartment.

Doubting Dowager, who was going from the toilet back to her seat, stopped by. She mused, 'Who's this woman? How did she get the birthmark on her cheek? Where is she going? How is she so beautiful? Is she married? If she is, what does her husband do?'

Without any of her questions being answered, she went to her berth and lay down lackadaisically.

'Sir, did you recognise me?'

'No.'

'I'm Lekha Nampoothiri.' He was shocked when he heard the name. He looked at her with respectful awe.

'Do you recall how, once upon a time, after her Smārthavichāram, Kuriyedath Thathri left this place forever?'

'I do. She went to Podannur ...'

'My trial is over today. I too am leaving.'

'How did you get this birthmark on your cheek?'

Following Carvalho to the First Class AC coach, she laughed, 'I was shot at by Lord Rama.'

The buffalo trader Zachariah was sitting in Carvalho's cabin. 'Sit down here,' Carvalho said to her.

'In those days, *Ramayana* was being telecast on Doordarshan. Carrying bows and arrows, all the boys of my place had turned into Rama. They staged wars all the time, shooting arrows made of bamboo. I got caught in the battle between Rama and Ravana. The arrow Rama shot that day gave me this permanent scar.'

'What role does a girl have in the battlefield?' Carvalho asked.

'Sir, Rama was fighting for his woman. Poor her. When it comes to the matter of women, Rama and Ravana are all the same.'

'Anyway, wait here for the time being.' He took up his chart and left.

All this while, Zachariah was looking at her with admiration. His lips quivered. 'You are more beautiful in real life than on TV,' he said, trembling all over.

The Western Ghats were visible through the window. The wind that had travelled down the ghats swirled around and raised dust devils here and there. It had started to get dark. He switched on the light inside the cabin. She was dazzled by the weak light.

'Ah, I've longed all this while to meet you at least once.'

She did not reply. Watching the fading light outside, she sat smiling.

'My name is Zachariah.'

'Mmm ...'

'May I lock the door?' He stood up.

'Ummm ...'

He closed the door of D cabin and latched it.

24

SAILING SHIP

The Arabian Sea, the scene of many violent historical clashes, kept moving parallel to the Sampark Kranti Express. Karamchand stood at the door, watching the sea. He wove his imagination into the undulating waves, the darkness of the water and the whiteness of the foam. The sea was swiftly travelling back in time, centuries into the past. He saw a ship sailing; it had stakes attached to both its sides on which human corpses were festooned.

This was the carrack of Dom Francisco de Almeida. He was on the way to win back the fort at Thalassery that had been besieged by the moplahs.[12] After he came to know that the Portuguese troops inside the fort were in great strife, starving with no food or water, he had set sail from Cochin. Seated on the ship, he was planning strategies to take back the fort.

Unaffected by all this, in the night, the slaves congregated on the deck of the ship. To kill time, they decided to hold a competition. Who among them had the longest organ? One by one they displayed their phalluses. A white man, one of the cannoneers, was the umpire.

Kariman released his penis from the confines of his worn-out loin cloth. When he did that, many of the others who stood smug and vain about their family jewels started to feel that in comparison, theirs was no bigger than a child's. The slaves had no hope that their organs would be put to any worthy use in their lives during their travels from one sea to another. The thought was enough for the organs to become flaccid, like serpents lowering their hoods.

All the while, the Portuguese cannoneer kept wowing them with tales of his conquests and sexual exploits. The lands he had visited, the body types of the women there, and the variety of their coital vocalisations as he buried himself into them. Inflamed by the stories, the slaves squirmed in their imagination. One by one, they withdrew into their dark quarters. They slept like cattle in the cramped spaces, one on top of the other.

The deck was cleared, except for the lookout on the mast and the sentries in the fore and aft. However, the severed heads festooned on the poles on starboard and port sides stared out into the sea with their bulging unseeing eyes.

Kariman stayed on. The memories of him frolicking on the seashores of Alappuzha tickled his loins and gave him a hard-on. Standing between two corpses, looking at the endless sea, he began to masturbate. The vessel started to pitch with the intensity of his passion. In his imagination, all the women of the land paraded themselves naked in front of him.

However, Kariman wasn't alone on the deck. Almeida stood behind him, sword in hand and a smile on his lips. With the cunning of a mischievous wild animal, he stood silent and unmoving behind him. The cruel captain watched the slave's penis become engorged and his eyes closing in the throes of an imminent orgasm. When it spurted, the sword came down in a flashing arc. Like the autotomous tail of a lizard, the truncated organ fell on the deck and writhed. Although separated from its owner, it hissed liked a serpent and ejaculated.

Looking at the writhing piece of muscle and tissue on the deck, Almeida declared, 'You've no need for this anymore.'

Kariman did not cry out. Biting down on the searing pain, he covered his loins with his hands. Betraying no emotion, he stood staring at his dismembered organ. When Almeida walked away, he bent down and picked it up. With a deadpan face, he kissed it. He then applied a poultice on the wound and dressed it himself.

It took many days for the wound to heal. In that time, he evolved into a minacious behemoth, an efficient machine ingesting food and excreting faeces. After the loss of Kariman's masculinity, Almeida made him his personal bodyguard. Kariman did not get rid of his amputated penis. He dried it, put it inside a small tin box and then tucked the box into his loin cloth. Whenever his body tingled, he would open the tin box, look at the shrivelled penis, kiss it expressionlessly, and keep it back in the box, restoring it to its old position.

When dawn broke, the ghost ship was bearing down on the fort. Cannon balls rained down on the moplahs who were laying siege. They scattered and fled from the precincts. Almeida's army disembarked on the shore now bereft of adversaries. Kariman was in the vanguard. Like an incarnation of Yama, he dashed around breaking heads and everything he lay his eyes on, spearing people like meat on a skewer.

They won back the fort. The last moplah standing was captured, and Kariman boarded the ship with a soldier impaled on his spear. He made an offering out of that hapless soldier to Almeida, who was seated on the cannon. With the little life that was lingering in him and blood pouring out of his mouth, the soldier was screaming obscenities at Almeida. When he finally died, he was commended to be the brightest face among the heads festooning the ship's deck.

The Sampark Kranti Express left Kozhikode Station.

Almeida's armada turned North, planning to capture Gomantak.[13]

25

TERRITORIAL ANIMAL

Bearing a cross-section of India, the train sped between the green mountains and the blue sea. It left mofussil towns, villages and ancient dwellings built with laterite stones in its wake. The day was ending, but so much had changed in the meanwhile. The contours of the land, the vegetation, the language ...

Karamchand thought about boundaries: 'How do boundaries form for language and culture? Which human habits lead to them? When a Malayali crosses over into Tamil Nadu, he does not mislay his language in Kanyakumari. Tamil and Malayalam are in a muddled tangle here. By the time he reaches Tirunelveli, the language is lost to him. If he walked further inland, he would be entering into a maze of unrecognisable Tamil.'

John's voice woke him out of his reverie. 'I'll show you some more pictures. This is my first tiger,' he said pointing to a male tiger on the screen. 'Karamchand, have you seen a tiger?'

'Yes. In the Thiruvananthapuram Zoo. Rani and Manikantan.'

John laughed when he heard it. He took out a book from his bag. Valmik Thapar's *Tiger Fire: 500 Years of the Tiger in India*.

'For me, India is the land of tigers.'

'That's true. India is the land of famous tigers. The Bengal tiger, Tiger Pataudi, Tiger Memon ... ha ha ha.'

'Which forests did they live in?'

'They were tigers among men.'

'I inherited the passion for tigers from my grandpa. I came to India with my father in 1974. To Ranthambore. My father being a renowned journalist, Fateh Singh Rathore-sahib had made all the arrangements for him. He was a legendary conservationist.

'In the late evening, we went deep into the forest in a jeep arranged by Rathore-sahib, accompanied by a forest guard. That was my maiden jungle trip. We parked where the forest road ended. Dreaming of the tiger, we walked between the trees that had started to shed their leaves in the autumn. Our camp had been set up near a waterhole. When night fell, we climbed onto the machan, hoping to see the tiger come out at night to drink water.

'It was one of the few waterholes that still had water. Rathore had kept its surroundings clean. We sat on the machan peering into the mysterious darkness of the forest. The dense foliage stopped the moonlight from creeping through. Trees seemed to graze the sky with a conceit of being witnesses to history. A few stars lay where they had fallen on the water. A wild, irrational fear consumed my father and me. Although birds were still singing, we were overcome by fear. We hugged each other and waited.

'"Will the tiger come?"

'The guard consoled us. "It should come. There's no water elsewhere in this forest."

'Midnight. There was a movement at the far corner of the waterhole. We focused our eyes. A huge beast pushed through the bushes and walked into the water. In a burst, the stars that lay on the water scattered and disappeared. When he saw the white stockings on the animal's legs, the guard said, "Gaur."

'A bison fattened generously by the forest. After drinking water, that black mountain roamed in the forest. Since I was waiting for the tiger, I wasn't impressed by the gaur. A procession of animals came and went—wild dogs, foxes, porcupines. Many such animals small and big.

'"We can be sure of one thing," the guard said.

'"What is that?"

'"There are no tigers in the vicinity." Father and I gave each other a disappointed look.

'The guard was from the forest; he was born there, he had grown up around animals and had now reached middle age.

'"Had the tiger been around, none of these animals would have come," he said. We went to sleep feeling safe and secure on the machan. Sometime in the night, I woke up hearing a frightful scream. Only then did I realise that it was a dream.

'Through the gaps in the dry leaves, drops of sunshine started to drip down. Tiny life forms started to emerge from beneath the layers of dry foliage on the ground. As we descended from the machan, a procession of white ants was on its way up. I watched the procession with keen interest. The ornamental tree spiders that had been clinging to the tree trunks now emerged to check if some prey had been caught in their webs. Nature has set in store such a smorgasbord of curiosities and mischiefs! While we were climbing down, a few white ants were killed, crushed between my father's palms and the tree trunk. Such tiny, inconsequential lives. They could not even cry out in their agony.

'My father joked, "I shall show you the tiger in the Jaipur Zoo. Be content with white ants for now."

'"For the jungle, a tiger is no different from the ant. One becomes food for the other," the guard said. Disappointed, we walked back. Daylight spread all around us. The forest took on a yellow hue. A herd of red muntjac deer trotted across our path.

'"Getting to see the tiger is like getting to see God, sir."

'A tree by the side of the trail swayed and its leaves rustled in the breeze. The monkeys stopped chattering and seemed to be listening keenly. Then they started to howl in a frenzy. The whole jungle seemed to be trembling with unease.

'"This animal has integrity. He will appear only in front of those who have a fervent desire to see it. When Rathore-sahib is out in the jungle, the tigers become like kittens. They walk around him, and rub themselves against him."

'Suddenly, the guard stopped. He pointed out to us the deep claw marks on the gum arabica tree in front of us. The sap was still oozing from them. There was the unmistakeable reek of urine.

'"Do you know what this is?"

'"No."

'"The male is marking its territory."

'"Do only males mark their territory?" I asked.

'"Do you think it could be otherwise? Have you heard of women marking out territories and founding a nation?"

'As soon as he said it, he pushed us both back with his hand. "Don't make a sound. He's close by."

'A movement in a thicket of bamboo. Two glinting, kohl-lined eyes were looking at us. Sheer majesty. The yellow sunshine slipped through the bamboo leaves and made lovely patterns on the tiger's body. Although he was watching us, there was no expression on his face. He bore a dignified languor. The insouciant hubris of having everything under one's control. A numbing fear crept up from the soles of my feet and froze my brain. My mouth went dry. The tiger shifted slightly. It pushed itself up using its front legs and stood up. He was not paying us any attention.

'He then turned towards us and let out a thunderous, guttural roar. It felt as if all the energy in the universe had converged at one point and exploded. My first photo of a tiger was taken at that nerve-tingling moment. Not on a camera. The picture was etched on my brain forever. Throwing one more look in our direction, he turned and disappeared into the undergrowth.

'I then took a picture of it with a camera.

'"His name is Ranbir," the guard told us. "Every tiger in Ranthambore has been named by Rathore-sahib."

'"It's a wonder he did not attack us despite our being so close. Why didn't he?" asked my father.

'"Wild animals attack only for food or in self-defence," the guard said.

'Karamchand, can you see the goosepimples on my arm? I have seen so many tigers after that day. How many thousands of photos I've shot! But none has thrilled me as much as this one,' John said with pride in his voice.

He then showed Karamchand a picture of a gum arabica tree. The claw marks were deep and distinct on it. Territorial marks. 'Crossing into its territory means either a fight to death or a quick retreat.' That was the third or fourth time he had said that.

Karamchand parted the curtains and looked out. Night had fallen. The train was slowing to a halt.

'John, there's a place in India where political parties leave their territorial marks on trees, walls and electric poles. Do you know it?'

'No.'

'It's Kannur, the station we're in now.'

The train cut its speed further. On the concrete signboard on platform no. 1, in its yellow and black combination, the word 'Kannur' was painted in three languages.

Kannur MSL 11 M.

Eleven metres above the mean sea level.

26

TIGER

The scene on the platform: a middle-aged passenger named Kuriakose was tussling with his heavy, oversized trolley bag, trying to squeeze it through the narrow door of the S1 coach. For a long time, the door frame and the heavy steel door resisted the attempts of his corpulent body to push it through. After he crawled into the coach following the exertions at the door, he practised some deep-breathing exercises to regain his equanimity. The compartment was ringing with the din the students were making. He became flustered again. Standing at the threshold, he fixed Elvindas with an angry stare and asked, 'Where's my seventeen?'

Elvindas pointed to seat no. 17. Steaming inside with the petulance of a middle-aged man, he bumbled his way between the students who were playing Antakshari. He snorted when he saw that the students had encroached upon his seat. They quickly vacated it for him.

After giving everyone a meaningful look, as if he was the monarch of all that he surveyed, he plopped down on the seat. Stuck on some letter, the Antakshari game came to a stop. However, the silence did not prevail for long. When the TTE appeared, Kuriakose bellowed, 'Is this coach meant for such devils?'

'They're young, sir. After a while, when all their energy is spent, they'll go to sleep. I've been seeing this all my life,' said Elvindas.

'People like you protect and spoil them. After sometime they'll start shouting slogans. They'll declare a revolution. What we need in this country is military rule. After that there won't be a peep out of anyone.'

The students did not understand the meaning or import of their conversation conducted in Malayalam. They restarted their game of Antakshari.

Nimesha Mehta approached Kuriakose. 'Sir, my seat is in the next coach; it's a lower berth.' He gave her a quizzical look. 'My husband's seat is here. If you can please move to that seat, my husband and I could be here together.'

'Bah!' he thundered. 'This is *my* seat.' He shoved the trolley bag beneath the seat. He chained it to the seat leg with a thick chain. He spread the neatly folded sheet on the berth. Then, spreading his legs as far as they would go, he installed himself on the seat like a plenipotentiary. As if he was the embodiment of irritability, he kept shaking his legs and flailing his arms. He swung his shoulders. He spread his arms like wings and placed them on the seat, palms down, as territorial markers. With his eyes, he drew an imaginary circle ring-fencing himself in. And in that ring, pulling up his legs under him, he sat in the lotus position.

He took his phone out and started to talk loudly into it. 'Hello, this is Kuriakose. Ah, yes, the same. Eight chappatis, two plates of chicken fry, four porottas, one beef roast, one-and-a half litre Pepsi bottle. Bring all this to S1. I shall not come down. You must deliver inside. Mark it.'

Nimesha Mehta rose from her seat. While walking to the next coach, she spoke to Elvindas testily, 'Sir, he is a tiger. If someone approaches him, there will be war. A warlord!'

Elvindas pointed to the picture stuck on the door of the coach. In that publicity poster of Rajasthan Tourism, a tiger, standing on its hind legs, upright against a tall tree, was clawing at the tree trunk.

Nimesha read the caption on the poster: 'Territorial Animal'.

27

THE WORLD OF STRANGERS

A common housefly that had lost its way buzzed around directionless in the cabin. Now it too was a passenger. With no self-consciousness, it was busy in two movements. However long and however much it flew, it could never go back. When he thought of the quandary it was in, Karamchand felt like laughing. In another time and place, it would have found a mate in an abattoir or in a fruit shop. The pair would have given life to thousands of flies.

Through the window, the sea and a fort jutting out into the sea were visible.

'What's the name of that fort?' John asked.

'That's the Bekal Fort.'

'Oho? Someone who's been to Golconda, Chittorgarh and Daulatabad can only see it as a miniature fort. Some of the railway stations are bigger forts than this one.'

A tiny station flashed by.

'Which station was that?'

'Kasaragod. The northern tip of Kerala.'

John started to search for Kasaragod on his laptop. Depending on the pictures on his screen, his eyebrows arched and eyes bulged. He was silent for some time.

'Have a look.' John turned the screen towards Karamchand. 'When I search for Kasaragod, I see photos of Somali children. How is that?'

It was true. They were photos of children with misshapen, disproportionately big heads; with contorted limbs; piteous faces with bulging, unfocused eyes. Like photostats of humans.[14] Karamchand cried inwardly. He did not respond. John took up *India* again. Silence grew and formed a bulkhead between them.

When he grew bored, Karamchand headed out of the coupé and walked towards the A1 coach. When he found Sameera's seat vacant, he occupied it. The train was crossing a river. On the adjacent seat was an aged couple. The discomfort of being caught inside an unfamiliar world was evident on their faces. Karamchand could sense that the cold air from the air conditioning was troubling the old man. What the man needed then was open land.

Sameera returned. 'I had gone to put more water in the river. Which river is this, man?'

'Chandragiri.'

'Where have we reached?'

'We're just about leaving Kerala.'

'Aiyyo, have we left Kerala behind?' asked the old man, parting the curtains.

'Not yet, but we soon will.'

'We're going out of Kerala for the first time.'

'Is that so? Where are you from?'

'Our house is in Elanthur near Pathanamthitta,' the reply came from the old woman.

'Where are you going?'

'To Delhi. Our daughter is a nurse there. Our son-in-law is there too.'

While they were talking, she opened their packed dinner. 'This is the first time for us in an AC train.'

When the smoked plantain leaf used to pack the meal was opened on the seat, the aroma of a whole village spread inside the coach.

'Had that guy in the jacket come by, we could've asked him to shift us to some place less cold.'

At that moment, Elvindas did come by.

'Sir, this place doesn't suit us. Can you shift us to an ordinary coach?'

The packed meal contained a small mountain of rice. With a finger, the old man carefully wiped up the grains of rice trying to flee the leaf plate and added them to the heap.

'George *etta*, that, unfortunately, can't be done. The computer has upgraded and installed you in the AC coach,' was Elvindas's response.

'My husband has the habit of snoring. That's why he's so concerned.'

When the smiling Elvindas moved away, George ettan sang, lowering his voice:

> *Deplorable is the cohort of inspectors, there's no*
> *gainsaying;*
> *Believed this train will bring an end to our tribulations,*
> *praying.*
> *All troubles were snared by the nets spread by the evil*
> *porters;*
> *Nothing will be lost but all should be weighed and put in*
> *the corners.*

The ditty made Karamchand and Sameera laugh.

'What song is this, George etta?'

'This is the story of our forefathers migrating to Malabar decades ago. Of their taking a bus till Aluva from there, changing to the train till Kozhikode, and ending up in various parts of Malabar.'

'It's a super song. Can you sing the whole thing?' Sameera asked.

'There's no need for all that. My sister-in-law's grandson has posted her singing this on Facebook. Just poke that thing with your finger.'

Karamchand searched for Ammachi's Song on Facebook. The search brought him to ammachi seated in this digital era, singing about the migrations of the forties. He saved the link for future use.

'Incidentally, Sameera, I discovered something wonderful. If trains hadn't been introduced, our famous Malabar migration would've never happened.'

'Karamchand, if there were no trains, we would've never met.'

'When man was made, an ever-spinning cogwheel was installed in him. That keeps him moving.'

Around the heap of rice were small packages. Each one opened to reveal a different vegetable.

While Karamchand watched, sautéed spinach jumped out of the open dinner and fled back to the village. It arrayed itself as healthy rows of spinach plants in a plot of land. The taro stem used in the curry stood by the parapet of the well and nodded its head. Raindrops fell and rolled off its water-repelling leaves. Karamchand placed the old couple in a tiled house on that plot of land. He thought that was the habitat best suited for them.

The couple started dinner.

'What do you do?' asked Sameera.

'Rubber tapping. Now that rubber prices have crashed, I have no work. My daughter told me that I can get a job as a security guard in Delhi. So, we're going.'

Karamchand planted rubber in a half-acre area to the west of the tiled house. He fenced it with screw pine trees. The rubber trees grew fast; a bamboo container tied to his waist, the old man went to tap rubber.

His wife was walking alongside him. 'Shall we buy a cow?' she asked.

'I too had the same idea,' he said as he tapped the rubber trees.

They opened a small package. 'It's game meat,' the old man said. An appetising aroma of the plantain leaf into which the still-warm meat had been dropped mixed with that of the meat and spread around them. Sameera started to salivate.

'Would you like some?' the old man asked Sameera. She looked at Karamchand. Both of them eyed the grilled game meat seasoned with wet ground coconut and red chillies.

A crazed sambar deer bounded into their plantation. It could have knocked down the old man who was standing beside the rubber tree. Shouting, he leapt back. However, by then the deer had collapsed. When he looked back, he saw his panting wife standing with a bloodied sickle in her hand. 'How did you reach so fast from so far?' he wondered. 'I ran to save you, not myself,' his wife said. 'If the forest officials see this, we'll be both hauled off to jail and spend the rest of our lives there.' They managed to drag the carcass home. They cut it up and cooked dishes with the meat. The rest, they pickled in ceramic crocks.

'To be honest, I have a craving for the meat,' Sameera said. The old man tore off a piece of the plantain leaf and handed it over with some meat on it. Sameera and Karamchand shared it. The newly pregnant woman's craving found its gratification thus. The passengers became busy with their dinners. The only sounds that were heard were the meals provided in the Sampark Kranti Express being masticated and pulverised. Like grinding machines, the passengers ground down the food with staccato crackling and gentler, steady state rhythms.

Seat no. 6 was empty. Karamchand parked himself there. Having reached a fork in their journey, the passengers closed their eyes to dream about the place and people they had left behind; their destination and the people they were going to meet there. Sleep refused to give Karamchand company. He sat at Sameera's feet, watching the flickering lights of villages. Sameera was stretched out and her ample frame had appropriated the lion's share of seat no. 5.

Karamchand was waiting for a special passenger who was expected to board from Mangalore. During that nerve-wracking wait, the boy with no history started to grow.

28

THE BOY WITH NO HISTORY - I

After the riots, the city was manifesting a mindset of the Middle Ages. A public trial was in progress. The roars of a delusional mob reverberated everywhere. Singing and dancing, people were headed to the public grounds as if they were going to a festival. Someone was on trial for treason. It was certain that capital punishment would be decreed and carried out. The whole city was heading there to watch and be exhilarated.

The police walked an old man to the grounds where the trial was being held. The mayor and other prominent citizens were seated in the gallery. The duty-bound police and officials were dashing around, performing their duties. School buses arrived and disgorged students. They had been brought to honour the mayor's decree that students should witness the execution. His rationale was that this would help instil and reinforce civic consciousness, righteousness and patriotism in the students.

On the previous occasion, the man who had been executed was one who had refused to stand up when the national anthem was played. It was only after he had been executed that they discovered he was handicapped.

'The last time it was death by hanging, remember?' a child asked his friend.

'The hangman of that day was fond of children,' another child said.

'The person to be executed had colourful papers festooned all over him,' a cute-looking girl commented.

'When he was dangled from the end of the rope and dropped, his writhing was fun to watch. It was as if he was dancing!'

'At that time, his relatives chanted aiyyo, aiyyo in a strange tune. That was fun too.'

'I wonder how they will do it today.'

'They will probably chop his head off?'

'We must be careful or the blood will spatter our uniforms. My mother will scold me.' The children continued their discussion.

The municipal council had only recently accepted the accountant-general's recommendation that hanging caused losses to the treasury and bullets were cheaper. Further, there was the added benefit of using the indicted people for target practice by the police. There was no doubt that this would energise the police and encourage them to hunt down more criminals. However, the municipal council also decided that on special occasions such as festivals, anniversaries etc., death by hanging would be conducted as a heritage ritual.

However, this was the first execution to take place after the recommendation made by the finance estimates committee, which had said that given the increase in the number of traitors at the current rate, and the price of a single bullet—100 rupees—the city would soon go bankrupt. It would be more economical, said the committee, to behead them with a sword.

The person to be executed was an old man. Even if no one had killed him, he would have soon died of his own accord. With his hands cuffed behind him, two policemen brought him to the centre of the public grounds. Age had debilitated him. He walked slowly but his head was held high. His eyes, full of intelligence, were sparkling. The screaming crowds fell silent. Judges, police authorities and administrators took their seats in the front row.

The two-year-old daughter of the mayor was babbling, attracting everyone's attention. She had been born after a long wait. Apparently, as per the democratic system, after the mayor's tenure, the citizens should elect this girl as their ruler.

From the crowds, a boy came forward. He opened a scroll and started to read out the charges against the accused. The city's policy required that a teacher should be charged and cross-examined by his students and a doctor by his patients.

The boy read in a voice that faltered with the tentativeness of adolescence.

'I am reading out the chargesheet against you. Charge one. You claimed that the history created now for our city, that it has an illustrious heritage, is bunkum. Our highly imaginative historians have churned out these books after toiling for countless days and nights.

'Charge two. You spread the calumny that the current mayor, when he was your student, was a dolt and a brute. Although this is sufficient reason for you to be given capital punishment, the third charge too is being read here.

'Charge three. In the documents found in your writing room, made out in your hand, you have stated that this city is a black dwarf star hurtling towards the primitive ages.'

The boy read the chargesheet in full. Then he bowed towards the old man and the crowd.

The old man stood with the usual beatific smile on his face. Their excitement having increased by a few notches, the crowd howled and cheered. The executioner stepped up, sword in hand. Its edge glinted in the sun. The crowd, panting to see the execution, egged him on.

'Our culture respects teachers. Even though he is a traitor, he is still a guru. Therefore, we shall all observe a moment of silence and pray for the salvation of his soul,' the mayor announced. The people rose to their feet.

The sword rose and fell. The old man's head tumbled to the floor and kept rolling, as if with a will of its own. A sardonic smile remained on its lips.

The crowds hailed the mayor. Children clapped their hands in glee. There was just one person in that crowd who registered his protest by stomping his long legs on the ground. He is a young man now, that protester. He is the young man with no history.

29

DISENGAGED

The Sampark Kranti Express entered Mangalore Station. The Malayalam heard in Kasaragod Station became more contorted and turned into Kannada-laced Tulu.

Suddenly, Karamchand noticed that Sameera had gone to sleep with her head in his lap. It had happened without either of them being conscious of it. Gently lifting her head and placing it on a pillow, Karamchand went out of the coach. Carvalho was outside on the platform. Elvindas and his colleague Ramkesh Meena stood a little further away. A lot of passengers were disembarking and embarking. A Marwadi was arguing with Carvalho. Karamchand did not pay them any attention.

Carvalho was trying to expel a beggar who had entered the coach through the vestibule. Trying to stop his expulsion, the beggar was bleating wretchedly. He was remonstrating in Marathi. The only word Karamchand could pick up from the stream of indistinctly spoken Marathi was 'Pandharpur', which sounded familiar. Carvalho was drowning the beggar's implorations with repeated bellows: 'Saale, maadarchod!'

A Railway policeman arrived and flung him out of the coach. Poking the beggar in the small of his back with his lathi, he drove him away to the farther end of the platform. Carrying a big cloth bundle, the man limped off towards the rear of the train. His plaintive cries that resembled the howls of a wild animal grew feebler.

Karamchand waited at the door of S6. Narendra Dabholkar, M73, Mangalore–Vadodara. Karamchand recognised him as he was approaching the coach through the crowd. Dabholkar was wearing a sparkling white kurta and pyjama. His light-coloured eyes transcended the thick lenses. There were stray black hairs in a head full of grey, as if they were somehow highlighting the greyness. He entered the coach. Karamchand watched him with respect and admiration.

The train started to move again. It gradually gained speed. There was a distressed scream from the end of the platform. '*Mera Pandharpur ... meri chhoti bachchi ... mera gaon ... aaahh ... aaah ...*' Ignoring the heart-rending wail, the train surged ahead. His pitiful cry travelled till the edge of the platform and toppled over.

The train looked like a moving city to those watching from afar.

Karamchand was now travelling on another train. He had to change many trains to be on this one. As he wondered where he should go next, he suddenly found himself in the Miraj Railway Station on a narrow-gauge line. A quaint train was waiting for him at the platform. An almost toy-train comprising four passenger coaches, two goods wagons, one milk tanker and one fuel tanker. An antique steam locomotive, panting and wheezing, was attached to it.

Without further thought, he entered one of the passenger bogies. His pockets were empty. The books in his bag had been read and reread. Hunger and sleeplessness had tired him out. His home had started to beckon him again.

While he stood alone and lost in the city centre a little while ago, he had a random yearning—if only a stranger would tap him on his shoulder and ask him why he was standing in the sun, and enquire if he had eaten anything, and when he answered in the negative, took his hand with affectionate authority and bid him to follow him. And when they were parting, hugged him like a brother. Nothing of that sort happened though. Like any other city, that city too was full of busy people.

When his thoughts moved from why no one was hugging him to why he wasn't hugging anyone, he felt like laughing.

The coach had very few passengers. All of them were farmers in soiled dhotis or shabbily dressed village women. As the train chugged on at a gentle pace, he let loose his imagination in the large swathe of sugarcane fields on the side of the tracks. He extricated a well-thumbed book from his bag and opened it to read.

The train stopped at a small halt station that had rails for pillars and asbestos roofing. Bougainvillea flowers looking like flames were spread on the roof. A shepherd with three or four sheep entered the train. The sheep also parked themselves on the seat beside him. Stuffing his decaying mouth with tobacco-laced paan, he too chewed, giving his sheep company. Karamchand kept gazing at them. The sheep and the man had the same features and the same expression.

A woman and her daughter entered and sat on the vacant seat across Karamchand. Like the sheep, they were also chewing the cud. They were spitting out chewed-out sugarcane pieces through the window. The woman was homely. She and her daughter conversed in rustic Marathi unintelligible to Karamchand and kept looking at him now and then.

Karamchand looked at the daughter from behind the book. Two curious eyes shone beyond the spine of the book. Now two unwavering pairs of eyes were locked on each other, but for no longer than a moment. The solitude that had been dogging him for a long time ended in that one moment.

He closed the book and kept it back. He had a desire to touch her. His feet crept up till they were next to hers. Their toes touched. She withdrew her leg as if she had touched a live wire.

Karamchand could see visions of an isolated village in her eyes. A small grass-roofed hut among the neem trees at the far end of a large tract of fields. Skinny cows chewing the cud, lying in the sun. One hen. A tall and lean old man with a hunched back who lay doubled up on a charpoy in the yard. A young woman fetching water from a remote well in plastic pots balanced on her head. The susurration of wind blowing through dry sugarcane leaves.

Someone's whistling from sugarcane fields. The cheeks of the girl blush; coyness adorns them.

The zamindar's son. Her lover.

The shepherd and his sheep got down at a subsequent station. Where will the girl get down? The thought that shortly she too would get down made Karamchand's heart flutter. He smiled at her. She returned the smile. Language that had become diversified beyond the Vindhya–Satpura ranges became an impediment between them. Yet they communicated with each other using the secret language that eyes understand.

Against his wishes the train rolled to a stop. The mother, followed by the girl, disembarked. Suffocated as if the Mandara mountain was weighing down on his chest, Karamchand ran to the door. Till now he had been lost in a world of his imagination. Another human being with whom he could communicate was close to him. A dreamy language beyond mere words suffused the space between them. She was already walking away from him. The train whistled. She turned back and looked. She was certain that he would be at the door. She smiled broadly, displaying her yellowing teeth, and then hastened her steps.

From the Himalayan heights of fantasy, Karamchand tumbled down to the depths of loneliness. The train disappeared into another sugarcane field.

He again heard that wretched wailing that yanked him back from the world of reverie to the present. '*Mera Pandharpur ... meri chhoti bachchi ... mera gaon ... aaahh ... aaah ...*'

'Trains have the cruel habit of seducing men and leading them astray,' Karamchand thought.

30

NOCTURNAL LIAISONS

24 January.

Midnight, when two days enter into a clinch and make love. When the earth has completed one more of its meaningless rotations. Karamchand felt that he was a tiny ant clinging to a circle that started with the wheels of the train and comprised the earth, the sun, the solar system, the Milky Way and the stars. The train was crawling on the crust of the earth like a millipede. An ecosystem that depended on its vicissitudes had bloomed and branched out like a canopy. When seen holistically, what kind of complex, compartmentalised prison cells have foolish human beings created in the name of systems? The nation is one such. Instead of sprouting like a plant and dying and rotting there, humans are immersed in pointless pursuits and fruitless experiments.

His thoughts zooming off on a wild ride robbed Karamchand of his sleep. Across him, Sameera lay asleep. He moved the window curtain to the side. In the moonlight, he saw her ample bosom rise and fall. Beguiled, he watched her inhale open-mouthed as if to fill her plump body.

Doubting Dowager woke up. A plastic mug in hand, she headed for the toilet. She paused by Karamchand's side and thought, 'Why is he awake? Does he also have acid reflux like I do? When he's awake at this time of the night, what are his thoughts? Is he a thief? If he is, what are the things he steals?'

She walked to the toilet. Karamchand started to feel sleepy. He rose to return to his coupé. Sameera's hand tightened around his own, without him realising it.

'Man, a penny for your thoughts,' she said sleepily.

'I was thinking about Socrates,' he lied.

'Oh, I know of him. Studied about him in Class 9. He was the guy who wrote a play named *Hamlet*, right?'

'No, someone who was forced to drink hemlock and die. Let me go sleep. See you.'

Sameera did not let go of his hand.

'You stay here. Anyway, there's a vacant berth.'

'But you snore.'

'Guy, sit down! I am bored and not able to sleep. And feeling cold too. Will you lie by my side and hug me?'

He pulled the curtain to the side. The sight of the world in motion outside entered their space. He lay down beside her. He pressed his warmth onto her shoulders. She had slipped back into a calm sleep. His warm breath fell on the curls on the nape of her neck. Pulling the corridor curtain close, they disappeared from the sight of the rest of the world.

'You are shivering because an evil design is lurking within you,' Sameera said. 'Lie close to me, I just need your warmth.'

Karamchand failed to find sleep. Two people who assumed life forms in the energy cycle that had no beginning or end were providing warmth to each other. He lay watching the sky outside. He watched the stars fly through the strands of Sameera's hair that lay across his face. Some strands hid a few of the stars. How inconsequential were the stars; the moon looked like a ripened mango ready to drop. She was snoring gently.

Karamchand touched her eyelids with his left hand. They were closed in slumber. The fingers slipped down her nose and reached her nostrils. Warm breath. The fine hairs on the philtrum and above the upper lip. Lips …

His hand shivered uncontrollably.

'Naughty boy,' she mumbled drowsily. He withdrew his hand as if it had touched fire. Body and mind, beast and culture faced off, locked horns and bellowed war cries. Electric impulses shot through his limbs and organs; his nerves throbbed and became swollen.

However, fear overcame every tumescence and arousal. The heat in their bodies went up immeasurably, unreadable by any thermometer. Blood-pounding desire leached into the marrow.

Fear!

Somewhere during the tussle between fear and desire, sleep arrived. When Karamchand woke up again, Sameera was awake.

'Did you go to sleep as soon as I lay down?'

'I didn't sleep at all.' He was stunned.

'I was involved in an experiment.'

'What kind of experiment?'

'Understanding if I would be able to lie next to a stranger cold and sober without undergoing emotional highs and lows.'

'What were your findings?'

'I leave that to your imagination.'

'Aha,' Karamchand sighed deeply. 'Let me go,' he said, looking at his watch. It was 4 a.m.

'Umm …'

Sameera accompanied him till the door. She stood holding the door handle, looking at the moon that was following the train. 'Where might have we reached by now?'

'Some remote village in Karnataka,' Karamchand replied.

She opened her bag, gathered some mustard seeds from inside and flung them out.

'What was that?' a puzzled Karamchand asked.

'Mustard seeds. There's a reason. I may end up telling it to you.'

Before reaching his coach, he had to pass through the Sleeper coaches. As he was passing through the vestibule, he looked down. Below him, the rail tracks were speeding backwards. Two bogies stay coupled together only on the strength of a screw coupling that could go out of commission at any time. Any big train can break up into many sections if there is a collision.

Karamchand was getting into S2 from S1. Suddenly the checkered steel plate under his legs moved out of its slot. There was a loud report. The train wobbled and shook more than usual. Before he realised what was happening, a large hole appeared in front of him. The engine whistle hooted three or four times.

The passengers were asleep. Since such unexplained loud sounds were expected in a train, no one woke up. The Sampark Kranti Express had broken up into two. The two sections decelerated and came to a stop. Clutching the handles of the vestibule, Karamchand stood at the threshold of the vestibule, still shivering in terror. He experienced the void that appears suddenly when a train splits into two. At that moment, a hand touched his shoulder. Startled, he looked around.

'Don't be shocked. This is common on trains. In other words, trains are designed and manufactured to be coupled and decoupled quickly.' It was Elvindas. 'Don't raise an alarm. If other passengers get to know of this, there'll be a hue and cry.'

Karamchand went to the door and looked out. A flashlight in hand, the assistant loco pilot was walking towards the bogie. The guard from the tail of the train shined his own torch. The truncated front section started to shunt back slowly. Karamchand went back to the vestibule and watched the front section roll back towards the remaining section of the train. As it got closer, he could make out a feminine form standing at the other opening, scared, pale and looking at the darkness with unseeing eyes.

He succeeded in recalling her name: Nimesha Mehta. After re-coupling the train, the guard and the driver returned to their respective positions. Shortly, a long whistle was heard and the train started to roll on ahead as if nothing extraordinary had happened. Through the vestibule which had become one again, Karamchand walked into the next coach. Nimesha did an about turn and walked on.

As he walked along, passing by the travellers stacked one above the other in the bays, he was reminded of crypts. On berth no. 7 in the S6 coach, the TTE lay asleep. From the name plate on the black jacket that hung from the hook, Karamchand read the name—Ramkesh Meena. He had enough time for a nap. The next stop was Madgaon.

None of the lights were on in the coach. Karamchand walked forward in the darkness. He saw a light at the end of the coach. When he reached there, he saw that the light came from Narendra Dabholkar's berth. His bald head shining, Dabholkar was reading in the dim light of the reading lamp. His thick lenses gave his face an ineffable majesty. Unwittingly a name appeared on Karamchand's tongue and slipped out in silence: Old Savant!

Karamchand sat down at the end of the seat. The old man raised his head and looked at him.

'The train split into two, didn't it?'

'Yes, but no one is aware of that.'

'What's your name?'

'Karamchand.'

'That's interesting. All right, how are you related to Gandhi?'

'Only as much as every Indian is related to him.'

'You know the connection that Gandhi has with trains, don't you?'

'Yes, from the point of him being thrown out of the train till Indian Independence. I've read most of it.'

'Once, during the Non-Cooperation Movement, he was travelling from Jorhat to Dibrugarh on a special train. At midnight, his train collided with a goods train. There were no casualties. After detaching the bogie in which Gandhi was travelling, the train resumed its journey. Only after it had run a fair distance did the driver and the guard realise that Gandhi was a passenger in the coach that had been left behind. They shunted the train back all the way and reattached Gandhi's coach. Our history includes such amusing moments.'

'Do you have any more such interesting stories?'

'Gandhi has written that the Railways had a role in spreading epidemics like the plague in India. Gandhi was the sharpest critic of the Railways as well as one of its biggest beneficiaries.'

'I wasn't aware of all this.'

'You should be. Having given his name to you, he has conferred some responsibilities on you too.'

Karamchand wanted to engage the old man in more conversation. However, seeing how immersed he was in his reading, almost as if he was meditating, he did not have the heart to disrupt it. He walked back, got into B Coupé and closed the door. John was asleep on his berth.

Karamchand downloaded the article written by Gandhi in 1908 in *Hind Swaraj*.

It must be manifest to you that, but for the railways, the English could not have such a hold on India as they have. The railways, too, have spread the bubonic plague. Without them, the masses could not move from place to place. They are the carriers of plague germs. Formerly we had natural segregation. The railways have also increased the frequency of famines because, owing to the facility of the means of locomotion, people sell out their grain and it is sent to the dearest markets. People become careless and so the pressure of famine increases. The railways accentuate the evil nature of man: Bad men fulfil their evil designs with greater rapidity. The holy places of India have become unholy. Formerly, people went to these places with very great difficulty. Generally, therefore, only the real devotees visited such places. Nowadays rogues visit them in order to practise their roguery.

Good travels at a snail's pace—it can, therefore, have little to do with the railways. Those who want to do good are not selfish, they are not in a hurry, they know that to impregnate people with good requires a long time. But evil has wings. To build a house takes time. Its destruction takes none. So the railways can become a distributing agency for the evil one only. It may be a debatable matter whether the railways spread famines, but it is beyond dispute that they propagate evil.

The English have taught us that we were not one nation before and that it will require centuries before we become one nation. This is without foundation. We were one nation before they came to India. One thought inspired us. Our mode of life was the same. It was because we were one nation that they were able to establish one kingdom. Subsequently they divided us.

I do not wish to suggest that because we were one nation we had no differences, but it is submitted that our leading men travelled throughout India either on foot or in bullock carts. They learned one another's languages and there was no aloofness between them. What do you think could have been the intention of those far-seeing ancestors of ours who established Setubandha (Rameshwar) in the South, Jagannath in the East and Hardwar in the North as places of pilgrimage? You will admit they were no fools. They knew that worship of God could have been performed just as well at home. They taught us that those whose hearts were aglow with righteousness had the Ganges in their own homes. But they saw that India was one undivided land so made by nature. They, therefore, argued that it must be one nation. Arguing thus, they established holy places in various parts of India, and fired the people with an idea of nationality in a manner unknown in other parts of the world. And we Indians are one as no two Englishmen are.

Only you and I and others who consider ourselves civilised and superior persons imagine that we are many nations. It was after the advent of the railways that we began to believe in distinctions, and you are at liberty now to say that it is through the railways that we are beginning to abolish those distinctions. An opium-eater may argue the advantage of opium-eating from the fact that he began to understand the evil of the opium habit after having eaten it. I would ask you to consider well what I had said on the railways.

India cannot cease to be one nation because people belonging to different religions live in it. The introduction of foreigners does not necessarily destroy the nation; they merge in it. A country is one nation only when such a condition obtains in it. That country must have a faculty for assimilation. India has ever been such a country. In reality there are as many religions as there are individuals; but those who are conscious of the spirit of nationality do not interfere with one another's religion. If they do, they are not fit to be considered a nation. If the Hindus believe that India should be peopled only by Hindus, they are living in a dreamland. The Hindus, the Mahomedans, the Parsis and the Christians who have made India their country are fellow-countrymen, and they will have to live in unity, if only for their own interest. In no part of the world are one nationality and one religion synonymous terms; nor has it ever been so in India.

I would ask you to consider well what I had said on the railways.

Before Karamchand lay down to sleep and pulled the blanket over himself, he wrote in his notepad: 'What extraordinary experiences I have passed through today, which a common man would consider implausible.'

He fell asleep.

'Where are you going, sir?'

Dabholkar raised his head and looked at Karamchand.

Karamchand said, 'I have heard of you.'

In reply, Old Savant only smiled amiably.

'To Ahmedabad.'

'You're a Marathi, aren't you?'

'Yes. I'm from Pune.'

'And in Pune?' This was an insubstantial conversation that could be terminated at any point.

'Budhwar Peth.' As soon as Karamchand heard the name of the street, a new dream migrated into his current dream.

Karamchand and his friend Amit Banjare were walking on the busy street of Budhwar Peth. Banjare was indefatigable. When asked why, his reply was, 'We banjaras are nomads. Walking is second nature to us. When you people congregated near river banks and gained weight from hogging, we gypsies walked the plains and mountains many times over. Now hurry up.' Karamchand struggled to keep up with him.

'Do you know there was a time when banjara women practised prostitution as a profession?' Karamchand envisioned an auxiliary army of banjara women who walked by the side of regular armies, working as comfort women for libidinous soldiers.

Budhwar Peth is a long street. It is the shrine where the city unloads its burden of lust. Both of them walked through the fort of lust. Standing in the ancient lanes and in front of decrepit buildings, women with painted faces beckoned them with lewd, come-hither gestures. It was Karamchand's first time in a red-light district. An exhibition-cum-sale of adorned bodies.

The street was overflowing with johns, common pedestrians and hawkers. Karamchand wondered where Banjare was finally taking him. Shortly he drew up in front of a painted board that read 'Carel's Brothel'.

'Read the board fully,' commanded Banjare.

'Carel's Brothel. Discount for Keralites. Estd. 1945.' An amazed and amused Karamchand repeated, 'Discount for Keralites.'

'Put your best foot forward. Pray to your family deities.' With an arm around his shoulder, Banjare ushered him in.

In the brothel parlour, on a sofa whose upholstery was in shreds, ladies of the night sat, trying to hide their sunken cheeks, wrinkles and other imperfections under a lavish coat of powder and makeup. Banjare took one of the chairs and sat down, crossing his legs. He had the aspect of a paterfamilias who had brought the baby for his baptism. Karamchand too took a seat.

Customers were coming in, and women were accompanying them up a flight of stairs. The walls were pasted with revealing pictures of Bollywood heroines. In between them were full-size photos of two men with forbidding looks. Karamchand was more concerned with finding out why a rebate was being offered to Malayalis.

A middle-aged man dressed in shorts and T-shirt came down the spiral staircase. He pulled a chair and sat across Karamchand and Banjare. Karamchand had only one question for him—the provenance of the discount for Malayalis.

'Look,' the man pointed to the first photograph. 'That's my grandpa, A. Carel. He was the first one to start a modern bordello in this city. For him it was humanitarian work too. Before him, this city too, like any town or village in Kerala, was a desolate land as far as matters of the flesh were concerned.

'Only after his arrival in Pune as an officer in the British army did he realise how sexually starved the soldiers he commanded were. He did not sit on his hands. He imported prostitutes from all over the world.

'As soon as the Second World War was over, to be precise, in November 1945, Carel's Brothel opened its doors for business. Today, the institution that was started with a Jewish prostitute—whom the Russians had saved from the gas chambers—and a South Indian woman, has one hundred and seventeen professionals, their ages ranging from six to sixty. It's one of great renown.

'My grandpa was an Anglo-Indian born in Kerala. Then, as now, Malayali men would stare at women, their tongues lolling like rabid dogs. My grandpa has told me that in his life he has not seen so many sexually deprived, lecherous men anywhere else in the world. How are men able to incarcerate women and molest them for months together? Therefore, this is the place for Malayalis to have their baptism. Half rate. A man who comes here should enjoy all the pleasures a woman can offer before he leaves.'

Banjare looked at Karamchand and smiled.

'The man in the second photo is my father, B. Carel. He started the school and a pigmy bank for the inmates. That was the time aged sex workers started to die from occupational diseases. He built a beautiful crematorium for them. With that, a girl born in this place had no need to depend on the outside world for any of her needs. Getting born was all that they had to do. Study here, earn here, deliver here, and die here. My name is C. Carel. The third generation. Do you want to know anything more?'

Karamchand chose a girl named Rathina. He was attracted to her Dravidian features, especially that look in her eyes. Holding his hand, she climbed the wooden stairs to the first floor. At the landing, a naked woman was seated on the floor. The sight of her nakedness, his first encounter, made him tremble. She was boiling mutton soup.

The first floor was divided into small chambers. There was a pervasive pong of sweat and seminal fluid in the corridor. From behind the closed doors of the chambers, hisses and moans, laughter and swearing could be heard. The frustrated male of the human species was venting his sexual energy.

Rathina and Karamchand entered a chamber and shut the door behind them. The desires that had been bottled up inside for years were surging out.

'Why did you choose me from among so many girls?' she asked him.

'Among all the girls I saw contentment only on your face.'

She gave him a disbelieving look. She started to undress. Karamchand quickly stopped her.

'No. I only need to talk to you.'

She looked surprised. 'Are you a journalist?'

'Oh, no! Many have written about your kind of girls.'

'Are you a writer then?' She spat out the paan masala that she was chewing into the washbasin. 'If you are doing a feature on me, you have to pay me more. Fifty rupees.'

'I'll pay.'

'If my photos are taken, it'll be a hundred more.'

'I don't need any photos. But, can I ask you something?'

'Umm ...'

'Why are you chewing paan all the time?'

'Ha, ha. That is my protection. Some of the regulars, old men, are more interested in putting my mouth to use. So paan masala is a kind of armour plating for me. Do you get it?'

Rathina sat next to him. He got a close look at her highly efficient body upon which myriad men had collapsed, sweating and panting. The hard water of the Deccan had corroded her teeth. She showed signs of premature greying. Her nail polish was scratched and she had dirt under her nails. Her left forearm had Telugu words tattooed on it. He found it amusing. He ran his fingers over the tattoo and asked, 'What's this?'

'Krishna.'

'Who's that?'

'My lover.'

Karamchand looked at her in surprise. 'What does he do?'

'Nothing.'

'Meaning?'

'The police shot him dead when he was on his way from Warangal to Dandakaranya.'

'Wha ...?'

'The police claim it was an encounter. That is far from the truth. Our wedding day was drawing close. He was in high spirits.'

'Hmm ...'

'And didn't Carel tell you that I was the most contented inmate here?'

'Yes.'

'That's true. Every man who comes is Krishna to me.'

Sounds of lovemaking could be heard from behind the cardboard partition.

'Yours is too bloody big,' said a feminine voice. 'Ha, ha, ha,' Banjare's laughter burst through the partition.

As the laughter rebounded off the walls, Karamchand shut the door on the second dream and returned to the first one. Narendra Dabholkar was waiting for him there.

'We shall discuss all this tomorrow morning. I have to give a speech tomorrow at Ahmedabad University.' The door closed on his first dream too.

Karamchand woke up and looked at his watch. He had not been asleep for even ten minutes. If that be the case, what is the duration of a dream? Time is so relative. He looked through the window. It was still dark. The train's presence now was reduced to a mere rhythm. Cleaving the darkness and as if trying to break the sound barrier, the train roared through an unknown landscape.

He pulled up his blanket and covered himself. Within minutes he was fast asleep.

THE STORY SO FAR

The emotional history of India includes that of the Railways too. The trains moved, creating the history of modern India and engaging with it.

The rail tracks did not mark India's surface alone; occasionally they went deeper into its antiquity.

John Brunton and his son William Arthur Brunton were in charge of building the rail line between Karachi—which was then a sleepy fishing village—and Lahore. During construction along the Indus river, they noticed that workers had fetched hard burnt bricks to lay as ballast for the tracks. While trying to find the source of the stones, they chanced upon the ruins of the prehistoric city of Brahminabad. They were the relics of a millennia-old civilisation.

The world was shocked by the great civilisation that subsequent excavations in that dead landscape revealed.

This is the story of how the Harappa civilisation was discovered.

To be continued ...

PART TWO

Herd Animal

Herd Animal

Once, a strange animal appeared in our village. Unsure where it had come from or where it should head out to, it wandered around our isolated village amidst three hills. It was a common, undistinguished donkey.

Those who travelled to Tamil Nadu and Sabarimala had seen the animal. It uncomplainingly bore whatever burden was placed on it. We had only seen it and read of it in stories. Having heard of its presence, many people came from everywhere to see the donkey. The donkey turned into a celebrity. It figured in everyone's conversation, it became the subject of every hair-splitting debate. All the discussions ended in one question: Why didn't any god or goddess make the donkey his or her mount?

The donkey did not involve itself in any of the debates. After chewing up and eating the rubber slippers it found on the way, it went into the bus shelter and curled up. Eventually, the decisive question arose—what was to be done with the donkey? A mad man adopted it, fed it grass and watered it, and mounted it. Wearing a crown of jackfruit leaves, he sat on it regally, whipping and driving it on.

Hooting and screaming, the public ran after the donkey and its rider. Spooked by the screams, the donkey set off on an uncontrolled run. The public did not give up. Eventually, the donkey and its pursuers fell into the village pond. That pond is now known as Kazutha Vizunthamkulam, in commemoration of the event.

Moral of the story: Asses who follow the ass will eventually fall into an asshole.

8.5k Likes   6.5k Comments   2.8k Shares

1

WATER BATTLE - I

The train had slowed down to tackle the dangerous curves in the valley. It was running late and the scheduled arrival time at Madgaon was long gone. The passengers in the Sleeper coaches were up in arms. There were raised voices from the B1 coach; the pilgrims were challenging someone weakly.

Karamchand woke up. He could hear the sound of feet in the corridor. The men knocked on the cabin doors, looking for the TTE. Karamchand emerged from his cabin. He asked Scraggly Beard, who was rushing by, what the issue was.

'There's no water in any of the coaches, sir,' he said breathlessly as he kept walking.

'Where is the TTE?' someone asked.

Karamchand pointed to Carvalho's cabin. They banged on his door. He emerged and was greeted by a volley of complaints, 'No water!'

'Is this a train or a desert?' someone railed.

Carvalho pressed the tap inside his cabin. Water gushed out. Yawning, he told those who crowded around the door, 'There's water.'

'We are not telling you about this coach. There's no water in the Sleeper coaches.'

Carvalho looked out the window. He was familiar with all the landmarks on the route. From the smell that came in, the sound of the wheels as they screeched or purred over the tracks, and the height of the trees, he could make out the area that the train was passing through.

Only as they were passing through Surathkal did he realise that the train was unreasonably late. The iron ore from derailed wagons dumped on the next track was telltale enough for him to know where they were passing through.

'I'll arrange to take in water at Karwar Station,' Carvalho assured them.

The name 'Karwar' made a coolness wash all over Karamchand. He remembered the summer when he had bathed in the Kali river that cut the Western Ghats in half vertically and cascaded down as a waterfall. Trusting Carvalho's words, the passengers made their way back to their seats. The parting shot of a passenger was, 'We'll only have to bear with this till Karwar. After that ...'

Karamchand washed his face in the washbasin inside their coupé. The bogies that house rich people have water. Light. Air-conditioning. Attendants ask after their welfare. Carvalho emerged again, now in his uniform. With nothing else to do, Karamchand tailed him. 'We TTEs have our morning walk in this fashion,' Carvalho told him.

He met Sameera in A1. It was apparent that she had woken up only a little while ago. He felt like something of an enigma was weighing on her face. The old couple was hunched up, swathed in their blankets. He went past them and kept dogging Carvalho's heels.

Doubting Dowager parted the blue curtains, poked her head out and wondered, 'Why do humans need all this water? Who discovered bathing? Why do humans bathe? In any case, humans will die one day. What's the difference between dying after drinking water and before?' She withdrew her head through the curtains. She belched, imagining the arrival of the tea vendor, buying the piping hot tea, blowing on it to cool it before drinking and abusing him that it wasn't sweet enough.

Meanwhile, in the adjacent cabin, a conversation was taking place. 'What's the ruckus about?' the retired teacher asked.

'There is no water apparently,' his wife replied.

'Water will be the main problem humankind will face in the future. There will be wars to get hold of water resources ...' the man said.

'Exactly! Twenty years back, we had never thought of buying water in bottles.'

'Where don't they have water?'

'Behind us. In the Sleeper coaches.'

'Oh ...' With a deep sigh they concluded their discussion about water. Pulling the blankets over themselves, all four of them resumed their interrupted sleep.

When they entered B1, the tour guide greeted Carvalho. 'Sahib, I have a few things to discuss with you.' He stood there as if he had something momentous to talk about.

Carvalho sat down on a side seat.

'Sir, I don't sleep at night. So many elders are sleeping, trusting me. Around 1.30 a.m. the train stopped in some remote village. A lanky boy ran up and jumped into the AC coach. He was wearing only a pair of torn shorts. I thought he didn't have the physique to cause anyone any harm so I didn't mind him. I stayed at the door; he too, humming a song.

'The train was passing another village. Grass roof huts could be seen in the distance among large cotton fields. I've been travelling on this route now for so many years. The train reduced its speed. I could see an open flame far away; it must have been a signal. The boy pulled the chain as soon as the train came parallel to the flame.

'By the time I made an attempt to grab him, the train had screeched to a stop. He jumped down and vanished into the tall grasses by the side of the tracks. Then the real scene happened. Men and women rose from the clumps of sugarcane and tall grasses like otters rising out of the water on *National Geographic*. They came in droves. They swiftly entered the coaches, filled their pots, and vanished quicker than they had appeared. The boy apparently was the infiltrator who had been sent to unlatch the Sleeper coaches' doors for them.

'Everyone was fast asleep. I was about to raise an alarm when I noticed that they had spared the AC coaches. I was relieved. We were not affected so why should I bring trouble to those poor people? It's water, after all, sir. Life giver, sir. Ram ... Ram ...' Before the second Ram ended, the old people took up the chorus and started to chant, 'Ram ... Ram ... Ram ... Ram ...'

Karamchand could not help smiling. The woman who only a few minutes ago had chased away a passenger from the Sleeper coach who had come to collect water from the air-conditioned compartment was chanting the loudest. 'After all, it's water, bhaiyya. Life giving. Our Ganga maiyya. Mother to us. Ram ... Ram ...'

Carvalho listened to everything with marked disinterest. It was apparent to Karamchand that water pilferage was a daily occurrence in that place.

They walked ahead. The passengers in the Sleeper coaches were agitated. Some of the passengers stopped Carvalho and vented their anger. As they passed the vestibule of the S4 coach, the door of the toilet opened slowly and a head which looked piteous and comical at the same time peeked out tentatively. The head asked, 'Sir, when will the water supply resume?'

'At Karwar Station. Please wait for another half an hour.'

'It'll come, won't it? I won't be able to come out unless I get water. You won't understand unless you're in my position. I'm trapped.'

Karamchand stifled his laughter and kept walking. The face that looked like a synonym for helplessness withdrew into the toilet. The door closed.

The middle-aged woman stopped Carvalho. 'Will it come, TT sir?'

'It will, madam.'

'Back in our Gujarat, all we have to do is open the tap. If you want hot water, you have it, if you want it cold, you can have that too.'

'Behn, I heard that once when the taps were opened there, blood flowed out. Is it true?' the man with the beard tried to provoke the woman. The comment forced her to lower her head and remain silent for a while.

The passengers in S6 were also shouting for water. Ignoring the commotion, Old Savant took out another book from his satchel and started to read.

The train was detained in some small station. As if heralding the torridness of the forthcoming summer, the arrows of sunshine attacked like tiny demons. Half-dry stalks of grass yearned for shade. The sizzling-hot rail tracks lay bare-chested in the sun. Emerging from his tiny room, the stationmaster gestured with his hand.

'It's a crossing,' Carvalho told the other TTEs. They returned to the H1 coach.

Karamchand stayed at the door, watching the sights. He saw a tiny wilted plant walking in search of water. It was exhausted from walking. It desired to grow luxuriantly in the cool rain.

Karamchand switched on his tablet. He started to doodle on it with his index finger. Doodles turned into words. He closed his eyes. In his mind, only he and the plant remained. The plant became an ache inside him.

The train was waiting at the platform. The passengers had got down and were strolling around lazily. A moribund mango tree was looming over the platform. People were breaking off its half-dried leaves and chewing on them. The station had only a small, lime-washed room and two broken-down platforms. Beyond the tracks lay heaps of iron ore unloaded from derailed wagons. Like the hacked breasts of the Western Ghats.

From the north came a whistle, emerging from the tunnel. The mouth of the tunnel was hidden by tangled dried vines, lending it an air of mystery. Smoke rose from the face of the tunnel, accompanied by puffing sounds. Sounding like the end of the world, a goods train, hauled by three diesel engines, trundled by. Karamchand stood at the door, watching the dreadful beauty of that moving mass of steel. He grew into a child at that moment. He started to count, 'One ... two ... three ... fifty-eight ... Oh my gosh!' Marvelling at the child in him, the goods train left the station.

Already three hours behind schedule, the Sampark Kranti started to move again. Karamchand walked to the front of the train. In S6, he sought out Dabholkar.

'Was there a passenger named Dabholkar on this seat?'

'There was an old man here. I'm not sure if his name is Dabholkar,' someone replied.

Karamchand waited for some time and then headed back to his own coach. He took John's *India* and started to read.

Camera in hand, John entered, interrupting his reading. He showed Karamchand some of the pictures he had shot during their journey. The picture of a plastic bottle thrown out in an arc into the Sharavati river out of the speeding train that itself was curved like a bow was beautiful. Karamchand felt respect for John's sense of perspective and his keen eye.

Karwar was still half an hour away.

They sat in the air-conditioned coach, watching the scorching wind turn into a firestorm on the top of the hills split by fury. Only those seated inside the coach had the impression that the earth was, by and large, cool.

2

THE BOY WITH NO HISTORY - II

He was now a young man. His shoulders were broad and strong enough to bear the weight of leading a city or even a nation. He was waiting in queue at the Gateway of India to take a boat to the Elephanta Caves. Pigeons were billing and cooing and fighting in front of the memorial that had witnessed the departure of the last British soldier from Indian shores.

A tall, old man wearing a fez walked towards the pigeons. They swarmed around him. He scattered grains from his cloth bag. Jostling for space, the pigeons pecked at the grains. Some of them took the liberty of perching themselves on his head and shoulders. After emptying the bag, he walked back. The birds followed him for some distance. He looked back once from the iron gate. Rays of unconditional love beamed from his eyes towards the birds.

The young man wished to touch the old man. However, by then he had disappeared into the crowd.

Battering the waves, the boat left the city behind. He opened his bag. He pulled out a bloodstained burkha and threw it into the sea. Bobbing up and down for some time on the water like the carcass of a large sea bird, it disappeared from view.

He had ended up in the riot-torn city by chance. All the streetlamps had been smashed, and the city lay in complete darkness. With its vision impaired, the city communicated through sounds. Muted sounds became residuum within the terrible silence. Sometimes it was the sound of glass being smashed that broke the silence. Mothers smothered the cries of their babies in the hollows of their hands. In the pitch darkness, the strident sounds of a wordless cry came close and went away. The city lay in darkness like a capsule in which sounds had been interred. The smell of blood was pervasive.

When he heard the moans, he went to the corner they were emanating from. The sounds came from beneath a streetlamp that had been vandalised a long time ago. Two rabbit-like eyes shone from under a heap of firewood. He saw only later the body clad in a burkha that seemed to be one kind of darkness hiding within another darkness. Two doleful eyes gazed at him imploringly.

He threw away the bamboo staff he carried for self-defence. He held her hand and helped her up. He asked her to remove her burkha. She must have torn off the carapace of her religiosity trusting the glowing, imperative look in his eyes. He hid it in his bag. Hand in hand, they walked through the city as it thinned into a slum and then into a swamp.

She was handed over at one of the thousands of shanties with plastic sheets for roof. A few people, wrung out by privation, were waiting expectantly there. That house had sounds—the sounds of hunger swallowing up the stomach. Naked children ran up when they saw her. They snatched her bag and ran to the corner of the hut. It contained a cutlet that she had saved up from the refreshments provided by the garment factory that employed her. The famished children shared it hungrily.

As he was leaving the shanty, a home to woe, an old man with a hennaed beard asked, 'Beta, if you are not Allah himself, then who are you?'

'Me? I am the boy with no history,' he laughed.

Retaliatory rioting had started in another corner of the city. It would be dangerous to walk in the city now, dodging petrol bombs, swords and exhortations to kill. He took out the burkha, donned it, covered his face and started an unhurried walk.

The world he saw through the burkha was a different world altogether.

3

WATER BATTLE - II

The train reached Karwar Station. The passengers in the Sleeper and General compartments, who were sweating and pining for water, tumbled out. When they tried the water taps in the station, they were aghast. Seeing Carvalho at the door of the H1 coach, a few of them ran to him. 'Weren't you the one who said we'll get water at this station?'

Carvalho descended the steps and opened the two-inch valve of one of the filling hoses. The hose was at the fag end of the water cycle that had sprung from the heart of the green carpeted Western Ghats, become a thread, a stream, a rivulet, the Dudh Sagar river, a river system, a cascade and eventually delivered it for human use. He waited, but no water came out. He brought the mouth of the hose to his ear. He could only hear the sobs of the Dudh Sagar river.

Things went south from that point on. The need for water coalesced individual passengers into a fighting unit. Those who appeared to be weaklings turned into violent warriors. A group of over a hundred sat down on the tracks in front of the engine. Another group gheraoed the station. The stationmaster was locked up in his room. They screamed in various languages. The screams soon attained a rhythm. The thirsty, infuriated passengers marched up and down the platform shouting 'WAA-TER, WAA-TTER' at the top of their voices.

Amidst the cacophony of people speaking in tongues, a voice rose above all. 'Do you know who is speaking to you?'

The passengers turned around to locate the source of the challenge. The owner of the stentorian voice was a titan, over six feet tall, and with a physique to match his height—the very same middle-aged man who had threatened Carvalho that morning in the H1 coach. All the other voices ceased as if they were switched off. He raised his fist and said, 'Do you know who I am?'

People looked at him in admiration. Like obedient lambs they gathered around him. A tiger roared suddenly. People moved back in alarm. It roared again. He extricated his mobile phone from his pocket.

'My name is Dvi. We want water. *Humko abhi paani chaahiye.*' His voice was loud enough to be heard by everyone. Returning the phone to his pocket, he told the crowd, 'It's a railway official.'

He climbed on to the ledge around a pillar of the station building and addressed the crowd, 'We need water, *now*. My dear fellow passengers, chance brought us together on this journey. Our journey should have been a pleasant one, if not a happy one. However, we are now in a state where even the fundamental need for water has been denied to us.' Even those who were shouting slogans fell silent and paid attention to him.

'Therefore, I tell you all this: stay with me, support me. I'll get you water. I'll be with you always and be fighting for you. I'll even die for you. If you support me, no power in the world can ignore our demands. Give me your blood and I shall give you water.'

The speech ended with a round of loud applause. The crowd hailed him in one voice. They forgot all about the water. They forgot their thirst. For now they had gained something more essential and rarer than water—a leader.

Right in front of Karamchand's eyes, a leader was born. The passengers hailed him again. Followed by his entourage of energised supporters, he went to hold parleys with the stationmaster who, along with the train captain, was locked up in his room.

The water tank was at the north end of the platform. Scraggly Beard, who had been trapped in the toilet, was the one who discovered it. A water bottle in hand, he ran to the tank. He was wearing only a lungi with green stripes. He had run out of the toilet after all hopes that the water supply would resume ended. He opened the tap below the tank. As water gushed out and he started to fill the bottle, the railway staff rushed up to him.

'Don't touch this water. This tank is only for the Railway staff.'

However, he was in no condition to heed threats and give up on his agenda. A staff member knocked down his water bottle. Scraggly Beard pushed him back. Some passengers came to his help. The tussle between the passengers and the staff became a tug-o'-war with each party moving up and down. Karamchand thought that the tempo of the snake-boat race songs was apt for the ding-dong battle that was taking place in front of him.

'Kuttanaadan punjchayilae ...' the passengers are pushing the staff.

'Thiththithaara thiththitheyy ...' the staff is getting pushed back.

At the height of the rough-and-tumble, the water tank came crashing down. Its top flew off and fell upon the tracks. As the two sides fighting over the water watched, it flowed down the platform in a minor torrent, over the edge of the platform and onto the tracks. The moribund stalks of grass between the ballast on the tracks hungrily sucked in the water. In a few moments, the rest of the water evaporated.

Meanwhile, the leader had stationed his retinue outside and gone alone into the stationmaster's room. He gave the bewildered stationmaster a death stare, smashed his fist on top of the metal table and demanded, 'Does this place have any system at all?'

'Sir, please sit down,' the stationmaster requested. The leader sat down beside Carvalho, then looked out. A rough-and-ready mob was waiting, bursting to do his bidding. He felt greatly impressed with himself.

'Tell us, sir,' the stationmaster spoke in Kannada-accented Hindi. 'If you set your mind to it, we can resolve the problem, here and now.'

'How?' The leader imperiously shifted in his seat. He crossed his legs, looked through the window and ensured that the mob was still there. He realised that he had moved up from the status of an ordinary passenger to that of a leader.

'We'll take in water at the Madgaon Station. On the Konkan coast, only the Zuari river has some water. You will have to wait till we reach Goa.'

The leader had enough sense to understand that he had no option but to wait till Madgaon and that if the trouble escalated, the police would be called in, the protestors arrested and removed and the train allowed to proceed.

He went out and addressed the mob again, 'My dear co-passengers, the Railway authorities have buckled under the pressure I brought to bear on them. Initially they had promised to fill water at Ratnagiri Station but, unnerved by the vehemence of our protest, they have agreed to have it done at Madgaon. Despite the new dam at Salaulim, at Madgaon the train will get water. I, Dvi, am giving you this commitment. You can trust me on this. I'll be with you all the way. Jai Hind!'

The mob clapped heartily and ostentatiously.

'Be that as it may, I need at least a bottle of water now,' Scraggly Beard bleated from behind the crowd. 'Or I won't be able to even walk. No, no, no, not to drink. How can I make you understand?' No one heard him. He and his private sorrows were drowned out by the clamour.

After the crowd received the assurance from the stationmaster, the guard who had been gheraoed was released. A victory procession was organised from the engine to the guard's room. His head held high, Dvi was at the head of the procession. He did not shout slogans now. Some men in the rally did, and others repeated after them.

Behind the guard room, Dvi got onto the footboard above the cowcatcher on the Wanderer. Raising both his hands above his head, he declaimed to the crowd bubbling over with excitement, 'Water is a right of the generations.'

4

OLD SAVANT

Twisting and turning, the Sampark Kranti rolled on, skirting the edges of the hills from which greenery had disappeared. Karamchand returned to S6. He wanted to pick Dabholkar's brains. The old man was looking out of the window. Karamchand sat down next to him. The old man smiled at him. The depth of his experience shone in the annual rings of the wrinkles on his face.

'What is the seminar that you said you were to attend?'

'Growing Nationalism and Black Magic.'

'Oh yes! It is a bizarre subject, though. The mind is now accepting of black magic and suicides. I have some doubts that I need to clear with you. Please instruct me like you are my guru.'

'You may ask. But first, I shall say this about a guru. The guru is a place where a sceptic unburdens himself. When scepticism ceases, contemplation ceases. Therefore, there is no need for a guru.'

'My questions may be childish. Many have given definitions for them too. However, since the time I met you, they keep cropping up inside me.'

'I like questions.' Dabholkar spoke like a grandfather to a grandchild.

'It's because your subject is nationalism and black magic that I had these doubts all of a sudden. Nation, nationalism, patriotism and all that. Let's start with your views on the nation. What makes a nation?'

'A nation is an open jail. Look, mobility is human identity. The nation is a shackle put on our ankles. Our movement is circumscribed.'

'Oh?'

'The nation is an open jail. Its vastness is what stops us from realising this. If your nation was a geographical area of a mere one acre, you would realise it immediately, that man is locked in by boundaries.'

'Okay, if that be so, who created nations?'

'Where is the doubt? Man did. Everything that is against the natural order has been created by men. Men are territorial animals. Have you seen the city's sewage collection points? Even a garbage bin will have a dog as its master. If another dog comes upon the scene, a fight will ensue. This same canine quality is what leads to the formation of nations.'

'All right, what about nationalism?'

'For the dog I mentioned earlier, the garbage bin is the source of its livelihood. Now consider a man as the owner of the garbage bin. He will embellish the garbage bin with stories. Believing those stories, other people will join him. They will write and sing paeans about the bin. People will stand to attention when they hear those songs. They will declare that their bin is the greatest bin in the world. They will fight for it and become martyrs for it. Nationalism is a Survivalogy that a dog doesn't have and that man has planted, tended to and cultivated.'

'What about democracy?'

'Democracy is dictatorship with makeup on. Fundamentally, it's a system where, wearing a mask, an authoritarian man puts on an act. Since all concepts created by man are products of his brain, that is their limitation too. Democracy and autocracy are two points on the same straight line. Even superstition and atheism are on the same plane.'

'Then?'

'Then, in the next stage of evolution, humans may transform into a better creature, and the superfluous, meaningless boundaries may disappear, and man may roam this earth with more freedom. From the millions of generations before him, he would have learnt the futility of accumulation.'

'What kind of human will he be?'

'He will be a nomad.'

Karamchand stood close to him. The train was speeding like a bullet. He picked up his phone. Dabholkar put his arm around his shoulder. The parched hillside was visible between the window bars. Karamchand clicked the shutter and that timeless moment was captured on the image sensor of his camera.

5

WATER BATTLE - III

Expecting a Skype call from Australia, Louis Fulton Carvalho was waiting at the door of the H1 coach. Whenever he saw the globe, he would smile inwardly, visualising his wife and children walking upside down Down Under. Once, he expressed his misgivings to a professor of geography who was a passenger: 'Sir, if the earth were to shake, wouldn't the Australians drop off just like that? Like overripe cashew fruits dropping down?'

The question baffled the professor. He gave Carvalho an hour-long class on earth's gravity, how the universe had no top or bottom, and how what goes up must come down. After listening to everything and nodding sagely, Carvalho said, 'Whatever it is, sir, if they do fall off into the void of space, the loss is all mine, isn't it?' That question struck the habitually garrulous professor dumb.

When the last bar of the mobile signal disappeared, Carvalho gave up his attempts to connect to Skype. Suddenly, the pantry manager came running and panted, 'Sir, some people have attacked the pantry. They have run away with all our supplies of mineral water bottles. Please call the police.'

Carvalho immediately dialled the control room number.

Fear quickly enveloped the Sampark Kranti Express. The passengers' faces reflected a dread that something untoward was about to happen. Those conversing stopped and fell silent. The news of the raid on the pantry had spread throughout the train. Doubting Dowager poked her head out and surveyed the silence around her. She wondered: 'Why this silence? Why do people make noise? Why do people fall silent? Why did God, who created singers, also create the mute?' When she felt relieved after asking all these questions, she withdrew her head.

Home to a silent dread, the train entered Madgaon Station. In place of Kannada, the announcement welcoming the passengers was in Konkani. The platform was full of policemen. As soon as the train came to a halt, scores of passengers jumped out and ran onto the tracks. They opened the filling hoses. Water squirted out of them as if from water cannons. The men bared their torsos in the stream of water. The day turned into a water festival.

Banging on the side of the bogies with their lathis, the policemen walked to the pantry car.

'We have managed to hold on to one of them,' the pantry manager told the police. Holding him by the scruff of his neck, the pantry workers brought the man to the door. 'He was the biggest troublemaker, sir,' they informed the inspector. The rioter was the hapless Scraggly Beard, who had been trapped inside the toilet since morning. He was still wearing a lungi.

'Get down,' the inspector bellowed.

'Sir, I've done no wrong. When I couldn't find water anywhere ...' He had much to share; however, overwrought and emotional, his attempts to speak became unintelligible squeaks and bleats. A policeman shoved him by his neck down onto the platform. He looked around piteously. Encircled by khaki uniforms and lathis, he trembled in fear. All the passengers were on the other side of the tracks, enjoying the water festival, and no one was there to see his plight.

'Please submit a memo, sir,' the inspector said.

Carvalho expressed his misgiving. 'Should we go to that extent?'

'Definitely. As a deterrent. No one should ever dare to do this again. This is the Indian Railways, nothing less. The Indian Railways!'

With the apathy of a government servant, Carvalho wrote out a handing-over memo and gave it to the inspector. Till then, Scraggly Beard was under the impression that all of this was make-believe; that after some intimidation and a warning, he would be let off.

However, by that time a vice-like grip had tightened around his neck.

'Please release me, you're hurting me,' he said. A wary smile still lingered on his face. The grip on his neck tightened further. Another hand was crushing his ribs.

'Aiyyo, sir, I've an interview in Mumbai tomorrow. Spare me please.'

As he was pushed away, a heavy police boot imperceptibly ground his foot into the platform floor. It was now evident to him that the police meant business. He started to cry. There were no compassionate listeners around. The leader was busy overseeing the filling of water in the coaches. He was now the leader of the victors.

When it was clear that his situation was truly hopeless, Scraggly Beard screamed at the top of his voice, 'You sons of bitches, you had better kill me ...' His scream was strangled by a policeman's iron hand over his mouth.

When the train started to roll slowly, Elvindas picked up the young man's bag from the seat assigned to him in S4 and threw it down on the platform.

'Hey police, what atrocity is this?' The voice, though weakened by age, was firm. 'The provision of water is a duty of the state. By bottling it, the commodification of water that should be freely distributed has been your handiwork. And yet you will jail someone who has taken a handful of water?' Wagging his walking stick, Dabholkar stood at the door trembling with anger. That voice of protest too was drowned by the sounds of the train and went unnoticed. The cries of the young man fell on the platform and shattered. The train picked up speed.

'Poor boy,' the middle-aged lady headed to Gujarat commiserated.

The bearded man joined in, 'He was showing some discomfort since the morning.'

'He was a brave boy and showed such daring,' said another man.

'If something has to be done, the youth have to be at the forefront.'

'How many people had to go to prison for us to win our freedom?' As Carvalho walked, listening to the conversation that had now reached the topic of Independence, he was feeling guilty. The young man was possibly the sole support of some poor family. If only he had been a little firm. He walked with his head bowed. He was aware that should anyone challenge him, he had no justification to give them. Yet, he wished someone would get angry with him. However, no one questioned him.

'Sir, please wait,' the middle-aged woman stood up from her seat. Although he was shaken, he stopped and turned around. She walked up to him. He stood ready to apologise on behalf of the Railways and cite his own helplessness, should she chide him. However, her need was far beyond all his expectations.

'Sir, can I take that boy's seat too? I want to sit with my leg up,' she asked, lifting up her saree and showing him her swollen knees. Carvalho's face turned red with rage. He gave her an angry stare. Perhaps due to the fierceness in his look, she returned quietly to her seat.

After witnessing all this, Sameera Fathima was uneasy. She was gently caressing her belly inside which a new life was taking shape. 'What kind of a world is my child going to be born into?' she asked Karamchand. His answer was only a laugh. 'Man, how far is Panvel from here?'

'About six to seven hours,' the reply came from Carvalho.

'I'm going back to my cabin.' Karamchand got up and went down the train.

John was reviewing the photos on his camera monitor. He twisted the screen towards Karamchand. A digital documentation of the events of the day from daybreak. Among them, a number of pictures narrated the wretchedness of Scraggly Beard. The crushing, vice-like grip of an ostensibly friendly policeman around his ribs had been faithfully recorded. After running through all the photos, John asked him, 'What was the issue?'

Karamchand replied shortly, 'It was a battle for water.'

6

SAILING SHIPS

Karamchand watched the Arabian Sea at Goa through the chilled window panes. Among the rising and crashing waves, he saw five sailing boats. Standing at the prow of one, the captain was looking at the city through a spyglass—Francisco Almeida. He was thrilled by the opulence of the naval city that had the Sahyadri mountains as its backdrop. The soldiers of the Vijayanagara Empire were patrolling the shores of Gomantak.

The previous day, a ship filled with pilgrims returning from the Haj had become his prey. As soon as he saw the ship from Makkah, the hostility that he had carried from Europe bubbled over in his veins. Commanded by him, the five carracks surrounded the vessel from Makkah. The pilgrims shrieked in horror at the sight of the vessels festooned with corpses speeding towards them. Hundreds of unarmed men, women and children.

Cannonballs from the five carracks fell upon the pilgrims' vessel. The wood splintered and the vessel started to break up. The terror-stricken passengers cried piteously. They called out to the Almighty as a last refuge. No one was around to save them. Standing on the sinking deck, they implored Almeida to spare their lives. Almeida watched in glee as they grovelled and pleaded. He ordered his soldiers to empty their arquebuses into the drowning people.

The sinking Haj vessel caught fire and continued to burn surrounded by the five carracks. A fiery death dance in the open seas. Screams that drowned the sound of the waves. As the wails of the accursed beings fell on his ears as music, Almeida sat on a bronze cannon, drumming on it, and thanked Jesus Christ. The stench of burning flesh was carried by the sea breeze. Drinking in the stench to his heart's content, Almeida continued to sit on the cannon.

'Vasco da Gama wouldn't have enjoyed such a soothing sight,' he said, smiling to himself.

Many of the pilgrims started to leap into the sea to avoid being burnt alive. With as much voraciousness as the fire, a parallel navy of sharks tore into the people. However, Kariman kept the sharks from feasting on one girl. She too had leapt into the sea from the burning deck but, before she hit the water, Kariman speared her and lifted her up using his powerful arms onto the deck of their ship. The girl was pregnant and near her term.

Almeida was sharpening his sword on the abrasive surface of the cannon. The next moment the sword went clean through her belly and came out on the other side. 'Allah ...' she let out a heart-rending cry and collapsed to the floor. Enjoying the moan as an unheard melody, Almeida pulled out the sword. Intoxicated by the headiness of that scream, he became one with the ecstasy. Still drumming on the cannon, he relished the ebb and flow of the girl's wails. The moans became weaker and weaker and finally died.

Almeida opened his eyes with a deep sigh of orgasmic satisfaction. After ensuring she was dead, she was undressed and strung up. An adornment of Almeida's carrack, she terrified other sea-goers. The five carracks sailed north, creating waves of terror.

Fishermen were the first to see the surging carracks. Rowing their catamarans and canoes, they sped towards the shore. Like a volley of gun salutes, the carracks fired cannonballs one after another into the heart of Gomantak. The fishing villages trembled in fear. Streets and houses went up in flames.

A swarm of five thousand soldiers in body armour, chain mail and holding muskets descended on the shores of Gomantak. The western borders of the Vijayanagara Empire eventually fell to Almeida, the plenipotentiary of King Manuel the Fortunate. When they entered the city, Kariman impaled with his spear the first man they met. Holding the screaming man above his head, Kariman walked as the vanguard for Almeida's troops, a sight that was enough to terrorise the denizens. They fled in droves to the mountains. The army looted and plundered. After thirty days of unbridled depredations, Almeida and his army returned to their ships. Throughout those thirty days, Kariman remained at the forefront like the God of Death, hoisting the rotting corpse. As a purveyor of death, the eunuch spread such dread in that land that the story of his arrival continued to be recounted for generations.

One of the carracks had a captain named Carvalho. After returning to the fort in Thalassery, he never went back to Europe. He kept a converted Christian woman as his concubine. His spermatic fluid irrigated many new vaginal canals. Illegitimate half-breed children were born, reminding everyone that colour is a memento of the seed. Dispersing, the clan spread all over the world, delivering their broods and commingling through inter-marriage. This captain of the Sampark Kranti, Louis Fulton Carvalho, was surely a splinter off that main trunk.

As ordered by King Manuel, Almeida returned home after handing over charge of Thalassery to Afonso de Albuquerque, a general admiral and statesman. He left on a single carrack and with only a handful of seamen. Unable to tear himself away from the sea, Kariman stayed with Almeida as his faithful manservant. On a vessel festooned with desiccated corpses, backed by the monsoon winds, they set sail on the southern seas.

Standing on the ship's stern, sometimes Kariman screamed fearfully. The cardinal points froze as his screams reverberated. The water sprites trembled in fear. He was a man and superman too. He had no past nor future. He had no qualms. He lived by what he saw. He fed his hunger by hacking and eating the shrivelled breast of the corpse hanging from the mast. His glories already a memory, the nobleman Almeida was now an ordinary sailor on the high seas with only the monsoon winds to aid him. He had no cannons, he had no soldiers, food was running low. If they could reach land, they would need to replenish their stock of fresh water.

Finally, they saw land. Tall verdant mountains came into view. A river flowing down the mountains into the sea could be seen. Almeida ordered the ship to approach the shore. Kariman and Almeida went ashore carrying leather water bags and headed for the water source. However, awaiting them was a group of cannibals. The aborigines met Almeida with a volley of arrows, which they shot hiding behind trees.

'I am the lord of the Indian Ocean.' He strode ahead shouting these words. A poisoned arrow pierced his leg.

'I am the plenipotentiary of King Manuel.'

Another arrow pierced his chest. His body started to become discoloured.

However, they spared Kariman. They lowered the bows and arrows that were aimed at him. What saved him was his complexion, darker than the night, a souvenir of the sperm that had given him life. They saw in him one of their brothers who had parted ways with them sometime in the past.

The aborigines hacked the limbs of the half-dead Almeida. Suddenly, Kariman came rushing and, with one stroke of his sword, sliced off the still-conscious Almeida's penis. He then screamed with such ferocity that everything around them trembled. The cannibals plucked Almeida's nails and pulled out his hair. They hacked and diced his torso. Almeida heard the music latent in Kariman's screams. The faces of the thousands of helpless people he had killed and thrown into the sea bobbed in the sky above him.

With their eyes closed as if in prayer, they too enjoyed the music of pain. Among them was an embryo, split in half.

Boiling water in a clay pot awaited Almeida. He was dropped into the water as diced flesh. One of the cruellest men in history, the lord of the Indian Ocean dissolved in the water and became soup. The aborigines drank him with relish. After keeping aside a wooden bowl filled with the soup, one of the aborigines asked Kariman if he wasn't hungry. He was hungry. He packed Almeida's penis in a leaf. He roasted it over the fire and ate it.

When a wicked man is born, a poisoned arrow marked for him is born along with him. And a hunter too, to shoot it.

7

DVI - I

The last man to board the train when it left Madgaon was Dvi. He ran alongside till it picked up speed. By the time he pushed aside the old man still standing and waving his walking stick at the door of the S6 coach and entered, the train had left the platform.

'Don't be outraged,' Dvi told the old man. 'The law will take its course.'

He walked to his own coach in the front of the train. A small group of passengers was following him. A young soldier travelling from Thiruvananthapuram to Ambala was close behind him. He had quickly turned into Dvi's bodyguard. He was taking occasional sips from a cola bottle in his hand.

'If you had given the slightest indication, I would have smashed that stationmaster's head.'

'I knew there was no need for all that. In the meantime, I'd already talked twice to the Railway minister,' Dvi replied, smiling. The mobile growled in his pocket.

'It's the chief secretary of Goa. He's calling, having heard of the ruckus.'

The passengers looked at him in admiration as he walked past them. His voice was loud and deep. His long strides showed determination. In no time, he had been acknowledged as a leader. He reached the S8 coach and took his seat. A group of young men hovered around him. The soldier was in the forefront.

After gazing out of the window for a little while, Dvi spoke, 'I've taken a decision.' The young men were attentive. They ached for action and appeared to be ready to beard any lion.

'Let's walk through the train from one end to the other,' Dvi said.

'Superb idea,' one of the young ones gushed.

'Like a tour, okay?' Dvi said.

'We're ready.'

'In that case, two of you should go ahead and announce my arrival.'

'I'm ready,' each one volunteered.

'For the time being, two will do. We're starting a game, okay? I'll select the two.'

Dvi tapped the soldier on his chest. He was proud that he was the first to be chosen. From that moment he was transformed. He threw out the cola bottle through the window.

'Among you, who all are travelling to Delhi?' Although many of them stepped forward enthusiastically, Dvi chose a dark Tamilian who towered above the others.

'You shall walk from the head of the train till the rear. If you meet any TTE or Railway police on the way, you should inform them of my coming. Especially, you should tell the conductor, Carvalho.'

Dvi tied a red ribbon around the heads of his chosen heralds. In an instant, that laurel made them distinct. A strip of cloth elevated them as partners in the divine dispensation of authority. Both departed to carry out their mission.

Their first stop was S8. The passengers looked on curiously as two men with a red ribbon tied around their heads appeared. Their initial thought was that the men were peddlers of back scratchers and other novelties. After walking up and down the compartment twice or thrice and ensuring that they had attracted sufficient attraction, they stationed themselves in the mid-section of the coach and clapped their hands loudly. The passengers fell silent, expectantly awaiting the next part of the show.

The two men stood with their backs touching. One of them started to read out the message that Dvi had written out for them. The other one repeated what was read out.

Dear Passengers,

We, the humble and respectful factotums of Shri Dvi, hereby announce and inform you that our saviour and the heroic leader who led us from the front in our righteous battle, when our train ran out of water and the Railway authorities ignored us, will now be touring each and every coach to meet the passengers and discover in person each one's grievances and resolve them.

This was repeated in all the coaches.

The amused passengers heard them out. Their responses were varied.

'Let him come, I have a few things to tell him. I should know if there's someone responsible for all these things,' the middle-aged lady in S4 said.

'Who's he?' Dabholkar asked in a mocking tone.

'Our saviour,' his emissaries replied.

'What are the problems that you are really facing?'

'Only when we enquire into them will we know what the problems are. Maybe there are no problems now. But what's the assurance that there will be none in the future?'

'Morons,' Dabholkar said, laughing.

The students in S1 catcalled them. Ignoring such fleabites, the emissaries passed through all the compartments announcing the coming of the saviour and finally reached the H1 coach. They met Carvalho there.

'We have come to announce that he'll be visiting all the coaches.'

'Who will?'

'Dvi-saab.'

'To discover for himself if anyone is facing any problems and to resolve them.'

Carvalho exploded. 'What am I here for, then? Bloody twits. If I feel the need for someone to supervise me, I shall send for you.' Taken aback by the outburst, the emissaries dialled Dvi's mobile number and handed over the phone to Carvalho.

Trembling with anger, Carvalho screamed into the phone, 'What did you think? That the train is the place for you to hold your dumb charade?'

'It's not what you think, sir,' Dvi's tone was placatory. 'I'm going to clean up the train. I'm going to make it a *swachh* train.'

'That's not a bad idea.' Those words seemed to have cooled down Carvalho. He smiled peaceably. 'If that's the plan, you have my wholehearted support.'

The emissaries departed.

'Are there bigger fools than these idiots? They are going to clean up a train on which Indians are travelling. A train of Indians who chew and spit as if there's no tomorrow. Ha ... ha ...' Carvalho spoke to Karamchand who was sitting beside him. 'Cleaning up the Ganges would be a cakewalk compared to this.'

While passing through the coaches, the emissaries looked as if they were walking through their king's vassal states. Although Dvi was waiting for them expectantly, he did not betray it.

'Sir, when are we starting the tour?' his followers asked. He gave them no immediate reply and remained lost in thought for some time. 'You all may go now. Come and meet me again in two hours. I'll tell you the next plan then.'

His entourage dispersed.

8

DEADWEIGHT

The train entered Karbude Tunnel, the longest tunnel on the Konkan Railway. It was one of the biggest construction projects of post-Independence India. Karamchand remembered E. Sreedharan, the Railway engineer who personified efficiency and on-time delivery. Trains and caves are alike. Caves evolved into trains. Where can you find a cave longer than a train?

Once, an Indian mountain and a British engineer got into a tussle. This was how it happened.

Colonel Barog was in charge of building tunnel no. 33 on the Kalka-Shimla Mountain route. His workers started tunnelling from both sides of the mountain. They were expected to meet each other halfway and complete the tunnel. However, Barog's calculations went awry, the alignment was incorrect, and they did not meet. He was censured by the government and docked Re 1 as penalty.

Dejected, he stood on top of the mountain. It was a face-off between his self-esteem and the majesty of the mountain. One cold morning, he went along with his dog to the mouth of the tunnel that was going nowhere. With the pine trees weighed down by snow as his witnesses, he shot and killed himself.

Another engineer was given charge. He too could not get the alignment right. The tunnel was finally built with the help of Baba Bhalku, a local diviner. Indians, who are wont to read history as fable and fable as history, discovered Barog's ghost haunting the tunnel. Even today, local citizens mention how they can hear him walking around, making calculations and shouting instructions.

When the train trundled through the tunnel, Karamchand stood at the door and hooted at the top of his voice. In the darkness, the hoots echoed back from various points in the tunnel. Hearing a feminine hoot behind him, Karamchand swivelled around to see Sameera Fathima.

She laughed. 'Why did you hoot?'

'I did it for the child in me. And you?'

'I hooted because I saw you hooting.'

'If we keep hooting like this, the next thing we know this will turn into a ritual.' Both of them hooted with laughter.

The next stop was Panvel where the Konkan Railway joins the Mumbai rail network. The Sampark Kranti would be reaching Panvel in a short while. Sameera took off the pullover she wore over her dress, folded it and put it in her bag. Karamchand was seated by her side. In front of the mirror, she combed her hair and tied it up. She took out a veil, covered her head, and became a Muslim. On Facebook, this was how her profile looked. She had an innocent look. Karamchand sent her a friend request. Stitching together whatever she had told him from the previous day, he created a narrative.

A Muslim family that is spread between Karachi and Kathiawar. A Zakir Hussain Seth from that family comes to Kerala to trade. He marries a local woman from Kodungallur. Sameera's grandmother has filled her daughter's memory with her own memories of prosperous times—warehouses filled with spices, boxes filled with currency and gold ornaments, qawwalis, silk clothes and kitchens redolent with the aroma of basmati rice and mutton curry.

Meanwhile, Partition happens. Trusting Gandhi, Seth decides to remain in India. His brothers choose to migrate to Pakistan. Gradually, business starts to fail. The boxes that held jewellery now hold cobwebs. Bankrupt and penniless, Seth falls ill and dies. Carrying her two infants, Sameera's grandmother flees to Madras. Sameera is born to Seth's daughter; marries a man employed in the Arabian Gulf and moves to Dubai. The wish to meet her brother living in Mumbai is what made her travel on the Sampark Kranti Express.

A train in India passes through diverse linguistic zones. When it arrived at Panvel, the Marathi language too arrived. The train eased by platform no. 1. Other express trains were arriving at or leaving from other platforms. The Sampark Kranti opened its doors for people to disperse to various corners of the city.

With a bag of mangoes in one hand and pulling a trolley bag with the other, Sameera came to the door of the A1 coach. Before she stepped down onto the platform, she looked back. Karamchand was standing right behind her. Her face betrayed no emotion. Bearing the aloof detachment that the middle-class can summon up, she alighted. The aroma of Kolhapuri mangoes that had suffused the coach too exited along with her.

Karamchand stood on the platform watching Sameera's receding form. As he watched her body sway and bounce as she walked, he became a mere male of the species. Suddenly, she turned, lifted her head and looked at him. She raised her hand and beckoned him. He walked up to her eagerly.

'*Edo*, I think I should tell you something.'

'What?'

'Didn't you tell me that we humans have only such sorrows that will go away if we so much as share it with others openly.'

'Umm ...'

'I walk around carrying an unbearable secret inside me. Should I tell you?'

'Tell me, I'll listen. And the secret will die with me.'

Sameera gave him a searching look. Sadness brimmed in her eyes. He also looked deep into her eyes. The burden of the secret seemed to have fatigued her eyes. She lowered her eyes. Her eyelids closed slightly. Eyes still downcast, she started to speak, 'Those two red stripes that you saw ...'

'Which ones?'

'In that pregnancy test strip.'

'Umm ...'

'Its paternity is not Salim's.' Karamchand felt as if he was levitating.

'There is a young Pakistani accountant in our office. The child is his.' Karamchand looked at her as if she were a mythical animal.

'It's possible that he is a blood relation of mine. Someone who lost his country of birth when an arbitrary line was drawn across a map. These mustard seeds were given by him. Wherever I travel in India, I'll fling those seeds as far as I can. He too will do the same in Pakistan. Have you seen a mustard field in full bloom?'

'Yes.'

'It's like a yellow blanket. From one mustard plant a thousand plants will be born. They all bloom at the same time. The whole continent will be covered in yellow. The boundaries will be erased. My child will run across them and play tag in many countries.'

She stopped speaking and looked into Karamchand's eyes. Her eyes looked calm after she had unburdened herself of the dead weight. She grabbed a handful of mustard seeds from her bag and handed over some to Karamchand. 'Wherever you go, you should fling them far and wide.'

Both of them threw the seeds towards the edge of the platform. Suddenly, a yellow field bloomed inside their minds.

She drifted away like flotsam on the waves of a sea of humanity in the station. Now bearing the dead weight that Sameera had divested herself of, Karamchand stood at the door of the coach, trying to catch another glimpse of her. His eyes briefly turned moist.

The metropolises are upturned maws of light. People disappear into them and turn into nobodies. The horde of people who alighted at Panvel was swallowed by Mumbai city.

'We are getting down here,' the retired teacher told Shaji, the young man. His wife and daughter counted their baggage and ensured that they had missed nothing. When no one was watching, the daughter slipped the towel provided by the Railways into her bag.

'Me too,' said Shaji as he readied his own suitcase. He returned the Kindle to his bag. Sometime in the night, his eyes had established contact with hers.

When the train came to a halt, he was right behind the family.

He brushed his leg against the small toe of the girl who was lingering behind her parents. She returned the compliment with a pinch on his toe using her own toes. She pulled out her mobile phone.

He whispered, 'Nine double four triple seven ...' She dialled the number. Beethoven trilled on his left chest. She saved the number as 'Sampark Kranti'. Close encounters of the revolutionary kind.

Alighting from the train, they went their ways into the city's maze. However, challenging their own caste predispositions, a girl and a man continued their friendship.

Lekha Nampoothiri woke Zachariah from a deep sleep. 'You water buffalo, wake up. It's time for me to get down.'

Both of them were stark naked. He looked at her with sleep-filled eyes and said, 'I dreamt everything all over again.'

'What everything?'

'All that you narrated to me.'

'Aha!'

'How many grandees and VIPs!'

'True.'

'Not to forget the judge with a mole on his dick!'

She started to wear her clothes. She became resplendent again.

'Aiyyo, I forgot something ...'

'What?'

'It's a bad habit we buffalo traders have ...'

She looked at him inquiringly.

'You know, we brand our buffaloes with tattoos on their rumps so that we don't lose them.'

'Umm ...'

She turned her back to him, pulled down her panties, and bent over. Using bright green ink, he drew two horns on her rump. She sidestepped a little. He buried his face between the horns and kissed her. Then he drew tattoos beneath her navel.

'Whoever sees this will be unable to get a hard-on and go to pieces. This brand is the title deed attesting that you are my sole property.'

Lekha Nampoothiri too disembarked at Panvel Station. Through the tinted window glass Zachariah watched her walk away like a flaming brand. The train started to roll. He opened another bottle and poured the liquor into his glass.

Bearing permanent territorial marks on her body and a womb that gave off buffalo spoor, Lekha Nampoothiri melted away into the big city's long list of grievances.

9

DARSHAN

Cutting through the packed slums between the Panvel and Vasai stations, the Sampark Kranti was running slow. The city was bursting at its seams on either side of the track. Many who had started their journey with the train had detrained. New passengers had replaced them, yet the crowd had thinned. The main reason was the agitation for a higher quota of reservations in Rajasthan and Gujarat. John sat watching the sights through the window. India, now shrunk into slums, invaded his senses.

When he pulled aside the curtains, the sight that met him were those of couples making out and humping in public. 'This is the exhibition wing of the Kama Sutra,' John said.

'What position is that?' John asked, pointing it out to Karamchand.

'That's the ānata, the cow position, entry from the rear,' he replied, laughing. He had witnessed these scenes whenever he had travelled on that route.

'What about this?' John pointed to an entwined couple.

'That's the cygnine coitus.'

'And this one?'

'Auparishtikam or oral sex.'

'You're a bachelor. How do you know all these things?'

'A bachelor's world is wide and free. It has dreams and experiments. A married man's sex life is circumscribed and limited to the daily exertion in the missionary position.'

'All right, since I have seen so much live action, I am giving up the idea of my pilgrimage to Khajuraho,' said John, cackling.

'You shouldn't. If you can visit Varanasi, you can visit Khajuraho too. Isn't *that* one among the many routes to salvation?'

The train gathered speed, as if trying to escape the annoyance of the slums. Standing at the door of the A1 coach, Karamchand cast a backward glance. The train looked like a stretched-out parenthesis. If placed upright, it would look more intriguing than the Eiffel Tower. Or it could be imagined as an upright millipede. The chimney of the Wanderer could be seen at the far end of the train. The thundering vehicle that had once connected various regions was speeding impassively like a tamed demon.

Varied sights of the city stole into the train. When moving from the city limits towards the city centre, the city keeps gaining in height. From huts and shanties, it climbs up into luxury apartments and condominiums. Once, Karamchand undertook a sea trip to the Elephanta Caves from the Gateway of India, where the city slips into the sea. After the tiring climb up the hill, Karamchand landed up in front of the three-faced Sadashiva. Out of nowhere, rain started to fall, girding the island. He stood in the pleasant chill, admiring the sculptures. Three expressive faces adorning one neck. Aghora the dreadful on the left half, the full face in the centre as the preserver Taptapurusha, and Vamadeva, or the feminine aspect on the right.

Karamchand sought and found a cave not frequented by tourists and sat down. In it was a broken Shivalinga. He gazed at it for a long time. He closed his eyes and travelled back in time, one epoch after the other. He slipped into deep meditation. At its culmination, his corporeal existence ceased and his whole body turned into a phallus.

When Karamchand opened his eyes, he saw a young woman by his side. She too was meditating. An erect phallus could be seen between them. Her body flowed above him like the Ganges in spate. Using his phallus as an oar, he rowed within the depths of the Ganges. He disintegrated in the abyss. He ejaculated. With the rain outside and the Shivalinga in the dark cave as their witnesses, they sat across each other, naked. Neither of them was surprised by what had happened. As a reminder that the body will always win over contemplation and penance, a rock phallus stood upright between them.

After getting dressed, when he was leaving, she placed a grape between his lips. Remembering her nipples, he sucked on the grape and climbed down the hill. By that time, all the crushing heaviness that his body and mind had accumulated had dissipated.

Karamchand noticed the imperiousness of the city for the first time while travelling on the boat to the mainland—after an organic growth, the eventual, terrifying face of a city. When, years later, reports of the terror attack on the city and the Taj Mahal Hotel reached him, he recalled the climb to Elephanta and the sex with the lingering taste of grapes.

John cut into Karamchand's reminiscences. 'Does this train go via Godhra?'

'Yes, someone going to Delhi through the west coast of India must necessarily pass through Godhra.'

'Umm ...'

'It's a railway junction, isn't it?'

'It's also a watershed in our history. There are pre-Godhra and post-Godhra eras and worlds.'

Unconsciously, conversation died between them and silence took a seat. Both of them were lost in their thoughts. Although they tried to chase away the futile thoughts that had infiltrated their brains, both failed. A sense of history and historical consciousness brings people to a state of helplessness.

Sameera Fathima was melding two sundered geographies within her womb. A child would soon be born to citizens of two nations.

Perhaps when he came of age, the boundaries would have turned to dust and disappeared. He may run across the unpatrolled borders at will. Like an ant scampering across the surface of the globe.

John had fallen asleep with *India* resting on his chest. The Sampark Kranti chugged past Godhra Station at a reduced speed. The burnt-out shell of the S6 coach was visible on the siding. It lay there although many years had passed since the conflagration. Karamchand had passed it many times in the past. Each time he had pondered over the power of a spark. The spark that had changed the trajectory of the country and sealed its fate. John wasn't asleep. Karamchand saw his pale eyes glinting in the sodium vapour lamp light from outside. He sat up, holding the book to his chest. Their eyes met despite the darkness.

'You Indians are past masters at burning people alive, aren't you?' Karamchand did not understand what he was leading up to.

'I'd told you about my trip from Lucknow to Jaipur. On that trip, my father had taken me to a railway station, a small one named Bharwari near Allahabad. When no one was watching, he placed a rose in front of a huge water tank at one end of the station and prayed. I didn't understand anything. How did a red rose come between my father and a tall steel water tank in such a remote place?

'He told me the story on our return journey to Allahabad. During the 1857 Sepoy Rebellion, a group of three thousand people attacked Bharwari Station. A number of steam locomotives were parked there. The funny thing was, the rioters were scared of these engines. The rustics thought of the fire-breathing, smoke-emitting thingamajig as the devil incarnate. They were afraid to approach the engine, so they pelted them with stones from afar. They believed that Satan should be chased away by stoning him.

'The railway station had a few British employees. They had only one way to escape from the attackers. Along with their wives and children, they climbed up the tall water tank. They made their families sit inside the water tank and kept vigil outside. When it was apparent that their guns would not be enough to stop the mob, they too hid in the tank.

'However, they could not remain there for long. The heat and smoke from the fire that the attackers had started below their sanctuary forced them out. Many of them leapt down and perished. One of them was my grandfather's mother. Her family were commoners who had come in search of work when the railway projects started in India. They had no enmity with the Indians. Indians are obsessed with arson. You proved that in Chauri Chaura too.'

'Not merely in Chauri Chaura. In Godhra, in the Gujarat riots, in the anti-Sikh riots, in anti- and pro-reservation agitations. I thought of this only when you mentioned it now.'

'Do you know the reason?'

'No,' said Karamchand.

'Your primary Veda itself has its origins in fire,' John said in half-jest. He lay down again on his berth.

Karamchand too fell asleep.

A terrifying nightmare made the panic-stricken Karamchand fall down from his berth. Camera in hand, John, as he meandered in his dreams, did not hear or see what happened. When he came to, Karamchand clambered back onto his berth and closed his eyes to dream once more.

10

NIGHT

A day dawns with the tenderness of a flower blooming. A day lies deep within the womb of another day. A new day is born as a black flower from within the recesses of the cave of night inside which darkness mates with darkness. At midnight, the day that is receding wants to touch the new day that is emerging. It will stretch out both its arms for an embrace. By then, shaking off the shackles of the dark night, the new day surges forward at the speed of light. The receding day becomes history.

The book of history is so bulky that minor details escape attention and become lost. The new day strolls out into the light. Light embraces it. At its brightest hour, the day preens itself. After giving birth to many lessons, parables and allegories, it too surrenders to darkness. It too disappears into the great tome of memories that desire to embrace the nascent day.

The Sampark Kranti Express was now detained in a remote railway station. Enjoying the breeze from the nearby woods, the passengers were asleep. Those awake dozed off occasionally and when they woke up, they were under the misapprehension that they had travelled far.

However, Dvi was not asleep. He was pondering how to exploit the situation when problems presented such opportunities. The station had a low platform. He walked towards the light at the north end of the platform. The station was sandwiched by woods on either side. A signal lamp was burning in front of the stationmaster's room. Its smoke had deposited many layers of soot on the asbestos roof and the steel supports. In varied forms, decades-old cobwebs adorned the steel girders. The station was a hundred and sixty-five years old. The stationmaster was asleep, his head resting on a century-old wooden desk. The room had signalling equipment and other accoutrements unseen in other locations.

Dvi rapped on the desk. The stationmaster was startled into wakefulness. The unexpected sight of a titan looming over him had him bewildered. He raised his head and asked, 'What?' He had a receding chin that resembled a Neanderthal's.

'Why has the train been detained?' Dvi asked. The stationmaster stood up. The initial disorientation had left him. He had at hand only two faded, shabby flags. One green and the other red—two pieces of cloth on which the authority of a system had been invested. He stood before Dvi, tightly gripping the flags. It gave him the confidence of holding a revolver. He drank a glass of cool water from the earthen pot kept on his desk. Before the last gulp of water passed his throat, he replied, 'The socially backward community is agitating in Gujarat for reservation. They are stopping trains, removing rail tracks and ...'

'All right, if that's the case, when will this train leave from here?'

'Too early to say. It may be rerouted via Jhansi. If so, it will take twenty-four hours more than the scheduled time. Even that's not certain. There's some talk of farmers starting a big rally in Madhya Pradesh. Generally, our farmers do not resort to vandalism. Fighting with the land all their lives, they have learnt to be forbearing.' After rattling off this much, he drank the remaining water in the glass. It appeared as if he had not met other human beings or conversed with anyone for a long time.

Dvi walked back. A wooden bench stood midway on the platform. It was covered in vines, as if it had no memory of anyone using it as a seat. He sat down on that bench. Some unrecognised night fowl flew over him, flapping its wide wings. It was an eagle, a mini version of a roc.

This station too had a backstory. A hundred feet below his seat was a war memorial. To see it one needed a vision that was turned inwards and an unbounded imagination. The earth had embedded within its innards the fossils of creatures and events that had happened thirteen thousand years ago.

An underground river used to flow beneath the now parched station. It originated on a hill on which bears and leopards gambolled before it turned into a tributary of the Narmada. Two tribes lived on either bank. Occasionally they used to fight over an animal or timber that the river would bring down the hill. The fighting that day was over a bison that the eastern tribe had speared and killed. Ten men from the western tribe were killed in the battle. One early morning, while dawn was breaking, all members of the western tribe crossed the river and attacked the other tribe sleeping in their burrows. All but one of them were massacred.

The survivor, a pregnant woman, was incapacitated. The injured woman was tied to a tree and left dangling. She gave birth in that position. However, before the child hit the ground, both the mother and child were dead. The mother and child turned into fossils and were embedded in rocks to eventually become subjects for carbon dating. Time covered them with soil and rock.

Seated on that bench, Dvi made a few calculations. The passengers would come to know about the delay only in the morning. By then, the train would have been diverted and on a different route. When they came to know of this, they would start protesting. After that, as with any other problem, they would reconcile to it. His role stood between problems and compromises. He decided to wait patiently.

The stationmaster was speaking to the porter, 'If the train doesn't leave now, it will turn into a serious problem in the morning. This station doesn't even have a tea stall. The passengers will attack me. I wish we could somehow leave.' That was when Dvi noticed the porter who stood leaning against the granite stone wall in his faded red shirt like a washed out mural. The nearest town was at least fifty kilometres from this remote station.

Seated on the station bench, when he was dropping off, he heard the guard's whistle and the hooting of the engine horn. The guard flashed the green lamp from the rear of the train. Dvi ran and jumped into the Sleeper coach. The train started to move though its route and immediate destination were unknown. At least it was moving. Dawn was another four hours away. He lay down on the berth.

That was when he noticed that the two minions from the previous day had not left him. They were asleep on the floor, with only a newspaper as their bedsheet. The red ribbon of authority still adorned their heads.

Dvi fell asleep.

11

THE ARMY

The Sampark Kranti was now running like a traveller who had lost his way. It did not have its old self-confidence or its speed. It knew its destination but not the route it had to take. It was retracing its route and heading back south. In between, if a decision was made, it would travel east and then north. The passengers had boarded the train with the belief that it would deliver them to their destinations. Now they were asleep, oblivious to what was happening.

The coaches started to come alive around 5 a.m. Those who woke up switched on the lights in the bays. Squatting or sitting on the toilets they scrolled through Facebook and WhatsApp, willing the world to come to them. The world appeared on their palms digitally. They had an opinion on everything under the sun. Through their 100 square centimetre screens, they launched their polemics into the web. Until someone who could no longer withstand the pressure in their bladder or their bowels banged on the toilet door, they would continue as squatters on the toilet seat.

When the pantry workers spread through the coaches with tea and announcements in their hoarse voices, the rest of the passengers too woke up. Kuriakose was one among them. As soon as he woke up, he started to rail at the pantry worker who was near him, 'What kind of a bloody racket are you making! Can't you let me sleep?' Inured to such abuses, the vendor stood by, gazing at him unperturbed.

Kuriakose stopped his invective abruptly and asked, 'Do you have tea without sugar?'

'No, sir,' the vendor replied equably.

'How will people like me get to drink tea? Go fetch some unsugared tea.'

The vendor left and returned with unsugared tea from the pantry. Kuriakose was pleased.

'How much?'

'Ten rupees.'

'Here's twenty. Keep the change.'

'No thank you, sir.' After returning ten rupees, the vendor left.

'*Chai, chai, masala chai, garam chai.*'

The youngsters in the coach had witnessed everything. The leader of the students stopped the vendor in the corridor and asked, 'Why didn't you react despite his rude behaviour?'

'If I react and end up arguing with him, my manager will terminate my services. My family will starve.'

'Where are you from?'

'Gwarighat in Madhya Pradesh.'

'I've heard of the place.'

'You would've. That's where Lord Ashwatthama is known to give audience.'

'Ha, ha. Have you seen him?'

'Not me. However, my grandfather has. Many in our village have had visions of him.' The vendor moved on to the next coach.

Some of the passengers started to notice that the train was not on its usual route. However, trains doing an about-turn was nothing new for them. They did not realise the import of the train reversing its route. Ignorance being bliss, they became preoccupied with their other interests.

The red-ribboners heard of the route change in the pantry. They rushed to Dvi and woke him up.

'Boss, did you hear?' Dvi feigned ignorance. 'Something's happened to our train. It's now reversed its route.'

'Oho?' For a while he acted as if he was thinking. Then he told his henchmen, 'Do one thing. Find out the details from that train captain, the baldy.' They left for the H1 coach.

Karamchand felt an indescribable emptiness. Sameera was the cause. He had dropped into his pocket some of the mustard seeds she had handed over before they parted ways. He threw some of them into the desolate countryside they were passing through. In his imagination, he saw the land blanketed in yellow. His heart had an empty chamber set apart for a lover. His romantic affairs were like flashes of lightning. The yellow-toothed girl he had met on the narrow-gauge train at Pandharpur was one of his crushes. Rathina from Budhwar Peth was another. And now Sameera. Such flashes of lightning that he wished would become his own dogged him on all his trips.

Although awake, he lay with his eyes closed. John was still asleep on the adjacent berth. Karamchand heard voices and hurried footsteps in the corridor. He recalled the water battles and connected the events of the previous day. He opened the door and stepped out. The beribboned henchmen were talking to Carvalho.

'Sir, why has the train changed its route?' In reality, Carvalho had noticed the change only when he was questioned in this manner. However, he acted as if everything was within his knowledge. He dialled from his mobile but the area had no coverage. He dialled continuously. The number of passengers around them kept increasing. Carvalho had to give them answers. However, unable to find inspiration for a plausible response, he was stumped. At that point, a loud voice spoke from the back of the crowd, 'Then, let me tell you.'

It was Dvi. He gave Carvalho a mocking smile. When they saw Dvi appeared unexpectedly, the henchmen bowed and wished him. Carvalho knew he could no longer afford to remain mute.

He started to stammer, 'Umm … what I, erm … was about to say was …'

'You don't tell us no nothing …' someone from the crowd yelled.

'Let me tell you this. I am not able to reach anyone on the phone. I have no means of communicating with the driver or guard or the stationmaster. Truth to tell, the last person who comes to know whatever happens inside a train is the TTE.'

Someone chose to challenge him. 'Looking at your uniform one can't say that.'

'Listen.' Dvi moved to the front of the crowd. 'The quota stir in Gujarat has turned violent. They are blocking trains. They are uprooting tracks and taking them away.'

'Aha! That means we are in a stew.'

'It doesn't end there. The dispute between the Meenas and the Gujjars in Rajasthan has escalated into rioting. They too are blocking trains. In short, western India is going up in flames.'

When he heard about the blockades and the rioting, Karamchand felt he needed to make some changes in his itinerary.

'The farmers in Madhya Pradesh.'

'The Naxalites in Dantewada in Chhattisgarh.'

'In Kashmir …' people in the crowd were filling in the blanks.

'What I need to know is this. How are you going to recompense us for making our journey miserable? You have to make amends! We need answers and till they are given, we are going to gherao you.'

Initially, when he heard the demand, Carvalho felt like laughing. 'Am I the chief minister or something of this train to be gheraoed?' he asked.

'We know you aren't. However, the need of the hour is for us to gherao someone. For that, conveniently, only you are here,' one of the henchmen shouted from the crowd.

Dvi had made his decisions. He called his beribboned henchmen to the side and gave them instructions. 'You shall go to the coaches and apprise all the passengers of the current status of the train. You should inform them of the agitation that I'm starting here. Recruit two men each from every coach and come back here with them.'

The henchmen bowed and left. Their evangelism started with the S1 coach. To get everyone's attention, they stood back to back in the middle of the coach. They bowed ceremoniously and greeted everyone formally. They issued a coordinated call for attention, 'Os!'

They now had everyone's attention.

'Dear passengers, we're here to convey our leader's message.' The passengers looked at them. 'The train has taken a detour from its usual route.' The passengers became more attentive. 'We have no information about when the train will reach Delhi. Having come to know of this, our leader is gheraoing the train captain. If you come to the H1 coach now, you can see for yourselves what's happening there.'

That was enough to trigger the passengers. A Punjabi and a Marathi came forward. The soldier tied a ribbon around their heads and conducted the induction ceremony. They saluted one another, 'Os!'

With two volunteers joining from each coach, their tribe swelled. Karamchand followed them.

The train was skirting a big dry lake in a valley. Karamchand looked out of the door towards the engine. Now Wanderer was right behind the electric locomotive. Two epochs were running hand in hand. The Sampark Kranti was now running counter to time.

Sowing lies, reaping fear and instigating the passengers through demagoguery, the beribboned gang progressed through the train. Some of the passengers proceeded to H1 to witness the action there. The transformation of the train into a centre of agitation was quick. The irate passengers thumped and kicked the walls of the coaches and shouted slogans. Gheraoed by Dvi and his henchmen, Carvalho was rendered impotent and listless. He could do nothing to counter it.

With sixteen volunteers from the eight Sleeper coaches, the henchmen marched to the H1 coach. The small platoon was a mere one hundredth of the passengers of the train. However, they were organised and the rest were individuals. The passengers viewed the beribboned army marching through the train with mixed emotions. Some with curious amusement; others with abhorrence and antipathy. And a rare few with dread for the imminent disaster.

'If an army is raised in a system where peace prevails, that a war will follow is a given. An army needs a war to survive,' Dabholkar said.

'Yes, but isn't this a contemptible situation?'

'They don't feel that way. If he gets a fully drilled, subservient army under him, even the Buddha will turn into a despot. Gandhi's language will be different. Gandhi has remained as the great and revered one for us because he did not assume the role of a ruler.'

The beribboned army stopped near Dabholkar. 'Os!' they screamed in unison. They rounded on him and mocked him. Then, goose-stepping, they marched ahead. When the tail of the army disappeared, Karamchand gave Dabholkar a meaningful look.

'In the beginning, the Nazis were a small group.' Old Savant sat with his sagely eyes closed.

In the air-conditioned H1 coach, Carvalho and the other TTEs stood covered in sweat. He was repeatedly trying to make calls. He was now a captive on behalf of the Indian Railways. Dvi was silent. However, like a pervading cloud of arrogance that overwhelmed the train, his presence could be felt palpably. Behind him, the crowd swelled like a choppy sea.

If the mob was a pyramid, Dvi was its needle tip. He was the sum total of smaller individuals with analogous thoughts. Hitler was not a single individual. He was the manifest form of millions of mini-Hitlers. Had Adolf Hitler not come up at that point in history, another man would have reached the pinnacle of the pyramid. Hitler was a historical inevitability of his times. When the body politic starts to fill with self-harming corpulence, Hitlers are born.

When the beribboned army reached H1, the crowd parted to make way for them. The passengers looked at them with make-believe awe and fear. They arched their backs and hailed their leader, 'Os!'

Dvi reciprocated, 'Os!' The meaningless word reverberated like an esoteric command.

Dvi addressed the milling crowd. 'Dear passengers, these eighteen men are your representatives. And mine too. They will talk to you on my behalf and to me on your behalf. They are the controllers of this train. When the right time comes, I shall save you from the miseries of this journey. At the moment, you may disperse.'

Heeding his words, many of the passengers returned to their coaches. Although a few demanded red ribbons, Dvi refused them.

Eventually, sixteen henchmen stood facing Dvi. The first two recruits stood on either side of him. Dvi raised his right hand and said in a booming voice, 'Os!'

'Os!' eighteen throats echoed as one.

Within the Sampark Kranti, the minatory sounds of command-control and implicit obedience resounded. That made the passengers dozing and lounging in air-conditioned comfort, enveloped by the upper-class sense of security, wake up with a start.

'Os!'

A mere eighteen men. Beribboned. With red ribbons.

Now they were an army.

12

COUP D'ÉTAT

What had begun as small, isolated protests had now become uncontrollable. The train sped along like a mobile warehouse full of belligerent sounds. Carvalho and the other TTEs accepted the passengers' ire on behalf of the Indian Railways. The three of them were now in the custody of the passengers.

The passengers were chagrined at seeing their travel plans go haywire. They protested. They decided that, by pulling the emergency chain, they were going to bring the 'biopsy section' travelling along the spine of time to a screeching halt at the next station. They saw the advance signs of the approaching station along the tracks that stretched like a timeline into the future. All the signals were green, vouchsafing the train an unhindered passage. As the train neared the station, one of the beribboned men pulled the emergency chain. The train stopped at the deserted station.

It was a single-room station, called Smritibhoomi, set amidst peanut fields. Some villagers arrived and stood on the platform. Although their clothes were shabby, they were colourful. The women had covered their heads and faces with brightly coloured dupattas. Infants thrashed about in small cloth cradles that the women slung against their bodies. They were a group of gypsy blacksmiths who had reverted to being nomads since the harvesting was over. With racially inherited blacksmithery running in their veins, they moved from place to place like migratory birds.

Unaware of which train had stopped in front of them or what its destination was, they clambered into the Unreserved compartments carrying their tools and bundles. They were certain that the train would take them to some new city and that city would provide them with sanctuary for some time.

Seeing the train stop at his station unexpectedly, the stationmaster came out of his tiny room. By that time, shouting and screaming, the passengers had leapt down onto the platform. They turned into a faceless mob and encircled the station building. With the security provided by anonymity, they pelted the stationmaster's room with bottles and stones. Signals were smashed. A sharp stone grazed the stationmaster's ear and hit the head of a draught ox in a nearby field. It collapsed. The mob walked up to the stationmaster, pushing their three detainees in front of them. They added him to their list of detainees.

Unable to reconcile himself to the sudden developments, the stationmaster had lost his power of speech. He collapsed in his chair. Sweat poured off his head like a cloudburst. His eyes bulged and his irises almost touched his glasses.

Dvi entered the scene looking like a noble leader. He walked authoritatively, with measured steps. He raised his arms and commanded the mob to remain silent. They fell silent instantly, as if they had been waiting for the order.

'What we need is a strong leader. What we lack is that. When the king becomes weak, we need to step in and become the king.' He stood on the cast iron bench in front of the station and declaimed. The beribboned army clapped without a break.

'I have a dream. I shall realise that. From this moment, this train shall be under my control,' Dvi looked at Carvalho, who only wanted to somehow escape from the hole he was in and nodded meekly.

'As of this instant, this train is the Mahabharat Express. I am its manager. I'll decide where and when the train should go.' The mob cheered him. The stationmaster regained his senses. He gave the signals for the train to proceed. The passengers ran up to the train and boarded it. Mahabharat Express started its journey.

Karamchand resumed his place in their cabin. John asked, 'What happened?'

'A bloodless revolution.' The power balance on the train had just shifted. 'A coup d'état.'

THE STORY SO FAR

When every man is a story in himself, a train that transports thousands of human beings is a chronicle. The story of no man ends on the train. However, at some stage, most humans assume the role of a passenger on a train that travels between one city and another.

Many tragedies that have shocked the nation occurred on rail tracks. Men and women who have perished prematurely in trains that collided, fell into rivers, and exploded, travel alongside the rest of us. Some of these disasters have changed the course of the country's history. A train is not a set of steel wheels that travels on rails, nor is it a toilet complex. It is a living, breathing piece of history.

Indian trains which have witnessed countless deaths occasionally have babies being born on them too. On the Sampark Kranti Express that left Thiruvananthapuram Station on 23 January 2019, a baby was delivered between the Alappuzha and Ernakulam stations in one of the Sleeper coaches' toilets. A nomad woman let slip the baby she had delivered onto the rail tracks through the open toilet.

An old woman picked up the child from the tracks and brought him up. He grew rapidly. It was imperative that he grow rapidly, for he was not a live human being. He was a dream. He existed only in the space where human conceptions of reality and time ended. He was a figment of imagination.

However, his existence was not merely in an imaginary world. He was present in Dandakaranya; he was present in Naroda Patiya; he was everywhere where humans are present. He was the disquiet of the man who is unable to intercede with history. His human form was a product of Karamchand's imagination. Like mini-Gandhis coalesce to form a Mahatma Gandhi, he was the embodiment of teeny-weeny dreams.

Is he here?

Yes.

Is he not here?

No.

Who is he?

He is you.

Imagine an invisible chain. The strangers who have sat in each of the seats, vacated them and disembarked from the train are part of that invisible chain they unknowingly helped to create. A humungous human chain with the links not touching.

This Indian train comprises unseen figments of imagination, unseen co-passengers who are victims of rail tragedies, people without a past, and even those who have no present.

To be continued ...

PART THREE

The Subversive Animal

KARAMCHAND'S FACEBOOK POST

The Subversive Animal

I have seen humans as a single creature that has sixty million pairs of limbs, as many eyes, thirty million bellies, as many genitals, and hundreds of millions of teeth. In a primal rhythm, the legs were moving in the same direction and the tongues were chanting the same incantations. At Prayag Raj, I sat on the sandy banks of the confluence of the Ganga and the Yamuna, watching thirty million people head for the Triveni Sangam.

It was the second day of the ritual bath at the Kumbh Mela.

From my seated position I realised that humans meant legs and their movement was their verity. The authorities who reigned in the layered echelons of akharas, the naked and armed Naga sadhus and common people countable only in millions were on the move.

What was propelling them, I wondered.

Stories. There is only one thing powerful enough to make sixty million feet march as one—stories.

If that were so, what if this magnificent creature, who bore seeds of subversion within himself, was provoked using fables?

My thoughts progressed along those lines. In the same instant, trampling the harmonious links built by men over thousands of years, millions of feet stomped ahead.

8.5k Likes   6.5k Comments   2.8k Shares

1

THE CONCEPT OF A WEAPON

Night enveloped the train. It became a small city plunged into darkness by a power cut. There was light was only towards the front. For viewers in the distance, the train was only a sound that moved bearing an inky darkness. The train in the night has a different aspect; it is a dark demon that gallops.

Dvi's kingdom was steeped in darkness. Now he was the master of that darkness. As per the reservation charts no new passengers were to board the train or disembark at the many subsequent stations. The beribboned henchmen too were asleep. Dvi alone was awake. He recalled a sentence he had written down in an old notebook long ago. 'The heights by great men reached and kept were not attained by sudden flight, but they, while their companions slept, were toiling upward in the night.'

The train was now in his total control. However, there were some dissonances that could not be ignored. For instance, the irreverent, mischievous university students. They were an inconvenience, not a threat. They did not have the capacity to plan or lead a revolution, or organise the common man. Still, they could be an excellent source of energy. However, since they were limited to only the precincts of the university they did not become subversive. Yet, no dispensation had the power to withstand that energy, should it breach the banks and surge out. The only solace was that they were within the family system and that too as dependents.

The future that stared at them and the loves they stood to lose would keep them from indulging in rash acts. They would never be an uncontained torrent. And while they disliked the Establishment and craved freedom, they could be silenced with some crumbs that appealed to their selfish interests, and by keeping them hopeful.

Yet, they may perhaps choose the path of protests. That may create some inconsequential ripples. They happen naturally at certain points in time. Ephemeral like the Mexican wave that spectators at a football game create when the game gets boring. Like the worm turning, they may try to stand up. However, very soon they would return to their previous state. The caterpillar's only role is to lead the way to the silence of the pupa's cocoon. By the time the wings appeared, it would have transformed into another creature. The student's rebellion was merely the worm turning in the interstitial sliver of time between two examinations. Society can only view them as children. It can only see their political aspirations as mere emotional outbursts.

However, there were also dissonances that could not be contained. In the course of time, those could turn into total revolutions. Dvi had no information about what was happening in the General, Unreserved compartments. The occupants were not in direct touch with other parts of the train. The passengers were farmers, factory workers and manual labourers—those who had little to lose. They needed dreams. They must be plied generously with dreams. For centuries, those in power have been doing that. It is the best dream merchants who turn into leaders.

The public sets out on the path of revolution when it runs out of dreams. Governments and monarchies fall when those who have nothing to lose start to revolt. All the time, the public must be made to feel that they had owned something, that they still own something, and will continue to own something. Without allowing them to coalesce, they must be kept in compartments. They should be inveigled into getting themselves snared by sentiments of racial and communal superiority. Above all, an easily identifiable, worthy enemy should be found for them.

At this stage of his rumination, some ideas took shape in Dvi's mind. He had commandeered a cabin for himself in the H1 coach. Two beribboned henchmen stood guard outside. He opened his suitcase and pulled out a rusty dagger in a leather sheath. It harked back to the Iron Age. It had a history of sliding into millions of hearts, drinking their blood and becoming corroded by it. Sometimes it touched the walls of the heart by penetrating the gap between the vertebrae. At other times, in face-to-face combat, it sliced an arc in the belly of the enemy. When it was sheathed and tucked into the waistband, even a dwarf turned into a colossus.

Turning it in his hands, Dvi examined the dagger. Even in the darkness, its sharp edge glinted. He kissed its handle fondly. Believing it was inadequate for his purpose, he slid it back into the sheath.

He pulled out another weapon from the suitcase. Gandeevam—the bow created by Lord Brahma. After Lord Shiva carried it for a thousand years; after Prajapati bore it for five hundred and three years; after Lord Indra toted it for five hundred and eighty years; Lord Chandra for five hundred years; and Lord Varuna for a hundred years, the divine weapon reached Arjuna's hands during the conflagration that burnt down the Khandava Forest. At the time of the Mahaprasthanika, Lord Agni reclaimed it.

The mini version of that apocalyptic weapon was now in Dvi's hands. He felt great pride. He held Gandeevam close to his chest. However, deeming it obsolete, he put it away.

Next, from another pocket, he took out a dusty pistol. It had the serial number 606824 stamped on its metal skin. It was an Italian-made Beretta M semi-automatic of 1934 vintage. In 1941, when the Italian forces had surrendered in Abyssinia, the commanding officer V. V. Joshi had gifted it to himself as a souvenir. Eventually, it fell into the hands of Jagdish Prasad Goel, a gun runner in Gwalior. Sold for Rs 500 and a traded-in jammed revolver, it reached Vinayak Nathuram Godse, a brahmin youth. A standard issue of Mussolini's army, the pistol passed through many hands to reach the hands it was destined to reach.

After the assassination of Gandhi, it was hibernating inside that suitcase. Its time had come again. Muah ... muah ... muah ...

Dvi polished the gun. He caressed its black body. He kissed its cold, dead barrel, and shoved it in his trouser pocket. He rose from his seat, silently slid open the door and went out.

What else has intervened and interceded in history as much as weapons?

What is this thing between humans and weapons?

Weapons have led to the modernisation of humans.

Holding the gun with its unquenched blood lust, he walked through the darkened corridor. The narrow path trodden by men with ponderous, unrealisable dreams and even greater strife. A stretched-out path that accepted sinners and saints with the same serenity. In the A1 coach, everyone was asleep. From the farthest ends of the coach, a man and a woman were snoring like an antiphonal chorus.

Suddenly, parting the curtains, a long lean neck came out. It was Doubting Dowager, with her vulturine, beady eyes. She started to wonder: 'The whole world lies in darkness. Will the light never return again? Oh, could such a thing happen? It may not. But what if it happens? What's this flashing through the darkness? Who's this man pussyfooting past me?' Reeling in a set of new misgivings into her brain, Doubting Dowager withdrew her head back behind the curtains.

Dvi walked through the Sleeper coaches towards the rear. Chatting on their mobiles, only a handful of people were awake. At night, trains are repositories of dreams where thousands of dreams bloom and mature in abundance.

He had only one purpose. Two eyes which shone brilliantly even in the inky darkness. They should be buried forever. Their owner will give birth to new concepts every moment. He will attack with weighty, portentous words. Dvi increased the pace of his walking. His destination was the S6 coach.

He arrived there shortly. The reading lamp of berth no. 65 was still on. In its dim light, he saw an old open book and phrases underlined in it. He saw a hand with wrinkled skin holding the book, and above, where the arm originated, an old man's face. The light that fell on those sparkling eyes was being reflected back a hundred times over. The light that framed the head like a halo elevated the seventy-plus years of experience to a level of sublime sagacity.

The eyes of Dvi and the old man met. The old man gave him a questioning look. Suddenly, Dvi bent down and touched the old man's feet respectfully. The old man pulled back his leg quickly.

'I beg your pardon. You do know that we are from a culture in which preceptors and elders are treated with respect, don't you?'

'Aha?'

'Are you afraid to die?'

'Who's going to kill me?'

'I will, myself.' Dvi took the gun out of his pocket.

'Do you believe that you can kill me with that pistol?' the old man asked nonchalantly.

'Your body isn't bulletproof, is it?'

'Ha, ha, ha, you're mistaken again. As much as you are not a single individual, I too am not one. Dabholkar is an idea. Concepts do not die. What about the weapon in your hand? It will corrode and become unusable.'

'The weapon is likewise, old man. This is no ordinary pistol. This gun took Gandhi's life. In that sense, you are a very lucky man.'

'You fool! Did Gandhi ever die? Ideas are a continuum. From one it will turn into another endlessly, evolve and go forward.'

'A weapon is the last word on anything. That aside, if you have just cause on why I should not kill you, state that. You are entitled to an impartial trial based on natural justice before being sentenced to death. State your case. You are now standing in front of the judge and executioner of this train. It's your providence that I am both.'

'Read out your chargesheet,' the old man said evenly.

'One, you instigated the students to protest against the establishment. Two, you spoke in defence of a treasonous water thief.'

When he concluded, Dabholkar laughed. 'I had anticipated this as soon as you raised your ragtag army. That you would end up before me in quick time. I know that your greatest fear is words.'

'These are silly rationalisations. They won't stop me from executing you. Death is the real solution. Therefore, this night, without bothering anyone else, I am executing the sentence.'

Dabholkar was leaning against the window. Dvi grabbed his neck with his left hand. When death appeared before him like a keening, terrifying spectre, the old man's eyes bulged in fear.

'Why are you killing me? Am I not old enough to be your father?' was his exact question as he tried to break free. That was also what Dvi, the twin-functionary, heard. Only after that did Dvi drag him down and had him lie flat on the lower berth.

With monstrous force he pressed the muzzle of the gun to the old man's chest. He pulled the trigger with his evil finger. The old man writhed once. A thin stream of blood traced the course of a river beneath the seat. Tucking the bloodstained weapon into his waistband, Dvi rose to his feet. Even after they were stilled, the old man's eyes sparkled as if set with diamonds.

Karamchand leapt up from his berth. His heart was thumping. He was sure that he had heard a gunshot and a cry. The fact that he heard them made them real for him. If thinking made one exist, its audibility made the scream exist. The scream was reverberating throughout the train now.

He did not tarry. Karamchand went out of the coupé and hurried towards the S6 coach. Dawn had not broken. The coach appeared to be deserted. He examined Dabholkar's berth. The bullet had passed through the middle of the berth. There were drops of blood on the floor. Karamchand became disoriented. His eyesight dimmed. He felt dizzy. He took out his mobile phone. The number of likes on the Facebook post did not matter to him.

The news of the murder came up on some online portal.

'*Rationalist Dabholkar shot dead ...*' Karamchand's hands trembled. '*Anti-superstition activist and Maharashtra's most vocal rationalist Narendra Dabholkar was shot dead by two youths on a motorcycle on the Omkareshwar Bridge near ...*'

The time-space continuum started to whirl around in front of Karamchand's eyes. Many places converged on a single point in time. Shaniwar Peth and Rajghat rose in front of him as one pillar.

2

THE BOY WITH NO HISTORY - III

The sound of a file rasp working on steel fell upon Karamchand's ears. A blacksmith seated in a corner of his brain was sharpening his tool. The sound of steel on steel. Heavy metal music.

Sounds everywhere, only sounds. Sight was blocked, obliterating even shadows. A thousand blacksmiths were using a thousand rasp files to sharpen a thousand steel bits. The brain had turned into a storehouse of sounds. The booming blast of the universe being recreated made him close his eyes.

Gradually, sight returned to his eyes that remained shut. At the summit of his brain a human form was seated with his head bowed. He was filing a rusty piece of iron to sharpen it. A heap of iron filings hid him from sight. Karamchand ran up to him and sat in front.

'Why are you filing all the time?' Karamchand asked. The man did not raise his head. Karamchand kept repeating the question, but the man remained engrossed in his work and kept his head bowed.

'Look here, the insufferable sound of your filing is giving me a headache. You must either stop it or tell me why you are sharpening this arrowhead.' The man did not raise his head but grunted as if he had heard the demand. Possibly because he was fed up with the repeated questions, the man finally replied.

'Listen if you must, I'm a hunter.'

'Why have you turned into a squatter inside my head?'

'The wild buffalo and the hunter can be found everywhere. Haven't you read it in the epics?'

'Yes, how are you here?'

'When a cruel or imposter despot is born, an arrow too takes birth. And a hunter to shoot that arrow.'

In that moment the rasping sound stopped. The coolness of peace descended. Tranquillity undisturbed by even a gentle breeze. Karamchand's head dissolved in the glorious silence of the Shanti Parva from the Mahabharata that emerged from a point in the future and streamed out. The image of the man who was a blacksmith and a hunter became clearer in his vision. That of the young man with no history and who needed to fear no man.

3

SEQUESTRATIONS

An announcement brought Karamchand back to the present. The train was standing in a busy, noisy station. He descended to the platform and stood amidst hawkers and their cries, the lights and the shadows, incapable of distinguishing between reality and illusion.

Vadodara.

The handful of turbaned men reminded him of imperial nawabs. Karamchand saw old man Dabholkar walking past him towards the exit, pulling his stroller bag. With one foot in the dream world, he looked at the old man in wonderment. The old man walked along the plush platform paved with polished granite and went out of sight.

When he heard the voice of the middle-aged lady from S3, Karamchand turned around to look.

'Lucky, I've reached Gujarat at last. There is nothing to fear now.' She sat on the bench and dialled her mobile phone. Pleased to see her daughter at the far end of the platform, she started to talk loudly into her phone, 'Beti, hasn't your husband come with the Innova?' From the sudden change in her expression, it was evident that the reply was not a palatable one. The bearded man was standing by, ready to assist her, 'What, didn't you say that he will come with the car?' The line was disconnected from the other end.

'Should I drop you?' the man asked the braggart.

'Ayy, not at all. Have you travelled on the buses here? No, right? They gleam like gold and run like cheetahs. If you look out of the window you can see glass-like roads. What if I have to wait here till 6 a.m.? I'll happily sit here on this platform. Can you find a single mosquito?'

'Then let me leave. My place is close enough to go by an autorickshaw.' He bid her goodbye after heaving her big, heavy bag onto the bench. She raised her hand and waved him goodbye.

Shortly a look of desperation came into her eyes. One of the blowflies that had been feasting on the faeces on the track flew up and started to buzz around her nose. She made no move to swat it away.

Leaving the woman to her devices, Karamchand walked towards the AC coaches. One of the hawkers handed over a paper packet to Carvalho. He opened and handed over some of the unshelled peanuts, endemic only to the black soil of Vadodara, to Karamchand. Each kernel was as big as a marble. While he popped them one by one into his mouth and chewed them, Carvalho took him by his shoulders and, giving them a friendly but authoritative shake, asked, 'Don't you sleep?'

'The heights by great men reached and kept were not attained by sudden flight, but they, while their companions slept, were toiling upward in the night,' said Karamchand breathlessly.

Carvalho quickly pulled his hands back from Karamchand's shoulders and asked in amazement, 'Who, really, are you?'

Karamchand skinned and popped two more kernels into his mouth.

4

MEMORABLE DEATHS

The train left the station swiftly and Karamchand started to chase it. Eventually, only where the platform ended could he leap and grab the handle of the S1 coach. In a flash he saw death loom in front of him. The irrepressible survival instinct in him transferred all the strength in his body to his arms and in one swift heave he was inside the coach. As he stood firm-footed on the steel floor, he realised that he had ended up inside not merely on his own steam. Another hand, which had helped him into the coach, had not loosened the grip on him.

'Why do you have to take such risks, bhaiyya?' asked the student leader from S1.

'I must ride on this train. I have been observing you from Ernakulam. I am watching everything that happens on this train as if it were a movie. Especially you all. Your bottomless energy. When you can't find songs as you play Antakshari, I become breathless. I have come here, unable to bear the tension. My name is Karamchand.'

'How did you reach here so quickly?' The sound of their conversation woke up the other students, who now joined them.

'I have some trepidations. Let me tell you the first among them. My dear young fellow, I've heard so many of your speeches on YouTube. The clarity of your thoughts; your voice which is yet to turn deep; the hair that catches the wind; and above all, the great hope that you give us all ...'

'So what exactly is your fear?'

'That you will be killed. I couldn't bear the tension while I was on the platform.'

'Bhaiyya, death holds no fears for me. For greater people than me have been killed in this country. However, your name, Karamchand, still raises hope.'

'I don't deny that. The second series of killings started with Narendra Dabholkar. Tell me something: Whose death was more significant? Gandhi's or Dabholkar's?'

The youth became pensive. The students stood listening to them. However, more than them, a rotund bald man in a safari suit was paying him keen attention—Kuriakose. After the first phase of the journey, he had shed his armour of brusqueness and had become friendly with the students.

'Dabholkar's death is more significant,' the youth said.

'Why?'

'Both were killed by the same forces. However, they died in two different eras.'

'Please explain, young man,' Kuriakose joined the conversation.

'Because, when Gandhi was killed, those who were obliged to justify it were a tiny minority. That was the reason why they subsided after Gandhi's assassination. They were in hibernation for decades, their fangs concealed and claws retracted. By the time we come to Dabholkar's assassination, their ideology had grown to a level where they could establish that his death was a necessity. After Gandhi's assassination, they became inert. However, Dabholkar's assassination led to a series of assassinations.'

'Yes, I was waiting for this reply. This is the cause of my fear too. I have another demand. You should fight in the next elections,' Karamchand said.

'For argument sake, let's assume that I will fight in the elections. But how will my brand of politics succeed in a society that believes Ashwatthama has reappeared; one which lays national highways to cater to Hanuman?'

The TTE turned up suddenly. Their conversation was naturally disrupted. 'Why's there a crowd here?'

'We were playing Antakshari,' Kuriakose replied. Elvindas looked at him in amazement.

'Sir, didn't you complain that the coach was too noisy?'

'That was a long time ago.'

Elvindas laughed and moved on.

One of the girls tried to restart the Antakshari that had not been interrupted.

'Which was the letter you had stopped at?' Karamchand asked.

'Aaa,' a girl with light-coloured eyes said.

'Shall I sing? It's a Malayalam poem.'

'All right, you may please do. It feels like I haven't heard Malayalam for a long time,' said Kuriakose and sat up erect.

Who is it that rocks me gently
Like a child in a cradle.
Sleep arrives; atop a trundling
Train hauled by memories.

Sudden, with a shudder
The night growls
Lurking, slowly takes aim
And lunges to devour the train
That swims across the river.

From the surging river,
Flares up darkness;
Water screams,
From the mouth of the gaping tunnel;
Sound shatters in the windpipe.

The broken metre pants,
And scatters in threes and twos;
Disjoints in lines and
Stiffens in mid pauses,
Swerves, buckles and goes off the rails,
Face down, descending, plunging, plunging ...

He traversed through a range of high and low tones and when he trailed off, the students broke into loud applause.

'Your Malayalam is like gravel being rattled inside an aluminium vessel. But this song had the lilt and tempo of a running train,' the light-eyed girl said.

'Brother, who has written this song?'

'It's not a song. It's a poem called 'A Train Set to Keka',[15] by a poetess called Anitha Thampi.'

5

DVI'S CHART

Smug after the assassination, Dvi sat alone in his cabin. The hubris of being able to repress things had given his eyes a hard look and arched his eyebrows. His nose stuck out like a finger enforcing a command.

Dvi now had the reservation chart that he had taken off Carvalho. He flipped through it. S6, 65, Narendra Dabholkar, M73, Mangalore-Vadodara. He drew a cross mark in red against the name. He searched for other similar names in the chart.

He found some old reservation charts under the current one. Carvalho had kept them as a part of a collection. He found these names in them. Then he flipped through the Waiting List chart. There they were. Their berths had not been confirmed so far.

1.   Govind Pansare

2.   Gauri Lankesh

3.   M. M. Kalburgi

He underlined the three names in red ink.

He also found names of people who had been booked for forthcoming journeys and were currently on the Waiting List.

1. Sunil P. Ilayidom

2. Perumal Murugan

3. K. S. Bhagawan

4. Kamal Haasan

5. Amartya Sen

6. ...

He was exhausted from underscoring names.

6

DIVISIONS

This was the third night after the Sampark Kranti Express had started its journey from Thiruvananthapuram. The stretched-out train, connected by buckle joints, rocked Karamchand to sleep with its rhythmic oscillation. The diverse people he had run into over those three days merged with his unconscious as diverse stories. Among them were the ones who had stories of their own and those who did not. And there were those who carried mighty tales inside them and walked around suppressing them, as if they had no stories to narrate. Linking all of them in a long story, the train continued its progress.

Watching John—the European who had connected with the miracle of India over three generations—sleeping in the parallel berth, Karamchand too fell asleep. His sleep, too, comprising countless people, was eventful. To be reborn in stories, they appeared in his dreams.

When the train split into two, Ramkesh Meena was asleep on berth no. 7 of the S7 coach. Sensing something untoward had happened, he rose from the berth, pulled on his jacket and rushed to the door.

By then, scaring him, the coaches from S6 onwards had lost their connection to the front portion of the train, and were rolling in reverse. This was his first such experience and unaware of what he should do in these circumstances, he grew nervous and started to sweat. Should he pull the chain? Should he leap out of the train and run? Should he scream? Should he record everything on his mobile phone and upload the video on YouTube?

While such thoughts were passing through him in a flash, the train came to a stop, having rolled up the rise at the 75th mile. With nothing propelling it, weighed down by its own mass, the truncated train failed to take the rise. The whistle could be heard from the engine.

Whoo ... whoo ... whoo ... whoo ... whoo ...

From his lessons at the Railway School in Tiruchirappalli, he recalled that the series of toots meant *'lambi gaadi choti ho gayi'* or that the long train has become short. During those days when there were no walkie-talkies or mobile phones, the loco pilots used to communicate with the train guards and stationmasters through coded whistle blows.

The passengers were fast asleep. He jumped down from the coach. This section of the track was not maintained for people on foot. Sharp thorny grasses grew on the side of the track, with thick bushes beyond them. What lay beyond was unknown. Birds woken up by the disturbance flapped their wings and trilled.

The red signal from the guard was visible about a kilometre away. In response, signals from the engine driver in the front could also be seen. The whistle sounded again. Shortly, the locomotive started to reverse slowly to join with its truncated part. From the track he jumped back into the train.

He had assumed that no one else would be awake. As if to substantiate that, the snores of the passenger on no. 17, the lower berth, could be heard. However, when he entered, he saw a girl standing at the other end of the bogie, staring fearfully into the darkness as the train rolled in reverse. On the outside wall of the toilet, to the left of the girl, was a strikingly beautiful publicity poster of Uttarakhand Tourism with snow-capped mountains and the tag line 'Valley of Solitude'.

As if to remind one that such islets of solitude can be found even in heavily crowded places, a sliver of light lay on the poster. For that small narrow isthmus between two bogies, what could be a better name than Valley of Solitude?

Another publicity poster was affixed on the wall of seat no. 7 in S7 reserved for TTEs: that of Sikkim Tourism with the picture of the summit of one of the Himalayan peaks glowing orange in the sun. It too had a caption—'Square of Hope'. Where could one find a better name for that small square of space where wait-listed passengers congregate?

The passengers who moved from one bogie to another would have to go past the Square of Hope and walk through the Valley of Solitude.

Nimesha Mehta was asleep on berth no. 65 in the S6 coach. An urge to visit the toilet woke her up. She tried to wake up her husband Feroze to accompany her till the toilet. Loath to wake up and much less to accompany her, he gave her a discourse on how Indian Railways are safe for women, turned to the other side and went back to sleep.

His discourse was not powerful enough to stop her urge to void. Nature hollered from inside her belly. She walked towards the toilets. Both toilets at her end of the bogie were locked from the inside. Through the vestibule she entered the Valley of Solitude of the S7 coach.

It was a lost valley. Two parallel steel tracks were fleeting past in a deep ravine between two hills. She entered the toilet and locked the door.

It was another world. Using inks in myriad colours, the male of the species had emptied the bowels of their minds on the walls. They were covered with depictions of multiple sex positions, with the annotations outnumbering the graphics. It was a netherworld filled with lewdness, politics, religious bigotry and empty braggadocio. She took pictures on her mobile. She tried to upload the photo on Facebook with the comment 'How much better is the Facebook wall' and feeling/activity 'Feeling pity for Indian boys'.

The train broke into two at that same instant. Shocked by the unexpected sound of the breaking apart, she exited the toilet and tried to walk to her coach. That was when she saw the S6 coach cutting and running away from S7 and receding into the darkness.

Realising even in that fraught moment that the links between the bogies were very tenuous, she stood in the Valley of Solitude and trembled, watching and listening to the sounds of the half-train disappearing into the blanket of darkness.

The girl Ramkesh Meena saw when he entered the bogie was her. He quickly went up and touched her shoulder as she stood petrified. Sensing a hand on her shoulder, she spun around, even more terrified.

'It's natural for trains to break apart and join back together. In other words, all the long trains are designed and built accounting for such happenstances. Do you understand?' He spoke in an authoritative voice. Her face showed relief and hope. Ramkesh Meena's fear also lessened when he saw the calmness return to her face.

'Come in and sit here calmly,' he instructed her. She went up to seat no. 7 and sat down.

'What happened, sir?' asked a man who had woken up hearing them converse.

'Nothing, trains make extra noise on this section,' Ramkesh lied.

Nimesha dialled her husband sleeping in the next coach. Outside, the assistant loco pilot and guard re-linked the train and returned to their respective stations. Shortly a long whistle was heard from the engine. The train started to roll again. With a deep exhalation, Nimesha expelled the fright that had balled up inside her. After thanking the TTE, she headed back to her coach.

She returned as quickly as she had departed. She looked agitated and spoke in distress to Ramkesh, 'There's a problem. The shutter has been pulled down. What am I supposed to do? Is this ghost train going to stop anywhere soon?' She smacked her head with both her hands.

'Please relax. I will get you into S6 shortly,' said Ramkesh and pointed to the vacant seat. 'For the time being lie down here.' However, she could not sleep.

As for Ramkesh, he fell asleep, using for a pillow a thick tome on history that he had been lugging around for the past one month intending to read it. If the train ran without interruption, the next station was six hours away.

When he woke up in between, he saw Nimesha standing in the Valley of Solitude. Her own compartment was only three paces away. She returned to the Square of Hope, holding the mobile phone that was tired from being dialled incessantly. She kept walking to and from the Valley of Solitude.

'What happened, Nimesha?'

'I'm not able to reach Feroze.'

'Don't worry, let him sleep. We are passing through forests where there's no network.'

She returned to her berth and soon fell asleep.

The train continued to run. When she woke up after a long sleep, Nimesha saw that the compartment was empty. Only she and the TTE were in the coach.

Ramkesh realised that three hours had passed after they had left Samjhauta Junction. There the train had split into two; one part had started travelling towards the west and the other to east. He felt a void inside when he looked at the disquieted girl seated in front of him.

The train's speed had picked up. Suddenly Nimesha leapt up and dashed towards the Valley of Solitude. Holding the handles at the edge of the vestibule, she screamed loudly. Ahead of her were rail tracks that seemed to fly out of sight. The surging train pulled her back.

At the acme of her panic, she stood trembling. On the horizon, where sky and land converged, the parallel tracks met, conjoined, mated, and turning into vapour, disappeared into the haze.

'Sir, where is S6? Where's my Feroze?'

The two sections of the train that had split were now 600 kilometres apart. In the moment that she realised it, from the square of hope, she went beyond the valley of solitude into the vast path where sunlight and speed were determinants of death. When it looked certain that she would leap out of the train, Ramkesh caught her.

'Nimesha, when we reach a proper station, I shall help you to get down safely. When there are a few hundred thousand ways for people to communicate, why are you so disturbed?'

She looked at him with hope-filled eyes. Her phone battery was fully drained and she felt completely isolated.

'Till then, keep reading this book,' Ramkesh handed over the book he had been using as a pillow. Some professor of history had left it behind in the train. The cover design in yellow showed a subcontinent and a woman split into two. With a burning heart, Nimesha, born as one of the last links in the lineage started by Zarathushtra, read the subtitle on the cover, 'The History of a People Torn Asunder'.

Karamchand wondered if there was another book such as this one. It was not necessary that a book on history as it was written originally with that title should be extant. However, when seated around round tables in third countries, paper maps of landmasses are bifurcated using rulers and pencils, people also get split into two. Many of the African nations were given straight borders or square shapes by men sitting in Europe. When a man called Cyril Radcliffe had taken the knife to India's map, the wails of thousands of men and women rose from every square inch on the ground.

Human history consists of separations and redemptions. Karamchand saw the dream about Nimesha when under the hangover of reading online about a Yazidi woman who was forced to eat her own child. The sex slave with the hazel-colour eyes who unknowingly ate her own baby had the same blood as Nimesha, whose forebears had walked to the east thousands of years ago and become civilised and enriched.

Ah, 'human', what a beautiful word!

7

THE LEGISLATURE

What are the basic needs of men, Dvi asked himself.

He himself provided the answers.

Food.

Sex.

Sleep.

Each animal needs these.

However, what is more important than these? Liberty.

When he thought of that answer, his brain lit up. He remained silent for a while and peered into himself.

If that be the case, what helps to maintain the system?

Fear.

Fear of what?

Fear that liberty may be lost.

What sustains the nation?

Policing.

No, the police are only an instrument.

Fear.

Fear of what?

Fear of the possible loss of liberty.

Isn't the right of speech included in that?

Definitely.

The right to eat the food one likes?

Most certainly.

To have sexual intercourse?

That too.

Isn't the fear that these rights may be lost that compels a person to abide by the system?

Yes.

So where does the loss of liberty happen?

Inside a prison.

In that case, the final question is—what sustains a system or a nation?

Jail.

Dvi looked out. Twenty-four hours remained for the Sampark Kranti to reach Delhi. It was roaring along in a deserted, arid region. As he kept watching, a child, emaciated by ingesting scarcity, flung a stone at the train. The sharp-edged flint was speeding towards Dvi's head. He swerved out of its way. It was a stone thrown in jealousy, admiration, frustration, disappointment, anger or wonderment at something beyond that urchin's reach. However, it did not have the power to wound the train.

Dvi quickly planned some moves. He WhatsApped instructions to his henchmen.

'Boys!'

'Os!' Eighteen impatient soldiers responded with their greetings.

'What sustains a system?'

'We don't know,' the responses came quicker than the question had gone to them. Ignorance is the primary quality to be in the ranks, Dvi smiled and said to himself.

'Then listen, jails do that.'

Eighteen smileys and eighteen applauding hands acknowledged it.

'So, shouldn't we be building prisons?'

Eighteen thumbs-up icons popped up on Dvi's phone.

'We shall turn a section of S6 into a prison. The rest of the compartment will be turned into a court and our administrative quarters.'

'Os!' The meaningless hiss had now acquired the power to represent the arrogance of their ever-increasing authority. The henchmen threw out the few passengers left in the coach. The bogie lay in an overwhelming silence that resembled the fearsome atmosphere of Auschwitz's gas chambers. Nine cells. Seventy-two chambers. The steel enclosures lay with their maws open, as if waiting for their prey.

Dvi's foot soldiers took little time to turn creative. On one end of the bogie, they tacked name boards on the doors of toilets turning them into 'Notified Jails.' The prison cells were ready. Dvi was amazed by the speed at which his plans were being executed. The eighteen henchmen stood before him awaiting his command.

'So, who are the culprits?' asked one who was drawing bars on a wall of the prison cell.

'Is there a doubt? Those who commit crimes are the culprits.'

'If so, what is a crime?' another henchman asked.

'Breaking the law is a crime.' The soldier—the first henchman recruited—replied, not Dvi.

Another one raised a point of order. 'If the law has to be broken, shouldn't we have laws first?'

'Yes. We can create as many laws as we want. That will help in netting us many criminals from many places. For example, the police install a traffic signal on a road which till the yesterday didn't have any signals. Those who have driven on that road unhampered till yesterday will face a new set of rules today. Those who do not obey those rules will obviously turn into culprits.'

The henchmen clapped.

'So, we assume you'll get busy making laws?'

'I'm promulgating the first law, listen.'

The henchmen, like fascinated children, were all ears.

'Every hour, our beribboned army will blow their whistles four times. That will be called the Clarion. When the Clarion is sounded, the passengers shall rise to their feet.' He explained the rules that the passengers had to abide by. The henchmen welcomed the new rules enthusiastically.

'What is the punishment for the lawbreakers?'

'What we usually do as a mob is to round on them and beat them to death,' one of the henchmen said.

'We have built the jails for this purpose, haven't we?' Dvi said.

'That's not enough. This is a high crime. They must be whipped,' the eighteen henchmen demanded in unison. 'My hands are itching,' each one of them said.

'If that's the case, the new law will contain all of these,' Dvi concluded, thrilling them.

In the train that was running with a new-found enthusiasm, the first law was discussed, drafted and passed. Shortly, the henchmen pasted the ordinance along the corridors of the train. The passengers seated in the train, which was now running in the reverse direction, stared at the First Law stuck on the walls.

The Clarion Observance Law, 2019 (C.O.L. 2019)
In order to reinforce unity among passengers and to enable them to exhibit their allegiance to the establishment, duly authorised beribboned representatives shall blow the whistle in the coaches every hour. This sound will be known by the name 'Clarion'. From time immemorial, we have known that the waves released by sound create positive energy in the human brain. Therefore, the following observances should be done by the passengers when the Clarion is sounded:

First Clarion: The passengers shall stand up respectfully.

Second Clarion: Touch the left ear with the right hand taking it around and behind the head.

Third Clarion: Bend down and use the left hand to hold the big toe of the right leg.

Fourth Clarion: Stand up erect. Inhale deep. Exhale.

All the passengers shall strictly observe the C.O.L. 2019. Those who fail to observe these procedures will face punishments such as monetary fines, whipping, and jail terms.

Exactly at 8 p.m., the First Clarion sounded in the coaches, piercing the ear drums of a community wallowing in the depths of laziness on a journey through the unknown. The passengers, who were preoccupied with various pastimes, leapt up as if a live current had passed through them. They stood erect like bushes whose tops had been pruned. An unnamed fear bored a hole through everyone's hearts like a high-bandwidth wireless information highway. No one looked at his or her neighbour. Everyone felt that they were being observed by unseen eyes. Irrationally, they lost trust in the person next to them.

A human chain was formed that ran from one end of the train to the other. A wave of fear passed through it. Everyone was present in the human chain. At one end was Carvalho. Doubting Dowager and the middle-aged villager couple were among the links. Hiding their indignation, the students joined the chain. Here and there, the beribboned henchmen stood facing the human chain. The only sound came from steel rubbing against steel.

Invisible to everyone, Dvi enjoyed the spectacle while seated elsewhere.

Exactly after one minute, the Second Clarion sounded. As if they had touched a live wire, those in the chain twisted their right arms around the back of their necks and touched their left ear. This time, although still looking grave, they stole sidelong glances at their neighbours to ensure that they were doing it correctly.

The Third Clarion sounded. The people in the chain who were solemnly holding onto their left ear leaned over to the right and touched the big toe of their right leg. The long chain of humans stayed bent, observing that strange ritual. When they had to arch down after many years, the bodies, whose physical exertions had been limited to expending themselves in the missionary position, started to creak in their various joints. In this position, accustomed as they were to staying erect all the time, popping sounds were heard from the vertebrae and discs in the spinal column.

As she stood in the human chain with her decades-old, kyphosis-affected spine, Doubting Dowager wondered, 'Isn't it enough if, instead of holding the left ear with the right hand, if the right ear is held with the left hand?' Then she found the answer herself. 'No, it's not enough, because the law states otherwise. However, the law is silent on whether the top of the ear or the ear lobe should be held.'

The Fourth Clarion too sounded. The passengers and staff straightened their aching spines in relief. After expressing it with a deep exhalation, they returned to their seats. Their responses were mixed.

'It's been such long time since I bent down.'

'I am proud that I bowed in front of the law.'

'I didn't dream that at this age I could bend down and touch my foot.'

'There is no doubt that this will boost our blood circulation. Someone like him will not frame a law like this unless there's more than what meets the eye.'

'How imaginatively has the law been designed.'

No one protested, no one demurred. A wellspring of discipline and obedience kept them chained together. They waited impatiently for the next clarion call.

Dvi waited in his cabin expectantly for the results of the clarion experiment. However, he did not betray his anxiety. Reports from all the coaches pegged the experiment as a resounding success. The henchmen WhatsApped him the legal points raised by some of the passengers. They were:

What should those who are asleep do?

Can left-handed people use their left hand instead of the right?

Must nursing mothers, pregnant women, senior citizens, invalid people etc., observe the regulations?

What is the beribboned brigade supposed to do?
Dvi replied to every query as follows:

Those who are asleep should wake up.

Left-handed people should become right-handed.

The law does not discriminate between able-bodied and pregnant women or aged people. Everyone is equal before the law.

The beribboned brigade members are observers. Their duty is to observe and identify transgressors and bring them before the law.

The passengers accepted the law with remarkable deference. For a moment, Dvi doubted that the C.O.L. 2019 would fail in its primary objective of creating culprits. However, in the same instant, the beribboned brigade brought before him a handcuffed, middle-aged man. After hailing Dvi with 'Os!' they pushed the man in front of him and stepped back. Dvi gave the man a questioning look. Fear had made his eyes bulge so that they were almost falling out of their sockets.

'Shall I start flogging him?' a henchman with a sinewy, even voice, asked for Dvi's permission.

'No!' Dvi said peremptorily. The henchmen stepped back. 'We follow a process for everything. You have the right to undergo a fair and just trial before you are sentenced.'

The middle-aged man was relieved. The eyes that bulged returned to their normal size. He believed that he was part of an organised system with a court that would listen to his side of the story.

The judge was a Brahmin with a broad forehead and was gifted with rampant baldness. Since he had drawn the *namam*[16] on the middle of his forehead, his face looked like it had been split in the middle. Dvi had discovered him in the AC First Class coach and appointed him as the judge. His sole qualification was his ponderous look.

Before he accepted the appointment, he had laid down some conditions. 'Once a law is made, it is freed from the lawgiver. The right to interpret it and to pass judgements on it shall be vested solely in me.'

'I give you my word that it will be so. There will be no interference of any sort,' Dvi announced. Only after that did the man shift to the court set up in S6.

The side lower berth in an eight-seat bay was the judge's seat. Sporting the *shikhi* on the top of his head as a symbol of haughtiness he had inherited along with his caste, the judge parked himself on the seat. The accused was stationed in front of him. Two whip-wielding henchmen stood on either side. When the urge to use them became insufferable, they squeezed the handles till their fingers hurt.

'When the First Clarion sounded, you did not show respect to the Clarion as laid down by law, indulged in wanton behaviour and insulted it. You, K. S. Sarvashaktan, M55, occupant of seat no. 63 in S3, have committed the crime of violating the system as per section no.1 of C.L.O. 2019. Do you plead guilty?'

Shaking his head to indicate denial and negation, the freshly minted culprit, a creation of the new law, looked piteously at the judge and pleaded, 'Your honour, when the sanctified Clarion was sounded as stated in your chargesheet, I did wish to stand up as a mark of respect and observe the decrees. It is also true that I was not able to do so.'

As soon as they heard it, the henchmen raised the whips. 'The accused has admitted his guilt. Why should the trial go on?' The judge gave them a forbidding look with his gimlet eyes.

'However, that was not due to any disrespect for the C.L.O 2019, your honour,' he continued. 'At that time, I was in the toilet, your honour. I was not in a state to stand up. In other words, had I stood up, there would be a situation where the Clarion would have suffered greater disrespect. Therefore, I pray most respectfully to the honourable court that on humanitarian grounds and in consideration of the mitigating circumstances, I may be discharged as innocent and absolved of crimes mentioned in the chargesheet.' Stating everything that he had to say in a single breath, the weakened man greedily sucked in air. His chest rose and fell like that of a frog's. He seemed to be under the misapprehension that he could reinforce his weak body that belied his name by breathing in deeply.

The judge fell into deep thought. Then he spoke, 'The law is silent on this peculiar situation inasmuch as what a man who is in the toilet should do when the Clarion is sounded. Where the law is silent, the judge shall speak. Therefore ...' he paused for a moment. He played with his shikha—starting with Manu, the primary lawgiver, a symbol of authority that had passed through many generations to reach him—a few times. He wiped the sweat from his Chanakya-nose. 'Therefore, invoking the noble concept of equality before law, as provided in section 11/24 of the C.L.O. 2019, the accused is hereby sentenced to the maximum punishment of fifteen floggings and one hour's imprisonment.'

Two henchmen took the culprit to the end of the coach. Many passengers had collected there to watch the punishment being meted out. The culprit was made to stand facing the prison door. Intoxicated by the power vested in him, the henchman raised the whip till the ceiling of the coach. His self-importance too touched the ceiling. As the executor of the supreme power on this side of the system, he took on the aspect of an executioner. He swung the whip.

'One ...' With a crack and hiss, the fall of the whip slashed Sarvashaktan's exposed back.

'Two ...' he writhed in stinging pain.

'Three ...'

...

'Fifteen ...'

When the whip fell silent, a wretched cry rose from him. He crumpled and sat down on the floor with the misery of having to bear the burden and irony of a name that meant 'omnipotent'. The henchmen immediately locked him up in jail.

The Clarion sounded again. The electrified passengers quickly fell into a line and linked up with each other. They learnt the drill quickly. It became part of their psyche. They became alert to the possibility of the Clarion being sounded at any time. Gradually, the long toot started to whistle inside their brains like the high wind of a hurricane. They could sense its curdled presence inside them even as they were eating, shitting, fornicating, conversing and quarrelling.

Dvi did not intervene either in the trials or in the sentencing. He sat in his secured cabin and watched animal fights on YouTube, his pastime. He had not had his fill of videos of lions and tigers fighting and mating. However, his favourite was watching the bulging, protruding, bulbous eyes of does as the lions buried their canines into their necks, their piteous bleats reminiscent of humans who have death staring at them.' Dvi enjoyed the agony of the death of others as he would enjoy music. At the height of their pain, he orgasmed.

He was watching a video of a pride of five lions and lionesses attacking a herd of wild buffalos. After isolating a female buffalo, they started attacking it from the rear. An agile lioness managed to sink its teeth into the buffalo's neck and hung on. When the helpless herbivore started to bellow pitifully, Dvi's excitement went up. He started to drum his fingers on his thigh. The herd watched one of its own being killed without any sign of distress. Their expressions reflected their apparent belief that they were powerless to intervene when destiny was in play. After watching the scene for some time, they moved away.

One of the male buffalos suddenly stopped in its tracks. It turned around and let out a bellow of extreme distress. The herd too stopped and turned around. 'This is not happening,' Dvi thought.

The buffalo pawed the ground. It shook its scimitar-like horns and galloped towards the lions. Hooking the lioness—which had still not let go of its prey—with one of its horns, the male tossed it high with incredible strength into the air like a rag doll. The lioness did a few somersaults in the air before it touched down, even as a group of buffaloes rushed in. The lions stopped roaring. The plains turned into a milling, churning blanket of black bodies. They stampeded over the five lions, pounding their bones into the ground.

Dvi's mouth ran dry. He switched off the tab. Although he leaned back comfortably, he was panting.

8

THE BOY WITH NO HISTORY - IV

Look, he is walking fast. Or, he has a reason to walk fast. Having been born in the first part of a novel against the backdrop of a train journey that would be completed in a mere three days, he was beholden to grow into an adult and travel all over India within that time. Many centuries ago, a man called Shankaran had undertaken such a trip. He, however, had a path of many years ahead of him, not days.

The young man with no history was starting on a journey. His destination was the Himalayas that loomed over an idea known as India, standing tall and shielding the north. That bright white curtain shines within his mind. From its flanks many rivers start off as thin threads, gain volume, tumble down the heights and irrigate the plains.

With his feet planted in time and space, he started to walk. On the border of the land of Cheras, he met an old woman. She was using a bucket fashioned out of an areca-palm spathe to draw water from a well. She wore only a single piece of cloth that reached her knees. The stone necklace she wore over her sagging breasts was swaying in time with the drawing of the water. He asked the old woman for some water. He sat at the feet of the old woman who was at least three centuries old. She poured water into his cupped hands and he drank his fill.

'Where are you going in such a hurry?' the old woman asked him.

'To the Himalayas,' he replied, pulling out a thorn stuck in his foot.

'And after reaching, what will you do there?' A hint of a smile appeared on the old woman's lips.

'I'll reach the summit of the snow-covered mountain and stand there for a moment.'

'And then?' The smile lingered on the old woman's lips. He had no answer to that question.

'You look exhausted.' The old woman made him lie down with his head in her lap. She caressed his head fondly and murmured softly:

> *Whether country, forest, ditch or knoll,*
> *O land! You are exalted where men are noble.*
> *Real vision is that which sees*
> *The One only, beyond the many;*
> *Real valour is of the person who has*
> *Conquered forever the senses five;*
> *Real learning is that which*
> *Grants you immortality;*
> *Real food is what you consume when*
> *You are fully liberated;*
> *And when you are not under anyone's command*
> *And you are neither a slave nor a servant.*

She placed her shrivelled breast in his mouth. He sucked hard on the breast, snuggling close to the old woman like a kit against its mother.

'This milk is enough for you to get through a whole century. All the same, keep this with you,' she said, gifting him a bag filled with Jñāna paḷam[17] to consume when he was tired.

'Who are you, granny with compassion in your hypnotic eyes, love in your words, and ambrosia in your breasts?' he asked.

'Avvaiyaar,' she said, her voice cool like the gentle breeze that blows down from the mountain.

He walked with long strides. As he did, he witnessed a group of migrants fleeing towards the south from the catchment areas of the Krishna and Godavari rivers. A migration that had lasted centuries. The scantily dressed people traversed plateaus and plains, driving skin-and-bones cattle before them and carrying emaciated children.

He continued on his own journey. A large army passed him, headed north. He asked one of the drummers, 'Who is your king? Whom is this army going to fight?'

The drummer gave him a surprised look. 'Don't you know? At the vanguard is the great Chola. The army is marching towards the Himalayas. When he returns after the campaign, he will be hailed as Gangaikonda Chola.'

The young man reached Kalinga via the southern trail and rested in the shadow of Mount Gandhamadana. The fragrance from the Kalyanasowgandhika flower that had dropped from the epic eased into his nostrils. He stood with his eyes closed. Suddenly, the ground under his feet trembled. The mountain peaks swayed. A heavy wind started and booming sounds made themselves heard. Without warning, the mace-wielding Bheema appeared before him.

'Where's this smell coming from?' Bheema asked. The young man pointed towards the summit of the mountain. Bheema walked off and the ground and forests trembled under his feet.

The heavenly fragrance that had enveloped him ceased. When the young man woke up, the air was thick with mineral dust. Gandhamadana was being transported in smaller heaps in dumper trucks moving in a line. The dumper trucks had the legend 'Vedanta' painted on their sides. When he started to walk again, he remembered, 'Vedanta. The end of Vedas. Ha!'

When he entered the land of the viharas, someone stopped him and asked, 'Who are you? What is your religion? What is your race? What is your clan?'

He answered all the questions with only one answer, 'I am the boy without history.'

As he walked, he became aroused. His undergarment ballooned. His penis swelled and became erect. He needed to divest himself of his load. He knew he would not be able to bear the load and keep walking any more. An overwrought body lags the mind. His pace slackened. A sinuous serpent rose up from his kundalini. It twisted itself around his body. The serpent of his own lust had subdued him. The juices surged in his throbbing, distended spongy tissues. Eventually he walked into a centuries-old brothel.

A naked girl who smelt of turmeric stood in front of him in one of the cramped rooms of Sonagachi. The sixteen-year-old's name was Maralekha. She arrayed on his sex-crazed body the tantric arts that her tribe had made their own through thousands of years' devotional service.

'You're Buddha and I, Prajnaparamita,' she said.

'You're Parvathy, I'm Shiva.' She made him sit on her lap. She filled his greedy mouth with her bountiful breasts. His body ascended to heaven. He found salvation through kama.

Like pollen in a hurricane, he continued his journey. Religions decayed over time. He skirted their suppurating wounds. With their lofty tenets putrefying and roots rotting, religions were becoming demented.

'My friend, high principles have been laid down for big people by even bigger people. For us ordinary mortals, with all our faults and shortcomings, an equally flawed and specious religion must be created. For that, a flawed and specious prophet must be born,' a drunk standing on a Buddha statue, pissing, edified him.

He saw another fleeing group in a boat caught in the doldrums in the Bay of Bengal. A people who had lost their nation, the Rohingyas. They were fighting for their lives, trying to keep themselves alive by breaking off and eating bits of wood off their floundering vessel that was carrying more people than it should have. Helpless human—to keep drifting is his curse.

Dusk had fallen. The young man with no history sat down beneath a pipal tree—an eternal witness to time—by the side of the deserted royal path. He was only semi-conscious. Water hemp grew luxuriantly all around him. He broke off a tender leaf, crushed it and let the juice drip down into his mouth. It set fire to his nerves and gave him a diabolical high. His body started to levitate. He forgot hunger and fatigue.

He was in a state of eternal youthfulness. His eyes were heaped with doubts—questions for which he could not find answers despite his continuing peregrinations. After many hours spent in that position, he espied another pipal tree at the other end of the royal path. He also saw a man with a careworn face seated beneath it. There was a halo around his face that was turning dim and clouded. He too had been watching the boy with no history for a long time. The boy was surprised and wondered who his observer in that isolated place was. They kept looking at each other for some time. It occurred to the boy that the man resembled the statue that lay stretched in the Ajanta Caves.

At some stage in his journey, the boy found himself in the cave that was covered by vines and other overgrowth. When he made his way wading through the darkness of the ages, he saw the luminescence emanating from the prehistoric stone. The Buddha was lying asleep, fully stretched out. He lay down next to the primeval stone. When he woke, he found a magnificent tiger sleeping next to him. He felt no fear as he lay between the Buddha and the tiger. Cohabitation had turned the tiger into a Buddha.

By some atavistic instinct, they both rose to their feet at the same time. They walked towards each other. Their minds traversed through strange thoughts. They sat down side by side on a flat stone.

'Who are you? Where are you coming from?'

'I come from the foothills of the Himalaya. Have you heard of Nepal?'

'Yes, I have. You are so fortunate. You can see the Himalaya all the time.'

'What do you mean fortunate? You look in any direction and all you see is the Himalaya mountains like torn pieces of white fabric. And bone-chilling cold! Anyone would get fed up.'

'Aiyyo, don't say so. All right, where are you going?'

'I? I'm going deep into the south. There's a place where three seas meet and their waves lap against one another. The sea where the waters provide salvation and turn into a phenomenon. Ah! The sea. What a magnificent sight it would be.'

'Ha ha ha ... it's nothing like that, my friend. Nothing of what you say is there, only water. What will you get by gazing at it? I live on the seashore. You are not going to get anything that I haven't got so far, or are you?'

'All right, what about you?'

'I'm going to the Himalayas.'

'And then?'

'And then nothing. My life's sole ambition is to go there.' When he heard that, the man who had come down the mountains in search of the oceans burst out laughing. The young man with no history too started to laugh. Neither could control their laughter.

'What's your name?'

'Siddhartha.'

'When did you start this journey?'

'Two thousand five hundred years ago. I became the Buddha on this journey.'

'That is good. Look towards that sea. Do you see a floundering boat there?'

'Yes.'

'That's a boat carrying Rohingyas.'

The Buddha looked at the boat. He saw wailing mothers and starving babies crying themselves hoarse.

He wept. 'I'm now the Futile Buddha. Let it be so. What is your name?'

'Shankaran.'

Try as they might, Shankaran, who sought the non-existent truth, and Siddhartha, who left his home seeking a solution for the miseries he witnessed all around him, could not control their laughter. Their mirth suffused for a long time the tranquillity that lay heavy in that wooded area filled with tall trees. When their laughter reached its acme, they attained enlightenment.

Finally, Siddhartha said, 'My home is calling me. I'm returning there. There, in my tiny kingdom, my wife and son will be waiting for me.'

'I have no one waiting for me, so I will head off somewhere else.'

They bade goodbye to each other and went their ways. Seated at a spot unmarked on earth by any one, at an unrecorded planetary conjunction in history, they recognised that every journey is a venture into the extra-terrestrial space to find the culmination of futility.

The young man with no history strode ahead on his long legs. He felt no fatigue. At that time, he heard the sound of a train close by—the music he liked most on this earth. He had grown up listening to the terrifying thudding of trains. Now the sound seduced him and dragged him along. When he crossed the shrubland at the edge of the desert, the train he was born in appeared before him. It arrived at the small, single-platform station in that desert and stopped.

He boarded the General Unreserved coach at the far end of the Sampark Kranti Express.

9

DESERT FESTIVALS

The memory of a roastingly hot breeze blowing from the Great Indian Desert welcomed the Sampark Kranti Express to Rajasthan. Carrying plastic water pots on their hips, a line of women stood by stoically, their faces covered with their sarees to save them from the crystal needles of sand grains stealthily carried by the wind. At one end of the line was a centuries-old living well. Water brought in tankers from some dam had been discharged into its empty, capacious belly, emptied by exploiting the last drop of the spring that fed it. The well would have been filled that day too.

Women spend much of their lives traversing the kilometres between their homes and wells, their spines bent from the weight of the pots, their heads bowed and feet blistered. Years pass in this tedium. And their entire lives too.

An Indian woman's waist and hip are designed to seat a pot of water. No, they are designed to carry a child with ease. If that is the case, the male of the species is cunning; he fashioned the pot in the shape of a child and handed it over to the woman.

Through that yellow terrain that had only thorny mesquite trees and peacocks, the Sampark Kranti Express sped like a blue bird. Perhaps because the blue colour reminded them of water, the women who were squatting beside the tracks to rest looked expectantly at the train.

They had a reason too to look on in anticipation. In 1892, Rajputana was in the grip of a terrible drought and famine. The scourge was closing in quickly, threatening to consume humans and cattle. That was when the trains appeared as guardian angels. The iron horses galloped in carrying water and victuals. The people of Rajputana deified the steam engines that rescued them during the famine and celebrated them in their folksongs.

The Sampark Kranti had stops at Kota Junction and Sawai Madhopur. The breeze that blew across the train, redolent with the smell of the desert, energised Ramkesh Meena. With nothing to do, daytime had become boring. To kill time, he had been lazing around in his berth, standing at the door, watching the plains roll by, counting the hours; now he was invigorated. By the time the train passed Mangalore, his ticket-checking duties would be complete. If some passengers boarded at Goa, Panvel or Surat—that happened but rarely—they too had to be accounted for. The majority of the passengers were Malayalis headed to Delhi and Chandigarh. Or there were soldiers headed to the Ambala cantonment and to Jammu.

Ramkesh Meena hailed from a small village named Binjari in the Sawai Madhopur district. It was not far from the Ranthambore Tiger Reserve. Traditionally farmers, they also doubled up as soldiers when kings ruled the region. They farmed wheat and mustard. Bringing up groundwater from the depths to the surface, they greened the desert. The skies that rained down only heat surrendered before them.

Ramkesh's first visit out of the village was after he completed his matriculation. It was not a normal journey that the villagers undertook—packing a meal of rotis, green chillies and sliced onions. He and his friends wandered wide-eyed in the courtyards of the old palaces of Jaipur. Travelling ticketless on trains, he discovered the boundaries of the Rajasthani dialect. He developed a craze for trains on those journeys. By the time he returned to Binjari on the seventh day, he had seen Udaipur, Chittorgarh—where his grandfather was a soldier in some king's army—Jaisalmer and even Ajmer, a favourite of Muslims.

When the Sampark Kranti was nearing Kota Junction, Ramkesh Meena appraised himself in the toilet mirror. He applied oil to his coppery hair and combed it neatly. He cleaned his face using face wash. Having finished preening, he resumed his seat. He had been married only a month ago.

Outside, on the scorched grass, the wind was bristling. Here and there, goats were grazing on the dry grass. To stop the kids from suckling, their dams' udders had been wrapped up in plastic bags.

'Kota,' John flipped through *India*.

'Once, I travelled by bus from this station to Chittorgarh,' Karamchand said.

'What's special about it?'

'The fort is known as a symbol of valour. Inside the fort is the memorial of Rana Ratnasimha's widows who committed *jauhar*[18] after his defeat by Alauddin Khilji. If you breathe in deeply, you can still smell charred flesh. However, that's not what I was about to tell you.' Karamchand fell silent for a while. John knew from their short acquaintance that those silences could be interminable so he tapped Karamchand to get his attention.

'It's about the small temple of Meera. I came upon this small shrine when I was wandering inside the fort. The ravages of time had smoothened the sculptures and yellowed them. I stopped in front of the shrine as if someone held me back. A young priest emerged from inside and said, 'This is the Meera Mandir.' In that one moment, I went back four centuries. A young woman with her eyes closed was walking, strumming a tanpura and singing Krishna bhajans. She did not notice jealousy attacking her in the form of a snake and poison. She did not hear the drum beats of the army or the crashing thunder. With the verses flowing effortlessly, she kept singing an epic song of love.

'When I looked through the tiny door at the small idol of Shri Krishna, I turned into Meera. Involuntarily, I started to sing the bhajans that had been lying frozen inside me for ages. The fort, its courtyards, walls, the idol and the small shrine dissolved in front of my eyes. My bones started to melt. Tears streamed down from my eyes. I drowned in the lake formed by my own tears. For the first time in my life, I experienced piety. I'd never passed through that emotion until that day.'

'True, everyone can't experience every emotion. For instance, a European woman will not be able to understand the bashfulness of an Indian woman.'

'When *Shakuntalam* is translated, that's what gets lost—bashfulness.'

The desert and the sky met at the horizon and looked hoary. The tranquillity of that dead landscape was shattered by the sounds of steel grazing steel. Fire could be seen in the desert in the distance. The flames and smoke rose to become a volcano. The breeze fanned it, spreading fear. It could have been a ball of fire that someone had thrown at the train. The passengers in the General and Sleeper compartments downed the shutters to escape the scorching fiery ball that seemed to be hurtling towards the train.

The train stopped at Sawai Madhopur. Ramkesh's family was waiting on the platform. When she saw him, a blush spread on his wife's face like a desert flower blooming. She was part of a small group comprising Ramkesh's father, mother and aunt. The elderly ladies from the village—guarded by primitive gods and where mustard grew—caressed his cheeks with their sunburnt hands. They gazed with pride at their son in the Indian Railways' uniform.

The train started to move. Holding Ramkesh's hand, the sound of tinkling glass bangles stepped into the coach. Ramkesh introduced her to everyone. Pointing to Karamchand, he said, 'Yeh, Karamchand saab. Likhnewala hai. He writes.'

Ramkesh and his wife occupied an empty coupé. Her face was covered with a red dupatta. Karamchand and John went to them to wish them. She served them sweetmeats fried in desi ghee. Opening their laptop, she played their wedding video. A colourful village appeared on the monitor.

A slim old man with a grey handlebar moustache, wearing a dhoti covering his skinny knees and holding a bamboo staff filled the screen. Ramkesh made the introduction. '*Yeh hamarey nanaji hai. Maharajah Scindia-ji ke fauj mein they.*'

Clad in wedding finery, Ramkesh was astride a white horse amidst his wedding party. By late evening, the wedding party reached the edge of the village, dancing and cavorting on the dusty path. The antique men and women lolling about on the charpoys in front of their homes blessed him. '*Bhagwan Ram tujhe bachayega.*' The screen was filled with brightly dressed villagers dancing to fast-paced music. All the colours in the universe had been turned into clothes. A universe of colours.

John copied the wedding video into his pen drive.

'Saab, actually when we were eleven, we were married.'

'Really?' John found it incredible.

'And then when we came of age, the wedding was celebrated.'

John and Karamchand left the coupé. Its door slid shut and was latched.

The sound of her glass bangles—she had bought them at a desert festival, her face bashfully hidden behind a dupatta—falling and breaking was heard.

KARAMCHAND'S FACEBOOK POST

India—the Book

Dear readers,

I am now aboard the Sampark Kranti Express, reading _India_. I have borrowed it off the chest of my co-passenger John, an Englishman, as he lies asleep.

From the time we started the journey, I have been observing how close the connection between John and the book is. He opens the book at every station that the train stops at. He reads the passages that have been written about that place. Sometimes, when he falls asleep while reading, the book will lie open on his chest. In reality, the book, with a jacket design of a fluttering saree on a blue background, is only a tourist guide. There are small descriptions of places of interest in India.

Somewhere in between, John fell asleep again. The thick volume was resting on his chest. I thought this was a condition that suited him best. For, within his heart too, I knew India would be found with equal intensity.

Even if it is a tourist guide, it has many observations that seem to touch upon the essence of India. While I was flipping through pages, I chanced upon an honourable mention it had made of Malayalis. The title above those four lines reads 'Kovalam Beach'.

> One of the most beautiful beaches in the world that should be on your list. While you are sunbathing be careful. There will be local people who come only to watch exposed skin. They will be either lurking here and there, or strolling aimlessly.

Look at that defining characteristic a publication that tourists worldwide depend on has stamped on the Malayalis.

Now I have closed the book and am gazing at the blue jacket. Deciding that India needs to be understood more without resorting to the written word, I am chanting 'In-di-a', 'In-di-a'. When I repeat them, these three syllables create a musical symphony in my mind.

As I watch, the people of the nation emerge from the page in a splash of colours. They express themselves in a melange of tongues. Stuck on one of the pages of time, this diversity is throbbing with life. The subversive animal with an innate instinct for conquests, forming groups and defending its territory was chanting three gentle syllables and stringing its miscellanies in a single thread.

My dear readers, I am closing this droll book called *India*.

8.5k Likes   3.5k Comments   5.0k Shares

10

SAMPARK KRANTI

The rain was embracing the barren lands. Dark clouds driven by the winds were discharging their load on the Sampark Kranti Express. Swirls of steam rose from the scorched, red-hot earth. The train had been detained at a deserted station. The young man with no history stood at the door of the compartment and towelled his wet hair. The rain started to slam into his eyes.

The occupants of the General compartment looked at him in amazement. Who was this guy who had boarded the train from this deserted station? A young man, six-and-a-half feet tall, with an astonishing physique. Watching the mountain of clouds rolling in from the horizon, he waited for the train to start moving. All his clothes were sodden. The train started; behind the curtain of the rain, villages started to run in the reverse direction.

He walked through the coach. It was packed with passengers unable to find seats. A group of gypsies that had occupied the vestibule sat loose-jointed amidst their large bundles. Two babies were sleeping back-to-back in a cloth cradle hung from a hook on the ceiling. Shabbily dressed men and women seated on the floor were chewing paan masala and spitting without a care. When the spray from the wayward rain started to hit them, a young gypsy man shut and locked the doors.

An eight-year-old boy got up from the floor and went to the door. He stretched his hand through the gap in the bars. Water filled his cupped palm. He pulled back his hand. He sprinkled the water on the face of his mother who was sleeping on the floor. Startled awake, she slapped him angrily on his back. He ignored it and stretched his hand out again. A wet leaf fell into his hand. The train surged ahead, leaving the rains behind. Sunshine started to lick the branches of the rain-soaked trees. The outer skin of the train soon became dry. Now only sunshine remained.

The boy still had his hands stretched out of the train. Suddenly something soft fell into his hands. He grabbed it and pulled back his hands. When he saw what was in his hand, his eyes lit up and his tongue throbbed. It was a piece of Kentucky Fried Chicken. That fried piece of chicken had flown out from the empty space between the hand and the mouth of someone travelling in the next coach.

He greedily licked the batter-pimple piece that looked like taste buds. He held it beneath his nostrils and inhaled its ethereal aroma. His mother watched him impassively. A girl who was sleeping, leaning against a bundle, was woken up by the appetising smell. Only a whitish piece of bone remained in his hand. She snatched it away. The boy had kept a small piece of meat hidden under his tongue. Praying that it would never run out, he kept sucking on it like a toffee. He stuck out his hand again. He dreamed of a piece of meat breaking free from someone's hands. From the other side, the girl too stuck out her pale hands through the gap in the bars.

Although He was travelling in the next compartment, those four hands remained stretched out like a prayer to a God who answered no one's prayers.

The passengers of the General compartment had become inured to the crowding inside. The ennui of the three-day journey showed on their faces. The young man with no history walked among them. He thought the train was like a social studies text.

He stopped near a small group in which one man was speaking and others were listening. On the wooden seat packed with people, there was a sliver of space that a person could squeeze into. He moved aside a handkerchief that lay there as a placeholder and sat down. The person who had been talking till then fell silent.

By the time the young man with no history could stretch his legs, the owner of the seat returned. Gripping his shoulder roughly, the man said, 'This is my seat, move!'

He smiled and got to his feet. The man was expecting him to fight. When the man saw the hefty young man comply without a murmur, he felt guilty. He tapped him on his chest and said, 'You can sit here,' after making some space next to himself. The young man sat down in that narrow space.

The conversation that had been interrupted by the entry of a stranger resumed. The narrator was a wrinkled old man with a long face, heavy grey moustache and yellow-tinged, tired eyes. He squatted on the seat, resting his head between his knees, hugging his spindly legs, and gesticulated as he spoke. Fresh soil from his fields and the smell of many years' vintage were clinging to his dhoti. His cracked heels and feet, reminiscent of parched lands, still bore the vestiges of the colours sprayed on them in the previous year's Holi. A walking stick that had propped him up for many years was leaning against the window. In its cracked self, it showed the privations of an entire village. Once acquaintance was made, he resumed his story.

'It was the fourth straight year of drought.'

The train entered a long tunnel. The eclipse started to swallow the compartments one after the other. In the pitch darkness inside the booming tunnel, the storyteller continued, 'Our cotton crop was completely lost. We had no grain even for our daily bread. How could we repay our loans? The bank staff and moneylenders started to harass us. We had hoped that the government would help us. We asked them to at least release water from the Murud Dam. But who listens to us? All the water was taken by the big industries.'

By the time he said that, the train was fully inside the tunnel. Darkness lay thick like the inside of a boa's intestine.

'At that time, my daughter's illness worsened. I had mentioned it before. She developed stomach pains from eating soil. We were habituated to eating grass and leaves. But soil! When we used to take the clay from the termite hill, add water, roll it into morsels and feed her, she would give us a helpless look. Avoiding looking at her, we used to sing—"Isn't earth everything, isn't earth the trees, aren't we the earth ..."'

He stopped talking for a little while. In that darkness no one could see anyone else. The young man with no history thought that darkness could not be the last word on anything and light would shine in the end.

'We could only see one way out. We decided to sell our bullock. The agent of the meat exporting company named their price. It should have fetched us at least forty thousand rupees; all we got was four thousand. By that time, our daughter's condition had deteriorated. When we reached the hospital clutching that money . . .' he burst out crying. In that forbidding darkness, in a frightful jugalbandi created by the wheels of the train and the narrow tunnel, his sobs prevailed.

'Haven't I seen you somewhere?' the young man with no history asked the narrator.

'Possible. You may have seen me on television.'

'Oh yes, in some of the channels. I remember now.'

'True, for a day I was the star for all the channels. The man who threatened to commit suicide after climbing up the huge pipal tree in front of the Vidhan Sabha. Yes, that was me.'

'And then what happened to you?'

'Don't you remember? Me jumping off the top of that tree that was high as the sky?'

'And nothing happened to you?'

'Nothing happened to me? That's funny! How did I die, then?'

Disarmed, the young man with no history sat before the farmer completely at a loss. Before him sat a dead man bearing witness.

'May I touch you? I can't believe my own eyes.'

'Why not?'

The train had outlived the eclipse. Squares of light started to enter the coach. He touched the farmer's arm. His fingers trembled and withdrew. He looked at every one of the passengers around him. Their eyes bulged, as if they were watching a terrorising sight.

'Why do your eyes hold so much fear?' the young man asked them.

'Young man, when you are facing death or when you see a lethal knife flashing towards your neck—only then will you understand. Friend, what do you think eyes that are staring at unexpected, untimely death look like?'

'So all of you ...?'

'We have all been killed. We travel with you persistently so that we are not erased from your memory.' It was a girl who spoke.

'I have seen you somewhere ...'

'Pushed down from the train ... I told you. You people who are alive, you have such short memories.' She laughed.

Another man took up the narrative. 'I was the first one to kill himself in Vidarbha. At that time, I had thought that if I died, the country would boil over and there would be riots. We are the ones who put food on your table, no? Nothing happened. After me, another two or three lakh farmers died by suicide.'

He was a mine of memories.

'My father would tell me. Son, everyone we think of as ours, our brothers and sisters, our children, our wives, they will all leave us. Because they have legs. Because they can walk. However, there is a group that will never leave us. Do you know who? Trees. All the water and whatever else we feed them, they will return to us as shade and support.

'My father had made me plant that neem tree. Finally, during the harvest season, realising that there was no one for me, I hanged myself from the first branch of that neem tree with a worthless heap of potatoes as my witness. Wasn't I the topper in Vidarbha?'

The coach had only two kinds of people—those who had died premature deaths and those who were waiting to die. He rose from that seat in the bay of ghost travellers.

'Why are you getting up?' Shifting to the side and making more space, the man who had given him the seat asked, 'How much space do we dead people really need?'

'Aw, nothing.'

'Please sit down. You look tired. I'll stand for some time,' he insisted.

'I have just returned from a journey. That's why I look tired. I'm leaving on another journey.'

'Where to?' demanded a twelve-year-old girl with a stoop, seated in a corner.

'From one end of this train to the other.' He walked to the front. From the corridor, he turned around and looked at them again. Dead people had been reincarnated as stories.

A snake charmer appeared in the corridor. He let out a snake from the basket and played the *pungi*. The snake moved its head in rhythm with the music, its hood open. The young man with no history stood at the door and looked towards the engine—the tall chimney that appeared to be speeding; glinting brass plates. The magnificent engine held him in thrall. Wanderer.

The Sampark Kranti Express crawled along the plains. A man and a woman squatted along the tracks where even the grass had been scorched by the sun. Many others could be seen squatting on the tracks emptying their bowels. That morning, the call of nature had turned into a bellow. An invisible wall stood between the men and women. Minding the tradition that had survived for centuries, neither of them breached that wall. There are private corners even in shitting fields. Their owners come at the appointed time, do their business, and go away. No one trespasses into spaces where strange chemicals create artistic installations and piles of shit resemble idols. They were also protected by invisible boundaries.

The squatting defecators, holding small pots in hand, watched the slow-moving train deadpan. The sight of the unexpected steam engine attached to the train made them lift their heads to look up. Some of them even jumped up and waved cheerfully.

The train stopped at the home signal that showed red.

The young man with no history climbed down from the General compartment. He walked along the bridge, on one side of which was a deep ravine with a small, dried-up lake at the bottom. Monkeys were swinging from the branches that grazed the roof of the bogies. Many of them who had tried to get too familiar with the train had lost their tails, or one of their hands, or ears. Although they tried to scare the man who was walking on the tracks, they gave up the attempt when they found that he posed them no danger.

The young man with no history climbed into the Sleeper compartment. It was a different world there, a page from a different book.

Although they were adjacent, they were separated by steel sheets. The young man with no history stood at the door. The floor was cleaner; the walls were not painted with paan-laced spittle; phlegm did not stick to the bowl of the washbasin; on top of it all, it was not crowded. Although tired and dishevelled, the passengers were clean and owned mobile phones that had WhatsApp, Facebook and myriad games installed in them. A majority of them were buried in their phones and travelling in a parallel world too. When they reached the station where they had to alight, the women used the mirror above the washbasin to apply make-up on their faces and put in place wayward strands of hair.

When a middle-aged man standing in the corridor brushing his teeth flicked his toothbrush, a drop of water hit the face of the young man with no history.

Two beribboned henchmen were present in the coach. The way they strutted around and talked down to the others gave him the impression that they were people with some authority. From the S8 coach, he walked towards the rear of the train. Some passengers were asleep on the upper berths. The cook in the pantry car was frying pooris for breakfast. The heap of pooris in the basket started to mount. The smell of boiled potatoes and heated mustard oil spread. He heard thunderous slogan-shouting from the directions where the aroma was spreading. He hurried towards the source of the commotion. The well-rhymed slogans were coming from the S1 coach, which was filled with students. The leader was a dark youth with a resonant voice, blazing eyes and uncombed hair.

The young man with no history saw dreams spark from his eyes as he led the sloganeering, thumping the damru in his hand and pointing his index finger to the heavens. He stood conducting a choir of outraged singers. He was the embodiment of the hopes and dreams of the youth travelling in that coach.

Like a collapsing volcano, his voice suddenly petered out as the young man with no history walked further away. Every coach had beribboned henchmen in it. As he kept walking, he could hear whistles. In an instant, a human wall formed through the length of the train. An unnerving silence rose in the midst of various sounds and the hubbub of conversation. Fear fell in line. He stood concealed and watched neurotic people breathe, bend and contort themselves as commanded by the whistles.

He passed through the Sleeper coaches and entered the three-tier AC coach. The air-conditioned coach was another leaf in the book of the Sampark Kranti Express. The passengers here were peaceable. Their voices were smothered by blankets. Weak-voiced prayers could be heard only from the pilgrims' coach.

As the young man with no history kept walking, a toilet door opened and a man and a woman emerged together. They demonstrated no embarrassment at running into another human being. She threw a slippery, used condom through the coach door from where the smell of boiled potatoes was wafting in.

He then remembered the four supplicating small hands that were thrust out of General compartment.

He passed through the 3AC coaches and entered the 2AC coaches—yet another leaf in the book. There was no visible separation between the 3AC and 2AC coaches. However, the two layers remained without commingling, like the waters of two oceans with different densities.

The silence in A1 was complete. Sound lay frozen in the chill. Covered in their blankets, the old couple sat hunched on the lower berth, sticking out like a sore thumb amidst the characteristic pompous snobbery of the coach. Like a village caught within a city. The sound of his footsteps made Doubting Dowager part the curtains and stick her head out. Her grey hairs fluttered in the corridor. Looking at him, she started to muse: 'Who's this? Why's he hurrying so much? Where's he headed?'

By that time the young man had passed her. Doubting Dowager withdrew her head.

He went into the AC First Class coach. He hesitated when he saw the carpeted corridor. The coach looked deserted, lifeless. It was an unattainable place. Unlike the other coaches, the silence was complete, authoritative and overwhelming. Suddenly, he saw another person walking down from the other end. He looked intimately familiar. The name also came to him.

'Karamchand.'

Yes, it is Karamchand. Travel blogger. He walked towards him to get acquainted. However, before he could reach him, Karamchand opened the door of B coupé and entered. Before the young man with no history could speak, the door was shut on him.

He waited at the door believing that Karamchand would emerge sooner or later.

11

DVI - II

Clarions were no longer being sounded at set times. They could be sounded at any moment. A chain of humanity formed as soon as they were heard. Eventually the stress and anxiety that they may sound at any time became entrenched in the passengers. An invisible despot and the Clarion that sounded on his orders resounded in their brains.

In the morning, half-asleep, the passengers who tapped open their WhatsApp were greeted by a new message. 'Dvi' was its caption.

DVI

Dear co-passengers,

One must assume that, by now, this question would have arisen in your minds: Who is Dvi? That is why this history is being recorded here. Who is Dvi? Why is he travelling on this train? What's the purpose of his reincarnation? What was his métier in his previous life? Who was he in his previous birth?

Read attentively.

He was born in a seashore village in the north-west region of Bharatvarsha. The village named Agravarshini was under the thumb of a rakshasa called Dundulan. On some nights, the rakshasa would rise from the middle of the western sea like a mountain. The sea would swell and a few villages would be destroyed by high waves. Many temples too were destroyed in this fashion. He used his scoop called Ajathavikritham to grab humans and cattle off the seashore and eat them. He kidnapped beautiful women, took them to his palace under the sea, debauched them till he could do no more and then killed them and ate them.

Unable to bear Dundulan's atrocities, the villagers started to pray to Lord Shiva. Their prayers were fulfilled. Dvi was born as the sixty-third son of a brahmin woman. He started to exhibit magical powers from birth. His tongue was longer than that of the other children.

It was the new moon day of that month. The sea was churning and a hurricane was blowing. Ships, including those launched by NASA that sailed on that route, were floundering. The needle of the Richter scale installed in Antarctica was stuck at 10.5.

Agravarshini village was trembling in terror, because if a child was born in that village, it was Dundulan's practice to drink its blood. Carrying her newborn, the brahmin woman started to flee. The miracle happened then. The newborn, not even an hour old, told its mother in a loud voice, 'Amma, take me to the seashore.' When she heard the newborn speak, the woman stopped running and started to wail.

'Matashree, this is our command.'

The mother did not tarry anymore. She suppressed her fear and sorrow and walked towards the seashore carrying the baby. By that time, using Ajathavikritham Dundulan had started to scoop up human beings from the seashore. The baby could see men and women lying and thrashing about like ants inside the scoop.

The miracle happened. The tongue of the baby carried on that mother's waist started to grow longer. It twisted around Dundulan's scoop. Dundulan, his head in the clouds, looked down. Within no time, Dvi's tongue that had grown longer than Anantha the serpent, coiled around the rakshasa, lifted him bodily and drowned him in the Southern Ocean.

That was the end of Dundulan's depredations. Agravarshini village danced for joy. From that day, there was only one mantra on the villagers' lips:

Jai Dvi, Jai Dvi. Jai Dvi. Jai, Jai, Jai Dvi.

After he read the message, Karamchand posted on Facebook:

On 1 February of last year, I was in a remote farming village in Uttar Pradesh, Vitnipur, about 100 kilometres from Naini and which can be reached only on foot. I arrived on a chilly night. My host was my friend Santosh Maurya, who prided himself on being a descendant of Emperor Ashoka.

I spent the night in a watchman's room, next to a buffalo barn, gazing at a Shivalinga kept on its mud wall on which 'Om Nama Shivaya' had been painted. In the morning, when I was searching for a latrine, Maurya sent me with his brother to the nearby fields. Mustard was in full bloom in the fields that were so fertile they could have grown even gold. With the mustard fields as a background, I took a selfie with my mobile camera. There were many other sights to see. Kol tribals who were heading to the fields with farming implements. Carts drawn by buffaloes. Huge haystacks. Lantana flowers that seem to have invaded the place.

When we passed by a house which had recently held a wedding, we saw a man tying a long bamboo pole with a red flag on the roof. 'That is the *shaadi ka jhanda*,' Maurya's brother pointed out. He was reading history at Allahabad University. The flag was meant to announce that the house had no more maidens to marry off.

I thought about symbolism then. Like the sindoor applied on a woman's forehead to declare that she was a wife now. A no-entry sign. How many varied symbols.

Passing a primary school and a small stream, I squatted near a small rise to do my constitutionals. My phone dinged and WhatsApp came alive. The world I was fleeing from had landed on my palm.

A video of an effigy of Gandhi being shot on Martyr's Day had gone viral on WhatsApp. Shouting 'Victory to Mahatma Godse!' a saffron-clad lady was firing the gun. As fake blood flowed out of the effigy, her acolytes were applauding her and hailing Godse. They were not very far from where I was.

Washing myself in a nearby stream, when we were walking back, I showed Maurya's brother the video. He watched it without much curiosity or agitation. When he saw blood coming out of Gandhi's chest, he pointed at it and said, '*khoon, khoon*' as if I may have missed it. In the video, a group of excited, fatuous young men took up a chant. I then heard the young man with me, in spite of himself, mumble along with them, 'Mahatma Godse ki jai.'

I, Karamchand, peered at the youth's face—baby-faced with soft lips and an incipient moustache and, on the whole, weaker than me. Yet, I felt afraid.

This is not Gandhi's India.

2.5k Likes   1.6k Comments   1k Shares

12

PUG MARK

Two contrasting undercurrents of fear and enthusiasm predominated on the train. Dvi had complete control. He sat alone in his cabin. Two of his trusted henchmen stood guard at the door. The sudden windfall of power and the abject servility of his henchmen stoked the innate lordliness in him. Every nook and cranny of the train passed through his mind. I am the lord of all these people. I decide their destinies. They are my guinea pigs. I shall lead this motley crowd like a shepherd leading his flock with his flute. They will stand and wag their tails before me. This empire will dance at the snap of my fingers. He started to type in the 'Red Ribbon' group on his WhatsApp.

> Communiqué 1
> Dear people, though we are travelling on the same train, we follow different faiths, hold them steadfast and dear, and are even ready to die for them. Therefore, in order to avoid inter-faith clashes, we are moving the followers of each faith into different compartments. Therefore, I am ordering the following classifications:
> 1. The S1 and S2 coaches are reserved for our Muslim brethren.

2. S3 is reserved for religious minorities such as Buddhists, Jains, Parsis, etc.
3. Only our Christian brethren will travel in the S4 coach.
4. All the other coaches are reserved for Hindus.
5. The arrangements in the AC coaches shall be overseen by me in person.
6. Execute the communiqué within the next half hour and report.

As soon as the communiqué was received, the Red Ribbon brigade sprang into action. As per their instructions, the passengers formed small groups. Their faith-wise segregation happened quickly. Those who were neighbours only a short while ago said salaam to one another and were separated.

After the initial uncertainty, they resumed their journey, making their own comfort zones in the allotted seats. When the realisation dawned that the neighbours were not different, they chanted the same hymns and worshipped the same god, a new love, like that for blood relatives, grew among them. They shared food. They discovered mutual acquaintances as they compared notes. Some even discovered blood relationships or via marriage. They started to think there were resemblances between them.

Once the initial flush of unity was over, differences started to crop up. Language was the first dividing factor. Differences in rituals was another. Gradually oneness disappeared and differences took over.

At that juncture, the second communique reached the 'Red Ribbon' brigade.

Communiqué 2

We see the need to extend additional protection to our women as they have to give birth to perfect children and enrich our nation. Therefore, you are hereby ordered to shift them to separate sections.

'Os!'

As soon as he received the instruction, the soldier, full of vim, rushed into action. When he dashed into the adjacent coach, a young couple pleaded with folded hands, 'Sir, not even a month has passed since our wedding. Please allow us to be together.'

'My wedding also was less than a month ago. For the sake of the nation, I've left her behind and come. Moreover, the law doesn't allow any leeway for couples. In front of the law a woman is what she is, a mere woman. Do you understand?'

He separated them. When he separated each man from his partner, he experienced a nameless glee.

With the third communiqué, the compartmentalisation of the train was complete. Each section represented a homogenous culture. Shortly after, the Red Ribbon brigade turned up bearing a tiger's pug mark as a stamp. They segregated each section, stamping them with the pug mark. Tigers roared in the section that had the inscription Death or War. The red pug marks bound each one as a territory mark of otherness and a barrier to fraternisation.

A community that in the not-so-remote past had given as much as they had got and yet fought shoulder to shoulder withdrew into their personal prison cells within the sequestered spaces of uneasy peace. When they wanted to revel in their caste superiority, in spite of it and unknown to them, a pang of guilt cropped up in them. A realisation that, evolving from anthropoid apes aeons ago, commingling and interbreeding, they are all travellers over the ages. The acknowledgement that the ejaculate that the ur man had flung liberally around spread like a contagion and they were reborn in many colours and shapes. An inner acceptance that no one has enough racial or caste superiority to celebrate.

There was only one person the henchmen could not sequester. This was Amanushi, a transgender. S/he too was a traveller of the Sampark Kranti Express. The henchmen tried to move hir to the women's section, but s/he resisted. S/he cursed them roundly in hir raspy voice. S/he became furious. S/he protested. Finally, when one of the henchmen tried to use force, intrepid, s/he used hir own muscularity to crush him and bring him to his knees. S/he remained impregnable as the henchmen rushed her. S/he lifted hir saree and exposed hirself to them. Shocked at the unexpected sight of the organ dangling between hir legs, the Red Ribbon brigade admitted defeat.

The Red Ribbon brigade allowed Amanushi, who was neither Hindu nor Muslim, neither male nor female, or rather who was Hindu and Muslim, male and female, to move about the train at will.

13

AMANUSHI

Before s/he joined the transgender hamaam, Amanushi was an object of ridicule in hir village. Whenever someone would sing a song mocking hir swaying hips, rather than beat him up s/he wanted to curse him to doom. When s/he saw that hir direst imprecations, instead of felling him, made him ridicule hir with greater gusto, s/he ran away from the village. S/he realised that no village had a heart large enough to accommodate hir. When s/he took a state road transport bus to Ernakulam and wandered around in anonymity, s/he was rather relieved. From the bus terminal s/he walked along the rail tracks and reached Ernakulam Junction Station.

The express train to Dhanbad was waiting at platform no. 1. The open doors of the train invited hir, who anyway had no place to go. S/he boarded the ladies' compartment where all the seats were taken and more. S/he sat down on the floor in a corner. S/he had no concerns about travelling to an unknown place. S/he only wished to be as far away as possible.

Tired, s/he soon fell asleep. In hir half-asleep state, off and on, s/he was conscious of people boarding and alighting from the train. When s/he woke up the train had left the borders of Kerala behind.

The coach was empty now. S/he had not woken up by hirself. A stranger had tapped hir shoulder and woken hir up. When s/he realised that s/he and the man were the only occupants of the coach, s/he felt nervous.

'Where are you going?' he demanded in a high-pitched voice in Tamil. S/he got up from the floor and sat down on the seat. 'Where are you going?' the owner of the squeaky voice asked again. S/he had no answer. S/he opened her arms out to show that she had no clue. The man took hold of her hands and said, 'That's not the way you gesture with your hands. You do it like this. This is the style in which we people do it.' He turned his hands in a peculiar way.

'My name is Saupanika. Will you be my friend from today?'

'I will,' s/he said.

'Then promise me.'

S/he held Saupanika's hand and promised. 'From today your name will be Amanushi.' Both of them moved closer to each other.

'But I'm hearing this name for the first time. In my place no one is given such names.'

'This is our world. We don't follow the conventions of the normal world.' Amanushi listened attentively. 'This is your second birth. We don't carry any old things. We are Aravani, the brides of Aravaanan.'

'Umm ...'

'Look, in its memory, a male body has vestiges of a female body. The two nipples that no one needs on the male body is proof of that.'

'What about the other way round.'

'It's there for sure! That small bud in female genitalia.'

'I haven't seen it. I don't have it.'

'They are the memories. Memories that once upon a time man and woman existed in the same body.'

'Where did you learn all this?'

'I keep travelling. I meet good and bad people. One of the men I met during my journeys told me about the memories of our bodies.'

Saupanika moved closer to Amanushi. Then without seeking consent, he pressed his lips on hers. They were lost in a long, protracted kiss.

'I'm hungry,' Amanushi said.

'Come.' Saupanika helped her up. When the train stopped at the next station, they alighted and boarded the Reserved coach.

'Walk with me, look at what I'm doing and do the same.' Amanushi followed hir. Saupanika clapped hands in a special rhythm. Amanushi followed suit.

'Arey bhai,' Saupanika stroked a man's cheek. After accepting the ten-rupee note he handed over, when they moved, a hand caressed Amanushi's bottom. When she turned around to snarl at him, he rubbed his fly and asked, '*Choosega kya?*' Saupanika turned around and swore at him.

The coach, which smelled of a miasma of stale sweat, paan masala, tobacco and mustard oil, was filled with north Indian labourers who were returning home for a vacation. Though it was built to accommodate seventy people, at least three hundred were packed in. Squeezing their way through the crowd, they entered the toilet and counted the collection. The majority of the money was in musty, torn ten-rupee notes. Saupanika had netted one-hundred-and-fifty rupees; Amanushi, two hundred.

They stepped out of the toilet into the arms of an uncouth, handlebar-moustachioed policeman. Even in that crowded coach, he stood in an empty square bereft of people. His aspect was sufficient to scare away people. With a lathi to boot.

'Who's this?' he demanded in Tamil, pointing to Amanushi.

'She's new sir, just arrived,' Saupanika replied.

'Come here.' He pulled Amanushi close to him with calloused hands.

He leaned against the door of the speeding train. He pulled hir hand down and pressed it against his crotch where a bulge was forming.

'Harder ... harder ...' Amanushi gripped his fly hard.

'Okay, you go now, I will catch you later.' They walked to the next coach.

The train reached Salem. They alighted, took an autorickshaw and were dropped at the bus terminal. They entered a restaurant.

'Look, we won't be welcome in every restaurant.' Amanushi ate two masala dosas. Her flaming hunger was quenched.

Their next destination was Koovagam. They boarded a bus. Saupanika talked throughout the journey. 'Our deity is Iravan, the son of Arjuna. His head was cut off in the battlefield of Kurukshetra and offered as oblation. We are all his brides.'

Amanushi was slowly eased into the mores and customs of her new life.

By late evening, they reached a remote village named Koovagam, one that turns into a town only during the annual festival at the Aravaanakovil. The village was enveloped in yellow, whether as dust, flowers, fabrics and garments or threads. The dusty road was full of people like hir. Amanushi felt elated as if s/he had reached hir kingdom. What if s/he got lost in the crowd? S/he stuck close to Saupanika. How does it matter if one gets lost in a place where one is a total stranger? Suddenly a man from a passing group ran towards hir, pressed hir breasts and ran away. Saupanika chased him, screaming, 'Scram, you fucking dog.'

There was joy everywhere. Saupanika flitted around renewing old friendships and acquaintances. S/he took Amanushi to a tree. S/he bought hir a yellow churidar-kameez. S/he threw away hir shirt and trousers forever and wore the churidar-kameez. S/he bought false hair and tied it on. She stuck firecracker flowers in hir hair. S/he turned into a beauty. 'How beautiful you are!' Saupanika pinched hir cheek. After applying blush, powder and lipstick they left the tree. In the twilight, they saw a couple passionately necking by the side of the dirt path. 'You should start today itself,' Saupanika advised her.

Holding a salver filled with flowers and fruits, they joined a queue. At the top of the queue was the minor temple and the idol of Aravaanan. Shortly s/he would be married to Aravaanan. In the night s/he would be Aravaanan's wife, Arjuna's daughter-in-law. S/he was overjoyed. A tree shade to remember, a kiss to recollect. An image to cherish and dream about.

Finally, it was hir turn. The priest tied a yellow thread around her neck. A bubble of ecstasy rose inside her and made hir throb inside. In the midst of ear-splitting sounds, Amanushi and Saupanika were separated.

A beauty pageant was being held on a decorated stage. Transgender persons, more beautiful than angels, were putting on a show. Amanushi kept walking. A few people were dancing around a firepit. Amanushi joined them. Dancing around in step with others, s/he reached the acme of ecstasy and then collapsed in exhaustion. Someone poured arrack into her mouth as s/he lay on the ground. S/he leaped up in intoxication and resumed dancing.

The dance ended sometime in the night. When s/he felt hungry she bought and ate koththu porotta from a street vendor. S/he had never experienced such euphoria in hir life. As s/he was making hir way to another venue of festivities, someone grabbed hir arm. When s/he tried to push him away, he exhibited the power of his masculinity. Eventually he seduced hir like a doe and led hir into the bushes.

The night wound down. As the sun started to rise, Amanushi noticed the dark looks that had spread on the faces of the intersex people around her. A night of festivities was now turning into a day of emptiness.

The day broke reminding them of loneliness and heartbreak as old as recorded time: Prince Aravaanan had been offered as a sacrifice to ensure the victory of the Pandavas at Kurukshetra. Koovagam had given up the aspect of a town and turned into a cremation ground. The widows of Aravaanan—his brides of a mere one night—hundreds of Mohinis, started to lament hysterically. The venue of the beauty pageant was now desolate. The fragrant night had started to reek. A sorry-looking wisp of smoke was rising from the firepit around which so many people had danced merrily.

Amanushi joined yet another long queue, the one to annul the union. Aravaanan's idol was being taken out in a procession from the temple. As the sounds of musical accompaniments drew near, so did the wretched wailing of the widows. The priest accompanying the idol was annulling the Mohinis' marriages. The priest approached Amanushi, who stood with hir eyes closed and hir head bowed. The dark, apathetic priest snipped the yellow thread with a small penknife. He smashed the glass bangles that resembled a rainbow on hir hands. Amanushi wailed like an orphaned child. No one paid hir any attention. Resounding with louder, more plaintive wails, Koovagam had turned into a widows' village.

The procession ended. The dream lover of the Mohinis was taken off the chariot and placed in the centre of the temple grounds. The embers that the acharya poured on him grew into flames and consumed him. His orphaned lovers beat their breasts and ululated. Under intolerable anguish, a town of one night turned into a town of the dead. Amanushi fainted.

Someone sprinkled water on hir face and revived hir. Smiling, Saupanika stood above hir. The pandemonium had subsided. The visitors were starting their return journeys in singles and groups. 'Shouldn't we leave too?'

'We should, but to where?'

'Come.' He helped Amanushi to hir feet. They changed their soiled clothes and boarded the bus to Salem.

They started to live together from that day. From their bases in Salem and Erode, they travelled on trains plying between Coimbatore and Tirupati, up and down. Their typical handclaps set them apart from others. Saupanika lived as a trans man; Amanushi the trans woman.

The happiness did not last long. One rainy season, when Mettur Dam had been opened, Saupanika fell into the Kaveri river and drowned. The Kongu Express was bouncing and bumping on the steel bridge. He was swinging from the door handle and trying to reach the adjacent coach. His head hit the steel girder and the impact threw him overboard. Kaveri carried him away and buried him in the trenches which find mention even in the Sangam Era scrolls.

Amanushi was alone. In a life spent moving from train to train, only the people she met there provided hir temporary company. The day Saupanika's corpse surfaced at Kallanai Dam, Amanushi dressed up as a man and boarded the north-bound Kerala Express. She returned dressed as a woman. That became the practice. Travel North as a man; travel South as a woman. She had done this for over a year on the Sampark Kranti Express.

Dvi's henchmen were trying to brand this Amanushi—with a history of such sorrows and torments—as a woman to corral hir in the women's section. After lining up all the eighteen henchmen in front of hir, she lifted hir saree, peeled off hir underwear, and asked, 'Tell me *chutiye*, am I a man or a woman?' The sight of two seasons on the same trunk stunned the henchmen. With that, Amanushi could not be tied down by any commandments.

The Sampark Kranti entered Mathura Station. Although there was no scheduled stop, the train moved at a slow, respectful speed, as if tipping its hat to the storied place. Shouting '*Mathura ka peda*', vendors jumped into coaches and leaped off when the coach reached the end of the platform.

Karamchand saw a magician on the platform enchanting his audience. He pulled a rope out of his bundle, flipped it, sent it up like a pole, and started to climb it. For Karamchand, Mathura Station swung back one-and-a-half centuries. He heard the sound of drums and shehnai. Crowned kings seated on elephants; troops of cavalry; British noblemen; buglers and trumpeters appeared before him in a vision—past days surfaced like a brightly rendered oil painting.

14

PARTITION

25 January

*At first, he could not place the origin of the rumpus. Then Karamchand
saw that the people who had been segregated and sequestered with the
help of pug-mark stamps were tearing down with destructive intent
the boundaries that were considered inviolable. There were battle
cries and they challenged one another. Sometime during the journey,
the despot, seated in an inaccessible, remote spot and controlling
everything, had lost his power. The henchmen who had sworn
unswerving loyalty had declared their own independent republics. The
thread of tyranny that held them together frayed and snapped.*

*Turning whatever came to hand into weapons, an uncontrollable
mob fought among themselves. Atavistic tribal instincts made them
scream war cries 'blood ... khoon ... khuna ... chora ... lohi ... irattam
... rakta ... raktam ... ragat ...' in many tongues.*

*Karamchand went to the door and looked out. In front of his eyes,
the Wanderer took on a life of its own and was transformed into an
ultra-machine with a thousand arms. It rose up in the sky, bellowed
and screeched. Its chimneys hooted. Steam surged out from its steam*

domes and steam chest. It stood like an aboriginal warrior and trembled with fury.

The electric locomotive that hauled a train with modern men in modern coaches from a different era stopped functioning. It stood helpless. Becalmed, the Sampark Kranti remained on the tracks at the junction where rail tracks from all corners of the country converged.

The warring people inside the train became nervous at the sight of the stalled train. Wanderer, with the energy gathered and latent in it for centuries, broke away from the Sampark Kranti Express. Leveraging its thousand autonomous arms, it skipped to the next track and disappeared. It returned quicker than it had vanished. It gripped and hauled off, one by one, the coaches from the rear of the locomotive without giving the terrified passengers time to react.

The power with which it crashed into the Sampark Kranti Express vaporised the train. The bogies became separated and isolated. They started to speed off in various directions on the tracks that met there.

Karamchand remembered Carvalho's words.

'Trains are built so they are easily separated and hitched. For those looking from the outside it will look like a single unit. However, it is not so. Though they are unnaturally linked using steel hooks that look strong, they don't have the strength to bear the impact of a sudden, unexpected collision. They get decoupled. Sometimes, one coach climbs over another. Coaches may turn turtle. They may fall into lakes and disappear altogether from history. It runs by burning within itself. It has life.'

Only when they were coupled together were the coaches in the train known as Sampark Kranti. Once freed from the train, the coaches ran helter-skelter on the tracks without direction. Carrying people from every human race, they wandered like tiny clans.

India's biopsy section had disintegrated into single cells. None contained India. The passengers, nurturing the disunity that grew beside unity, continued to travel upon the belly of the subcontinent on a journey with no end.

The Sampark Kranti was finally on the outskirts of Delhi. John was getting ready to alight. Before shutting down his laptop, he had another look at the latest photos. Moving images of the last three days scrolled in front of Karamchand. At the outer signal of Delhi city, the train rolled past blackened alleys and slums. A plethora of tracks swerved, merged, demerged, veered off, ran parallel. It was a congress of rail tracks. The corridor through which trains from villages and mofussil towns entered Delhi.

On either side of the slowly rolling train that did not stop at Nizamuddin Station, dreaming of past glories, the descendants of the Muslim kings and emperors who ruled India five centuries ago eked out an existence in shanties made from beaten tin plates. All that remained with them to gloat over past glories were thinly-attended qawwali soirees and mughal biryanis. A pasquinade by history.

In these streets, notwithstanding their disparateness, small mobs strung together on the single string of communalism were likely to turn up with no warning, screaming slogans and wielding staves.

Only the previous day, a procession had been taken out in those killing fields by people wearing blue shirts and Ambedkar masks, shouting, 'Neel salaam'. Do we need any more cogitation to understand that Dalit politics will decide India's future in the coming times? Aren't the dissonant sounds that break out here and there manifestations of this?

While alighting from the Sampark Kranti Express, Karamchand was unsure which side to join at this point of planetary conjunctions when time and history had gotten mixed up beyond recognition. Notwithstanding that he was one half Gandhi.

As he was closing *India* to place it back in his bag, John stopped for a moment as if he had another thought. After autographing the first page, he handed over the book to Karamchand, who accepted it happily.

India
Publishers: Lonely Planet
Price: US$ 34.99

When the pedestrian overbridge flashed by, John put an arm around Karamchand and gathered him close. Without wasting the opportunity, Karamchand clicked a selfie. He decided to post it sometime or the other with the caption 'Meeting of Continents'.

John alighted at Hazrat Nizamuddin Station. His yellow colour and stroller bag disappeared into the crowd. The train started to crawl again between the snaking tracks. Karamchand lay on the berth with *India* open on his chest.

There was a knock on the door. Startled, he jumped off the berth. A young man stood at the door. A six-plus footer, with a strong physique and commensurate vigour. He bowed his head and greeted Karamchand.

'Sir, can you give me your telephone number, please?' Karamchand gave him a questioning look. 'I read your travel blogs.'

Karamchand felt gratified upon hearing that and he wished there were others around who could have heard it. Karamchand gave him his phone number.

The Sampark Kranti stopped on platform no. 11 of New Delhi Station. Karamchand alighted, holding his bag. He sat on a bench on the platform and watched the stationary train. The other passengers who alighted were hurrying towards the exit. They blended in with the colourful, teeming crowds. Once out of the railway station, they would lose the status of passengers. They would become solitary men and women. Tongas, rickshaws and Ubers would bear them as solitary fares. They would end up in some flat or lane or kothi as nobodies who leave for work cursing the extremes of climate and masking themselves against the smog. The short-lived friendships that cropped up during the journey would end up in goodbyes. What would the people have presented themselves as during that short period?

Doubting Dowager too alighted. Cursing the cold, she swung her arms to warm herself. Watching the streaming crowds, she mused, 'Where are all these people going? Won't they crash into one another, stumble and fall if they keep walking like this? Why do so many people come to the cities? Can't they stay back in their peaceful and scenic villages?' After all these thoughts, she gave thinking a break. And then she thought, 'Why should I know all these things?' That led to an epiphany. Dropping on the platform the bundle of doubts that she had lugged along through the journey, the old woman melted into the crowds of Delhi. Her brain having been clarified by the journey, many halos shone around her head as a sign of her consecration.

As Karamchand watched, Dvi, cackling with laughter, passed by along with a small group of people.

A diesel engine detached the coal-fired Wanderer from the Sampark Kranti. The dead locomotive was shunted to the yard. The following day was Republic Day, and steam locomotives would be paraded. India was still an independent, sovereign republic, capable of celebrating the day.

Carrying the passengers travelling to Chandigarh, the Sampark Kranti resumed its journey. Karamchand got up from his seat. Standing at the coach's door, the young man wished him. He held up his phone and gestured to Karamchand, who took the call.

'Do you recognise me?' the young man asked.

'Who are you?'

'I'm that boy with no history.'

Karamchand looked at him in astonishment. He felt like touching the young man. However, that intangible emotion quickly left him.

'Do you know what my name is?' the young man asked.

'No.'

'Karamchand.' When he heard the name, Karamchand's eyes shone. In that rare, magical moment, when imagination and reality got into a clinch and created mischief, Karamchand stood stunned, lost to himself and the world. The young man continued to talk on the phone.

'Sir, let me say one more thing. Stop writing travelogues and write a novel. You have a wonderful imagination. Here you are, seeing someone who doesn't exist.'

Karamchand took his photo on his mobile. Then he realised that the face that appeared on the screen was his own.

'You are probably my imagination. Or perhaps, possibly my dream. If it's said that I think therefore I am, then because I think, you are there too.'

Karamchand waved his hand towards the vast emptiness.

The Sampark Kranti wiggled its tail for the last time and left New Delhi Station. Karamchand stood and watched the train. What a grand procession of events had happened inside that train.

And yet, for those looking at it from the outside, it was only a train.

ENDNOTES

1. Aum, I praise Agni who is the purohita (priest) of the yagya (sacrifice); its ritvij (priest performing sacrifice at proper times); the yagya which is offered to the Devas.

2. Vishu, a harvest festival, falls on the first day of the Malayalam month of Medam, usually either April 14 or 15 of the Gregorian calendar.

3. One chukram was $1/28^{th}$ of a Travancore rupee.

4. One of the low castes of Kerala.

5. A volunteer suicide squad of Nair warriors who tried to reclaim the right to preside over the duodecennial Maamankam festival for their king of Valluvanad.

6. A quotation from Sree Narayana Guru.

7. Mannathu Padmanabhan, a social reformer and freedom was the founder of the Nair Service Society.

8. The infamous Wagon Tragedy during the Malabar Rebellion in which 64 out of 100 prisoners loaded into a sealed wagon died of asphyxiation.

9. In Hindu mythology, the river bounding the netherworld or purgatory.

10. In Smārthavichāram, an inquisition of Nampoothiri women who commit adultery/fornication, an adulteress who accepts the charges is dehumanised and referred to only as a 'thing' or object, i.e. inanimate.

11 Father.

12. Muslims of Malabar are called moplahs.
13. The ancient name of Goa.
14. Victims of the Endosulfan pesticide tragedy.
15. Keka is one of the poetic metres in Malayalam literature.
16. A tilak worn by adherents of Vaishnavism. It represents the feet of Narayana with Lakshmi in the centre.
17. The mythical fruit set as the prize for a race between Lord Muruga and Lord Ganesa.
18. The practice of mass self-immolation by Rajput women, children, and retainers to avoid capture, enslavement and rape by an invading army.